She thought she wanted things to stay the way they were. Friends.

She could almost see the words forming on his lips, so she rushed in with the first thing that came to mind. "What would you like for dinner tonight? Never mind. I'll take care of it. All you have to do is select the wine and uncork it."

Josh ran his finger gently along the side of her face. "Emma…"

"After dinner I'd like to take the dogs for a long walk and watch the sun set from the granite rock. How does that sound to you?" she continued in near desperation.

"Emma…" he began again.

She knew she was jabbering on, but couldn't seem to control it. "If I'm going to make dinner, I should get started."

"Emma, listen to me—"

She was ready to interrupt again, but he forestalled her by closing his mouth over hers in a long and achingly tender kiss.

Dear Reader,

Welcome to *Sanctuary Cove*!

In my acknowledgments, I noted that *Sanctuary Cove* serves as an inflection point in terms of my editorial partnership. It is also the start of a new miniseries, set in the fictitious town of Sanctuary Cove in the Adirondack Mountains region. My last three releases comprised my K-9 trilogy, following the lives and loves of three San Diego Police Department K-9 officers. Although I'm thrilled to share with fans of the "trilogy" that it has now officially become a series, since there are more K-9 books to come, I enjoy variety in my writing and wanted to offer some to my readers.

While striving to write stories that are both emotionally and intellectually satisfying, I like to have my characters tackle some real-life, relatable issues, and you'll find this to be the case in *Sanctuary Cove*. For those of you who've enjoyed getting to know the furry, four-legged characters in some of my previous books, with hero Josh Whitmore being a veterinarian and heroine Emma Meadows a passionate advocate of all creatures, you might find an animal character or two in *Sanctuary Cove* that'll also capture your heart.

If you would like to use *Sanctuary Cove* for your book club, you can find discussion questions on my website, www.kate-james.com.

As always, I would love to hear from you! You can connect with me through my website above, at www.Facebook.com/katejamesbooks or Twitter.com/katejamesbooks, or mail me at PO Box 446, Schomberg, ON, L0G 1T0, Canada.

Happy reading!

Kate

HEARTWARMING

Sanctuary Cove

—

Kate James

HARLEQUIN® HEARTWARMING™

Recycling programs
for this product may
not exist in your area.

ISBN-13: 978-0-373-36827-3

Sanctuary Cove

Printed in U.S.A.

www.Harlequin.com

Kate James spent much of her childhood abroad before attending university in Canada. She built a successful business career, but her passion has always been literature. As a result, Kate turned her energy to her love of the written word. Kate's goal is to entertain her readers with engaging stories featuring strong, likable characters. Kate has been honored with numerous awards for her writing. She and her husband, Ken, enjoy traveling and the outdoors with their beloved Labrador retrievers.

This book is dedicated to the late
James Ingram,

beloved husband of Paula Eykelhof and
father of Emma Ingram.

Acknowledgments

Sanctuary Cove serves as an inflection point for me. It's midway through the development of this story that Paula Eykelhof, my editor since I started writing for Harlequin, passed the baton to my new editor, Kathryn Lye. Paula is renowned in the publishing industry for being an editor extraordinaire and having worked with many, if not most, of the biggest names in women's fiction and romance. I was truly privileged to have had the opportunity of working with Paula until her retirement at the end of June 2016. Paula, I cannot begin to express my appreciation to you for how much you taught me and for the great pleasure it was to work with you.

CHAPTER ONE

RAIN BATTERED THE sidewalk as Emma paused under the canopy by the entrance to the post office. She pulled the hood of her windbreaker low over her forehead and made a quick dash to the parking lot. Even so, she was drenched by the time she climbed into her SUV.

Poetic justice, she thought, that the sky had burst open while she'd been inside, arranging to send the signed agreement of purchase and sale back to Richard. That last tenuous link to her former fiancé was now irrevocably severed. As of the end of the month, the house she and Richard had planned to live in after they got married would belong to someone else.

Emma had picked up the envelope containing the documents just a couple of hours earlier, while weak rays of sunshine were still fighting their way through the thickening clouds. Richard had sent only the agreement—no note, no transmittal letter. What had she expected? "So sorry it didn't work out? It was fun while it lasted?"

There was no personal connection what-soever.

Perhaps it was better, more honest that way.

Emma shoved back her hood, splattering water everywhere, including on her copy of the agreement, which she'd left on the middle console.

"Great. *Just* great."

She wiped off the moisture before tossing the document on the passenger seat. In a gesture she knew Richard would've said was indicative of her inability to control her temper, she tugged the elastic band from her ponytail and pushed her sopping hair back from her face. When she started the engine, the sudden blast of cold air against her damp skin had her fumbling to shut off the air-conditioning.

What a difference a few hours and some miserable rain made.

Her wipers swished wildly as she pulled out of the parking lot. By the time she turned off the highway onto Otter Creek Road, her headlights were useless through the dense sheets of rain and swirling fog. The plump drops of water caught and tossed the light back at her.

Out of deference to the dismal weather, she kept her speed to a crawl as she wound her way along the gravel road toward her cottage.

With the next swipe of the wipers, a flash of color caught her attention.

She'd just convinced herself that her eyes had been playing tricks on her when she saw it again.

"Oh, my God," she whispered, as she eased her SUV to the shoulder behind the gray-and-red form sprawled at the side of the road.

Yanking the hood of her windbreaker back over her head, Emma hopped out of the vehicle and rushed toward the animal. A low growl had her slowing her approach.

She couldn't be sure if the animal was a dog or a wolf, but she knew he needed medical attention for the deep gash in his hind leg and by the odd angle at which that leg protruded from his body.

"Shhh. It's okay. I'm here to help. I won't hurt you," she murmured.

The animal pawed the ground with a front leg and twisted his head toward her. Keeping her distance, Emma stepped forward in an arc and eased into his field of vision.

She knew she couldn't move him, not only because of his size, but also for fear of aggravating his wounds. With the persistent growl, weak as it was, she wasn't certain he'd let her get that close.

But she had to do *something* to help him.

She reversed, slowly at first to avoid startling him, then ran back to her SUV. Grabbing her cell phone, she searched for the contact information for the local veterinarian she'd saved in case she needed it for her Alaskan malamute, Max. She found the after-hours emergency number and pushed Send.

Heedless of the rain, she paced impatiently beside her vehicle as the phone rang and rang. "Come on, come *on*. Pick up your phone."

On the sixth ring, her persistence paid off. A deep male voice answered.

"Is this Doctor..." She had the number programmed under *veterinarian* and couldn't remember his name. It didn't really matter. "Are you the veterinarian?"

"Yeah. Doctor Whitmore," he responded. "Joshua Whitmore. What can I do for you?"

"My name's Emma Meadows. There's been an accident. A dog—or possibly a wolf. He's been hit. He's bleeding and his leg's broken. But he's alive and he's in a lot of pain." She knew she was babbling, but she couldn't help it. Animals were her soft spot. She walked back toward the dog as she spoke, and with a sinking heart noted that the feeble growl had been replaced by whimpers and shallow breathing.

"Where are you?" The veterinarian's voice had an edge to it.

"Otter Creek Road. Just south of the highway."

"I'm on my way. I should be there in ten to fifteen minutes. Stay with him. Try to keep him calm but do not, *do not*," he repeated, "touch him or get too close to him. Injured animals can be unpredictable."

JOSH DISCONNECTED BEFORE the woman had a chance to respond. He hoped she would heed his caution. If she was negligent enough to hit an animal, she might be foolish enough to put herself at risk, too, he thought unkindly.

Having been in the shower when she'd called, Josh ran a hand through his wet hair.

It wasn't often he was in a bad mood, but after the long and grueling day he'd just had, topped off by Crystal playing more of her catty little games, all he'd wanted was a hot shower and a cold beer.

It didn't look like he was going to be getting that beer anytime soon.

He silently cursed the woman for more than likely driving carelessly in the rotten weather and causing a helpless animal to suffer the consequences. Josh tossed the phone on the bed and dropped the damp towel that had been wrapped around his waist on the bathroom floor. He tugged on a pair of jeans and a sweatshirt, pulled on a rain slicker and jammed a New York Yankees baseball cap on his head.

Hurrying downstairs, he paused to ruffle the fur of the yellow Labrador retriever stretched out on the rug in the kitchen. "I'll be back as soon as I can, Winston," he said to the dog. "Hold down the fort, will you, pal?" he added as he grabbed his keys off the hook at the back door and rushed out into the dreary night.

He spared an irritated glance at the recent—and decidedly obscene—graffiti on the side of his garage as he sprinted to his Yukon, which was parked in front of the veterinary clinic that adjoined his house.

He hadn't recognized the woman's name, so she must not have been a local, he decided as he climbed into his truck. "Careless weekend cottager," he grumbled under his breath and turned onto the highway. The Adirondack region had more than its fair share of them, in his opinion.

IT DIDN'T OCCUR to Emma to wait in the dry comfort of her vehicle. Thrusting her phone in her pocket, she moved closer to the animal. As he didn't show any immediate signs of hostility this time, she cautiously knelt beside him. His head jerked toward her and he strained to emit a warning growl. Although a moan was the best he seemed to be able to manage, out of respect for the large white teeth that flashed in the glow of her headlights, Emma slumped back on her heels, putting a little more distance between them.

"It's okay," she soothed. "I know it must hurt terribly. Help is on the way." Uncertain whether it was the words or her tone that caused it, she was gratified that he settled, but his breathing had become even more labored.

"Oh, no, you don't. Don't you give up!" she urged. "Hang in there." Disregarding the veterinarian's cautionary words, she held her hand out to let him scent it. Through slitted eyelids, the dog stared at her and sniffed her hand listlessly. Appearing to have passed the test, she reached forward slowly to stroke the matted fur of his neck.

He emitted a soft whine and shifted his head a fraction. Although his eyes were dull, he held Emma's gaze a few moments longer before his eyelids drifted shut.

Continuing to pat him gently, Emma prayed

fervently that he would have the strength to hold on until the veterinarian arrived.

And where the heck was *the veterinarian?*

THE HEAVY RAIN made the trip longer than Josh had anticipated. Driving in the nasty weather hadn't improved his disposition. It was nearly twenty minutes from the time he'd hung up the phone to when he spotted the black, late-model, luxury SUV parked on the shoulder of Otter Creek Road. And the woman huddled on the ground in front of it, stroking the animal. A set of choice words raced through his mind. It would be her own fault if she was bitten. Pulling up behind the BMW X5, he grabbed his medical bag and climbed out of his ancient Yukon.

The woman was hunched over the still form of the animal, as if trying to shield him from the worst of the downpour with her own body. There was a sadness about her—evident in her posture, the slope of her shoulders—that tore at his heart. When she glanced up at him with shimmering eyes, huge in her pale face, something shifted inside him.

He hoped he wasn't too late. That he wouldn't be deprived of the opportunity to save the animal. For the animal's sake, as much as the woman's.

"Josh Whitmore," he said when he reached her, and extended a hand.

"Emma Meadows," she responded in a voice so soft, the rain nearly drowned her out. "Thank you for coming." She briefly placed a chilled and wet hand into his, then inched back to make room for him.

She seemed so fragile, so distraught, but she wasn't his problem, he reminded himself.

Josh lowered to one knee and noted immediately the dog's labored breathing. The animal was still alive, as he'd hoped, but he wasn't certain if that was a blessing or a curse, depending on the extent of his injuries. The dog's hind leg had sustained the worst of it. He had a closed fracture, meaning the bone was broken but the overlying skin hadn't been pierced. There was a large laceration on his flank, too. Josh needed to find out if there were additional internal injuries. Those would create the greatest risk. He pulled a syringe and a small vial out of his bag, and administered a sedative.

Giving the drug a chance to take effect, Josh ran his hands along the creature's torso. He was relieved that he didn't detect any other obvious signs of trauma. He quickly dressed the cut to stop the bleeding. Next, he splinted the leg temporarily, so he could transport the dog to his clinic without exacerbating the break.

Having done all he could for the dog right now, Josh turned his attention to the woman.

She was soaked. Her long blond hair was plastered to her head despite her hood. He was three inches over six feet, but they were nearly eye-to-eye, kneeling beside each other. Disheveled as she was, he was struck by her beauty. She had large, almond-shaped eyes, the color indiscernible in the muted light, a small, straight nose, sharp, well-angled cheekbones and a generous, wide mouth.

A mouth that at present was frowning at him.

Josh ignored the frown. Not so easily, he also ignored the sudden tug of attraction. He tried to imagine what she'd look like if she smiled, before he reminded himself that slick city girls weren't his type. Crystal had taught him that lesson well.

Emma interrupted his thoughts. "Is he going to be all right?" Her voice broke on the final word.

Josh felt an unexpected need to comfort, but he couldn't lie. "His leg's in bad shape. He's lost a lot of blood. I'll know better once I've had a chance to properly examine him."

She nodded slowly. "Is it okay to move him?"

"I don't have a choice. I've immobilized the leg so he should be fine. His best chance is for me to get him to my clinic and ascertain if he has any internal injuries."

"How can I help?" she asked, as they both rose. She was tall, probably around five-ten, he guessed.

Josh swiped at the water dripping from the brim of his cap and gestured toward his truck. "Open the back, if you don't mind. The latch is on the bottom. In the center. There's a blanket in there. Spread it out so I can put him on it." As she was about to move away, he touched her shoulder. She swung around, her eyes meeting his. He felt that tug again. "Take this, too, please," he added and handed her his medical bag.

Josh lifted the dog as gently as he could, carried him to his truck and placed him on the blanket. "I'm going to help you, pal. Just hold on a while longer, okay?" Time was of the essence, especially if there were internal injuries. He turned to Emma. "I'll do what I can," he assured her.

"I'll follow you. I know where the clinic is."

He hadn't expected that. He'd assumed she

would've considered her penance done and head home—glad to get out of the storm.

"I won't get in your way," she said quickly before he could respond. "I just want to know he'll be fine."

Definitely *not* what he'd expected. Josh pursed his lips and nodded slowly. "All right, but try not to hit anything else," he said, as he climbed into his truck. He immediately wished he could've bitten the harsh words back. He wasn't a mean-spirited person, but there was something about her that poked at him.

CHAPTER TWO

EMMA SCRAMBLED INTO her own vehicle and made a quick U-turn. As she followed the diffused glow of the Yukon's taillights, Josh's departing comment registered.

He thought *she* was responsible for the dog's injuries! She was more likely to drive off a road and into a tree than hurt an animal.

It didn't matter what the judgmental veterinarian believed, Emma consoled herself, as long as he saved the dog.

She spent well over an hour in the veterinary clinic's reception area.

She'd hung her windbreaker on the hook by the door to dry. There was a coffee machine on a counter, and she took the liberty of preparing a pot. She sipped the cooling coffee from a paper cup and listened to the metallic clang of instruments from behind the closed door of the examination room. She could also hear the quiet murmur of the veterinarian's deep voice, although the words were indistinct. The fact that he *was* talking to the animal, whether he was heard or not, pleased her. It showed compassion. That emotion was in stark contrast to his harsh treatment of her. Maybe he was one of those people who was good with animals and not with humans, she mused.

When the examination room door finally opened, Emma was on her feet by the time he stepped out.

She observed again—with an uneasy feeling—Josh's quick perusal of her that she'd noticed at the side of the road when they'd first met. But she also saw the weariness and the unmistakable worry on his face.

He'd removed the baseball cap he'd worn earlier, leaving his dark hair curling just above his collar. He wiped his hands on a damp towel as he approached her, and she saw the towel was streaked with red.

Too much red.

Emma felt her stomach clench. She pressed a hand over it and tried to ignore the blood-soaked towel. She moved forward hesitantly. "How is he?"

"He's still heavily sedated," he responded. "I'll keep him that way overnight, but he's doing well under the circumstances. I surgically inserted a metal plate to repair the fracture and stitched up the laceration. It looked worse than it was. There's no muscle damage. There are no signs of internal trauma or bleeding. If I'm right about that, he should recover fully."

Emma blew out the breath she'd been holding. She took another step toward Josh. "Can I see him?"

"Sure." He moved to the side, allowing her to walk by him and into the examination room, and followed her. Emma would have sworn she felt his gaze on her and it caused the back of her neck to tingle.

Ignoring the sensation, she noticed the stainless-steel examination table, scattered with instruments, gauze and soiled cloths. Her stomach tightened once more, nausea churned and she quickly looked away. Then she saw the dog through an open door.

He was sleeping peacefully on a thick blanket in the corner of the room, his head pillowed on a folded towel.

Relief washed over her and tears welled in her eyes. She turned away from both the dog and the man while she steadied herself. Once her emotions were under control, she asked, "Can I touch him?"

Josh shrugged. "The sedative will keep him asleep for hours. Go ahead."

Emma crouched in front of the dog. She

reached forward and gently stroked his head. "Aren't you handsome? And you're going to be as good as new in no time," she whispered. Glancing up at Josh, she asked, "There won't be any permanent damage?"

Josh nodded. "There shouldn't be. He'll need time to recover, though. After that he can gradually get back to normal activity."

Emma turned to the dog. "Hear that? You'll just have to take it easy for a while, but you'll be fine," she said reassuringly, speaking her thoughts out loud. "How could someone have done this to you and just left you there?"

She continued to stroke the dog gently for a few more minutes before rising.

When she looked at Josh, she noted his furrowed brow and wondered what she might have said now to annoy him. Regardless, she was grateful for what he'd done. "Thank you, for saving him."

"It's my job."

Her gaze slid to the dog resting on the thick blanket and makeshift pillow, obviously having been placed there with thought and care. Just because Josh was lacking in social graces didn't mean that she had to be. She smiled. "I believe it's much more than that to you."

"It's what I do," he said curtly and escorted Emma back into the reception area.

She retrieved her windbreaker from the hook by the door and reached into a pocket to pull out her wallet. "How much do I owe you?" she asked.

He shook his head. "No charge."

"But—"

"No charge," he repeated. "Consider it my good deed for the day."

"Oh. Well… Thank you." She put her wallet back into her pocket and pulled on her coat. "What will happen to him once he's better?"

"I know most of the dogs around here. I don't think he's local. I'll try to find his owner."

"Is he a dog, then?"

"He appears to be, but he probably has some wolf in him, too."

"And if you can't find his owner?"

Josh's protracted silence worried Emma. She immediately thought of an animal shelter—or worse. "I'll take him," she said quickly. "If you can't find his owner, I'll take him."

Josh narrowed his eyes. "One step at a time. First, I'll make sure he's okay and try to locate his owner. If that doesn't pan out, and if his temperament allows, we can talk about finding him a new home."

Emma opened her mouth but ended up

huffing out a breath. What Josh said made sense. "Can I check in with you to see how he's doing?"

"Sure." He lifted a business card from a small wooden stand on the counter. "You seem to know my after-hours emergency number." As he offered the card to her, a quick grin lit up his face. The sharp planes and angles were transformed with its potency. "My office number is on there, in case you don't have it and want to catch me next time when I'm not just stepping out of the shower."

She studied his appearance for a moment. He had a wide, sturdy chin, an appealing nose with a slight bump, as if it had been broken at some point, strong, well-defined lips and perfectly straight white teeth. He was tall, with a solid, athletic build—broad shoulders, narrow hips and long legs. The sleeves of his sweatshirt were pushed up, revealing well-muscled arms. The thought of him in the shower made Emma blush.

Their fingers brushed as she accepted the card, and the contact sent a quick jolt through her system.

Stuffing the card in her pocket, she walked to the door. With her hand on the doorknob, she held his gaze. "Thanks again for what you did tonight. I'm sorry to have interfered with your evening. I'll be in touch to check up on the dog."

THROUGH THE GLASS insert of the door, Josh watched Emma head back into the storm. As tired as he'd been after treating the dog, it surprised him that the first thought he'd had seeing her in the reception area was that she was dazzling. In the harsh lights, he'd easily been able to make out the color of her eyes. They were gray. A deep, silvery gray.

Although he had always appreciated physical beauty, he'd never considered it his sole or primary focus. As such, he'd been astonished to feel another raw and powerful pull of attraction—especially in view of the situation. With Crystal's most recent little escapade, hadn't he just sworn off women for the time being?

Yet the tug was undeniably there.

Then he remembered something that had struck him as strange. When she'd been petting the dog, she'd said something about how someone could've hit the dog and left him. Josh had assumed that *she* was the one who'd hit the dog. What had he really had to base that on? Having seen her with the animal, her anguish apparent, it was likely he'd misjudged her.

She'd also offered to take the dog. Evidently, there was more to her than what met the eye.

He smiled as he walked back to his recovery room to check on his patient. It occurred to him that he was in a distinctly better mood than he had been before he'd ventured out that evening.

CHAPTER THREE

EMMA'S NIGHTMARES WERE MUDDLED. Richard, with his arm around an attractive brunette in a sundress, as Emma stood transfixed on the opposite side of a busy NYC street. The two of them laughing at her stupidity for believing he'd ever loved her...thought herself *worthy* of his love. The star-speckled evening gave way to a raging storm. A dog was lying injured and helpless at the side of the road, looking at her, imploring her to save him. As Emma's anxiety and desperation became nearly unbearable, a tall, dark-haired man materialized through the sheets of rain, dry and unruffled, to save the dog—and to save her. When he touched her shoulder, then ran a hand along the length of her drenched hair and whispered that everything would be fine, she jerked awake, disoriented and breathless.

Sitting up, she reached for the bottle of water she habitually kept on her nightstand. After taking a long drink, she let out a heavy sigh and rested her forehead in the palm of her hand.

Max, her Alaskan malamute, was immediately beside her. His solicitousness dragged her out of the lingering daze of the nightmare. She gave him a hug and, noticing her bedside clock, rolled her eyes. It was only ten after five.

She swung her legs over the side of the bed. It would be hopeless trying to fall back to sleep. Looking out the window, she was pleased to see the sky had cleared.

"How about we have breakfast and go for a long run?" she asked Max.

Recognizing the words *breakfast* and *run*, two of his favorite things, Max danced with excitement until Emma got dressed and they headed downstairs.

The sun had gilded the sky an intense pink and gold by the time they ventured outside. The air was cool, and she welcomed the bite of it against her skin.

A flagstone walkway, flanked by gardens, made a sweeping arc around the southerly perimeter of the cottage from the back deck to the front porch and toward the parking area. Butterflies flitted and bees buzzed from bloom to bloom. The sights, the sounds and the sweet and spicy aroma of the flowers lifted Emma's spirits.

A large and fit dog, Max loped easily by her side as she jogged up the driveway to where it crested before it sloped down again to join Otter Creek Road. She stopped and turned back. Her view was mostly unobstructed to the cottage, and where the property dropped off steeply to the small lake beyond it.

With the stillness of the air, the deep blue surface of the water was as smooth as glass and mirrored the wispy white clouds scattered across the sky. The vista from here never failed to take her breath away. It reinforced for her how right her decision to leave the city and move to her cottage in Sanctuary Cove had been.

She closed her eyes and inhaled deeply, filling her nostrils with the earthy smells of wet soil and recently trimmed grass, before she and Max sprinted away.

It was past nine thirty by the time they returned to the cottage. After showering, Emma called the veterinary clinic. She was told by the woman who answered the phone that Josh was finishing with a patient and would take the call in a minute, if she wanted to hold.

When he came on the line, Emma immediately asked about the dog.

"He's doing well." Josh's voice sounded pleasant. Even friendly. "Were you able to dry out from all the rain?" he asked.

Emma thought of the wet clothes she'd peeled off when she'd gotten back to the cottage the evening before and had yet to toss in the wash. "More or less," she said. "Is it all right if I visit the dog?"

There was a brief hesitation. "I'd prefer if you'd leave it for today. I want him to get as much rest as he can to regain his strength and help the healing process."

Emma gazed out the window at the bright sunshine and tried not to feel disappointed. Had she been counting that much on seeing the dog? Or...? No, it couldn't have anything to do with the veterinarian.

"Are you still there, Emma?"

"Oh...yes, of course."

"How about a counterproposal? If you don't have plans, have lunch with me and I'll update you on how our boy's doing."

She could hear the smile in his voice. His offer flustered her. "Ah, thanks...but I'm sure you're busy and—and I have a number of things to do today."

"Maybe some other time, then?"

"Maybe," she said noncommittally.

After hanging up the phone, Emma leaned

back in her chair. To her astonishment, she'd been tempted to say yes.

And what *had* kept her from agreeing? She'd avoided people since she'd arrived at her cottage nearly two months ago. All she'd been focused on was healing her wounds, and her work. What there was of it anyway.

She couldn't keep living like a recluse indefinitely.

Josh was being friendly, that's all. But even if he *had* been asking her out, where was the harm in it? With their house sold and the papers on their way back to Richard, that last connection to her ex-fiancé was gone. Thinking of Richard reminded her why she wasn't interested.

Feeling her old insecurities bubble up, Emma was in no mood to concentrate on the brand proposal she'd been contracted to do. After she'd been let go from her job with communications giant Tyson, Myers and Smith, one of her former colleagues had put her in touch with the owner of a small but growing media relations company. In-house resources at Pinnacle Communications were at full capacity and they needed help. She'd agreed to freelance for them, but now she questioned the wisdom of doing so. Yes, the money had been a contributing factor to her decision. She couldn't live on her savings and the proceeds from the sale of the house indefinitely.

But she didn't know if she had the confidence in herself anymore to be able to do even the basic work that was expected of her. The brand proposal was a perfect example. A year ago—make that three months ago, even—she would have polished off the assignment in a day or two. Fast forward to the present, and she'd been struggling with it for a couple of weeks, and her deadline was looming.

And thinking of Tyson, Myers and Smith, where she'd worked for the majority of her career, most recently as a senior executive, brought her thoughts full circle to Richard, reporter Daniel Leighton and the assignment for Senator Alan Morgan that had resulted in her losing her job.

Emma brewed a pot of tea, poured a mug and settled in an armchair in the great room.

Senator Morgan was arguably one of the most high-profile politicians in the country next to the president, and it was a well-known fact that he had his sights set on the White House. Richard, a criminal defense attorney, had been working with the New York senator to address allegations of corruption that had been made against the senator regarding the award of a substantial armaments contract to American Freedom Munitions, a midsize contractor. As questions arose regarding the company's qualifications, one reporter in particular, Daniel Leighton of the *New York Advocate*, began an investigation into how the company had been able to win the contract in the first place. In view of the persistent media interest, Richard had convinced the senator that he needed outside communications expertise.

On Richard's recommendation, Senator Morgan had offered Emma's firm a lucrative retainer for Emma to handle all media inquiries related to the allegations. If the situation escalated to the point where the senator's reputation was challenged openly, she had also been expected to manage crisis communications—one of her specialties—to protect and defend him. When she'd accepted the assignment, she'd had no idea about the extent of the senator's involvement. If Richard had known, he hadn't been forthcoming with her. And—as she'd later discovered—that wouldn't have been his worst transgression where she was concerned.

It was Daniel Leighton who'd shown her the copies of the checks that he'd claimed were evidence of kickbacks.

Emma's ethics were such that she couldn't

continue with the assignment under the circumstances. When she'd discussed it with Richard, he'd ridiculed her. After all, he was a criminal defense lawyer. Who had she thought he defended, if not the guilty?

From that point on, things had gone from bad to worse. Richard had felt that her terminating the contract with Senator Morgan would reflect poorly on him, since he'd recommended her in the first place. He'd seen the Morgan contract as a way to cement his bid for a partnership with his law firm, and he'd been adamant that Emma needed to keep working with the senator.

She couldn't do it. She couldn't lie on behalf of a client and—even ethics aside—do the job she was hired for, if her client wasn't truthful with her. The net effect had been that Richard had left her.

Within days, her boss, the managing partner of Tyson, Myers and Smith, had told her about the elimination of her position. He'd tried to convince her that it wasn't about her performance and it wasn't personal. He'd said that it was about workload and a matter of having to cut costs. He'd said all the right things, but in her heart Emma knew better. The senator had pressured her boss to let her go.

In hindsight, Emma recognized that accepting the assignment had been the beginning of the end—with Richard and her career—and ultimately had precipitated her move to Sanctuary Cove.

Well, at least something good had come of it.

She was thankful that she hadn't succumbed to Richard's insistence while they were together that she sell it.

Finished with her tea, she took her mug back to the kitchen.

No, she didn't feel up to working on the brand proposal, but she didn't want to work in the yard, either, where she'd been restoring the gardens. She poured herself more tea and retrieved her laptop from her office.

She'd purposefully avoided checking the New York news feeds for a while. It had been almost an obsession to stay current with what was happening with the senator and the allegations when she'd first moved to Sanctuary Cove. For weeks after her arrival, she'd searched online and read snippets about the ongoing investigation, and the categorical denials of any wrongdoing from Morgan's office. There had even been an interview with Richard, where he condemned the media's attack on the senator. Each time she saw a new article, a painful knot formed in her stomach and hurtful memories resurfaced.

She'd ultimately forced herself to stop following the case and resolved to put it out of her mind. She'd been reasonably successful.

Until now.

She set her laptop on her dining room table and did a quick search of recent headlines. Months had passed since her fateful meeting with Daniel Leighton, and she still couldn't find an article from him about Morgan and the kickbacks related to the AFM contract.

Strange, Emma thought. Daniel had all that information he'd shared with her, yet he hadn't written anything about it. She'd been in the business long enough to know how it worked. If you had a story that big, you wanted to get it into print as soon as possible before someone scooped you. Yet Daniel *hadn't* gone public with what he had.

An uncomfortable feeling crept into her belly.

Could those copies of the checks Daniel had shown her been fake, as Richard had suggested?

The discomfort in her stomach intensified. *Think. Think.*

She tried to recollect everything she knew about Daniel. Senator Morgan and his chief of staff had portrayed him as unscrupulous, opportunistic. Nothing in her background check corroborated their view. In fact, everything she knew about Daniel pointed to just the opposite.

If she accepted the senator's position that Daniel wanted to discredit him, why would a reporter who had built his career on a reputation of journalistic integrity and meticulous research choose to mount an unwarranted, unsubstantiated attack on a prominent politician?

Was there something more at stake for Daniel?

Emma watched a hummingbird dart around outside, then hover to feast on the nectar of a crimson bee balm.

Was it possible it was all about Daniel trying to reinvent himself as a political reporter, a position he'd been promoted to shortly before the allegations surfaced? Was he simply trying to advance his career?

Emma tapped a fingernail on the side of her mug.

The senator's characterization of Daniel didn't fit. Her research and her instincts both told her Daniel was not the type of reporter who would misrepresent the facts or fabricate a story. And why would Daniel have lied to *her*? Had he somehow seen her as a pawn to further his cause?

No. None of that rang true.

But if Daniel hadn't lied to her, why was there no story?

Was it possible Richard had been right... about Daniel *and* about her? *Could* Daniel have misled her? And by misleading her, precipitated the events that caused her world to crumble?

"Oh, my God," she whispered and squeezed her eyes shut.

It was unthinkable...

CHAPTER FOUR

EMMA HAD ANOTHER restless night. She woke exhausted and with a miniature construction crew gleefully hammering away in her head. But the insistent pounding hadn't been enough to banish the nagging doubts about Daniel Leighton.

After swallowing two painkillers, eating breakfast and taking Max for his morning walk, she felt marginally better. She poured more coffee into her mug and took it to her office. Max followed her, stretched out next to the chair and was soon snoring softly.

If only her life was as tough as Max's, Emma mused with a weak smile as she started up her laptop and opened the brand-proposal document. She sipped her coffee while she reviewed what she'd already done. Getting to the end of the document, she placed her mug on the coaster with more force than she'd intended, the smacking sound startling Max.

"Sorry, sorry," she said to him and tried to tamp down her frustration.

The proposal was mediocre at best. It lacked originality and pizzazz. Thank goodness she didn't have to have it complete until the end of the month.

Maybe Richard had been right, and she just wasn't suited to work in her chosen field—even on a part-time basis and without final creative approval.

Had she ever been good at it? she wondered.

Yeah. Sure, she tried to bolster herself. She'd been in demand, had been promoted several times at Tyson, Myers and Smith until she'd reached the highest position she could without becoming a full partner. She'd been recognized with an award—communications professional of the year—twice!

But now...

She stared at the computer screen. She'd been insistent with the owner of Pinnacle Communications that she didn't want her name associated with the work. She'd do it on a ghostwriting basis.

If that wasn't an indication of lack of confidence in her abilities, what was?

The owner had agreed to her condition without much discussion. He'd said it was because he wanted her on board regardless. Staring at her screen, Emma decided to start fresh rather than fix the stale ideas in the existing document. She tried to immerse herself in it, but soon realized it was futile. Frankly, she had no idea how to differentiate the athletic wear manufacturer in an already crowded marketplace. Instead, she decided to work outside.

She mowed and weeded and pruned vigorously for hours, all the while thinking about Daniel Leighton, Morgan and, of course, Richard, and all that had happened. By the time she stopped midafternoon, she was exhausted but in a much better frame of mind.

She'd been jumping to conclusions. She couldn't have been wrong about Daniel and what he'd shown her. She was positive that he was scrupulous.

There had to be another reason he hadn't gone public with the information he had. With resolve, she pushed the matter out of her mind again.

She showered, and dressed in faded jeans and a yellow T-shirt. In deference to the heat, she bound her hair up in a high ponytail. Her stomach growled, reminding her she'd missed lunch. While she ate a sandwich, she thought about the injured dog…and the veterinarian.

She considered calling Josh at the clinic but rejected the idea. She wanted to see for herself how the dog was. She didn't want to give Josh the opportunity to talk her out of it again.

The clinic closed at five and it was nearing that time when she parked her X5 in front of it next to a green Toyota. She was struck again by the size of the building. Granted, it was a combination of Josh's home and the clinic, but the clinic was a relatively small addition. The main house itself was large and rambling. While there was no obvious symmetry, the wood and stone of the façade complemented each other and the surrounding landscape.

Josh was behind the reception counter with his back to Emma when she walked quietly inside. He was preoccupied with a computer sitting on a side table. The only other person in the room was an elderly lady, cradling a white toy poodle.

Josh dragged his fingers through his already mussed hair, and continued to fidget with the mouse.

"I'm sorry to keep you waiting, Mrs. Fields," he said, without glancing back. "I'll have your invoice ready in a minute."

"That's all right, m'dear. Take your time. I don't mind waiting," Mrs. Fields replied. She stroked the poodle's wiry fur and gave Emma a wide, toothy smile.

The computer finally prompted the printer,

and Josh let out a sigh. As he grabbed the invoice he'd just printed, the telephone rang. He placed the invoice on the counter for Mrs. Fields to review, then snatched up the receiver and turned. His gaze collided with Emma's, and a slow smile spread across his face.

Her heart rate quickened and she forced a smile in return. She waved to him, then at a loss with what to do with her hands, she tucked them in the front pockets of her jeans.

Josh greeted the caller, but his eyes remained steady on hers.

She met his stare with an odd mixture of discomfort and excitement. There was no denying Josh's appeal, but appearance wasn't everything. His personality probably left a lot to be desired, as he'd been temperamental and unpleasant the night they'd met.

Her smile faded, and she ran her tongue over her suddenly dry lips. She immediately regretted the gesture, when Josh's gaze dipped down and his smile turned into a grin. And that grin alone made it difficult for her to breathe.

In what she hoped looked to be a casual move, she went to the display shelving at the far side of the room to examine the pet foods the clinic offered for sale.

She knew he was still watching her by the

heat of his gaze on her shoulders and an itch along her spine. She lifted a can of dog food, pretending to examine its label, and listened to Josh conclude the phone call and turn his attention back to his client.

"Here's your credit card, Mrs. Fields. Try not to worry about Muffy. She's perfectly healthy and should stay that way for a long time."

Emma marveled at the charm and warmth in his voice.

"Enjoy the rest of your day and please give my regards to your sister," he said.

"I will, of course. Dottie should be in soon with her Ginger. Bye, now," the gray-haired lady said as she walked out.

Josh flipped the hanging sign on the door to Closed.

By the time Emma turned to face him fully, he was leaning casually against the door watching her.

Her heart rate kicked up another notch, both surprising and annoying her. She struggled to not let it show. "I hope I'm not catching you at a bad time."

"Not at all. Mrs. Fields's Muffy was my last patient for the day. The clinic is now officially closed. Thankfully," he added with a relieved smile.

"Bad day?" He looked tired and his clothes were just a little rumpled. She felt herself soften toward him.

"Not really. Just an exceptionally busy one. We were booked solid, and Sherri, my assistant and all-around miracle worker, was off today. That means I had to do all the paperwork, too—not my favorite task."

"If you're busy, I won't keep you. I just came to see…" Emma hesitated, wishing she knew the dog's name.

Josh stepped toward her. That lazy smile and those warm brown eyes sent her pulse skittering.

"No problem. Our patient's doing much better today." He motioned toward the recovery room. "Let's go see him."

As they entered, the large dog gazed at Emma with guarded eyes. She remembered Josh's warning about the unpredictable behavior of injured animals and glanced back. "Is it okay to touch him?"

"Go ahead. Our boy seems to have good manners." To prove his point, he crouched down and let the dog sniff his hand before Josh stroked him. He checked the dog's pupils and gums, then moved to the side to make room for Emma.

She knelt beside Josh and held out her hand.

The dog raised his head, sniffed obligingly and his tail thumped against the side of the cage, causing a metallic clang. "He looks good...considering what he's been through." She smiled up at Josh. He was so close, she could smell the clean, fresh fragrance of his soap, see amber specs in his brown eyes and the faint stubble on his face. Hurriedly, she turned her attention back to the dog. "So he's going to be fine?"

"There's no reason he shouldn't be. His condition is stable. He's healthy other than for his injuries, and I'm no longer overly concerned about the possibility of infection."

Emma nodded, but kept her gaze averted. "Have you been able to find his owner?"

"No. I've asked around, contacted other veterinary practices in the area, put a posting online. No one seems to recognize him, and he's fairly distinctive."

Through lowered lashes, she looked at Josh again. He'd shifted to his other knee and was even closer, their faces only inches apart. "If, ah..." She struggled to remember what she'd wanted to say. She transferred her weight to her other side, putting more distance between them. "I meant what I said before," she replied. "I'll take him if you can't find his owner."

Before Emma realized what his intention

was, he tucked a loose strand of her hair behind her ear. She jerked back as if singed.

"Sorry," she murmured although she had no idea why she was apologizing.

SURPRISED BY HIS own action, Josh tried not to think of how smooth Emma's skin had felt. Yeah, it had been impulsive of him, but she'd overreacted to his touch, as evidenced by the way she'd pulled away and the shocked expression on her face.

He straightened the dog's bedding and refocused his thoughts. He, too, was concerned about what would happen to the dog. He couldn't keep him at the clinic indefinitely. Once healed, the dog would need exercise and room to roam. He needed a loving home.

He'd dismissed Emma's offer to adopt the dog when she'd first made it, considering it a knee-jerk reaction, perhaps driven by guilt, when he'd believed her to be responsible for his injuries. Clearly, she'd been serious.

"He's a large dog, Emma. He'll require space and considerable exercise. He might also need some training. If he's part wolf, there might be a degree of unpredictability about him as well, and he might have an instinctive prey drive that could make it challenging around other, smaller animals."

Watching her, Josh was struck by the many shades of gray her eyes could be, as they transformed from the color of storm clouds to a luminous silver. He felt the powerful pull of attraction again, and it brought Crystal and her antics to mind. Even so, he couldn't keep his gaze from lowering to Emma's lips as the corners curved up, and all thoughts of Crystal receded.

"Oh, I'm aware of the space and time demands of a large dog," she said with a chuckle. "I already have a large one. Max, an Alaskan malamute. I suspect Max would enjoy the company."

Josh had been so absorbed wondering how her lips would taste, he'd nearly forgotten what he'd said to her. Something about big dogs. Oh, right… "Okay. We'll see how things go. We should let our patient get some sleep now." He rose and held out a hand to help Emma up.

There was a slight hesitation before she placed her hand into his. He noted the skittishness in her eyes before she withdrew her hand and took a step back.

There was a shyness about her—an uncertainty—that seemed inconsistent with how beautiful and, by all indications, intelligent she was. She made him think of a delicate bird, injured in some way. He'd never been able to ignore a wounded creature, but it wasn't just that with Emma.

"Thanks again for taking such good care of him," she said, interrupting his musings.

When she glanced down at the dog and his tail wagged again, Josh could just about see her unease dissipate.

"Is it okay if I come back to see him?" Her smile lit up her entire face.

Stunning, he thought. The dog could make her smile with a simple flick of his tail and *he* made her nervous. "Anytime you like."

She studied the dog thoughtfully. "He needs a name. Even if you find his owner, we need to call him something for the time being."

"What do you suggest?"

She narrowed her eyes. "How about Theodore? Theo for short."

Looking down at his patient, Josh considered. "Meaning God's gift? From the Greek, right?"

"I have no idea. It just came to me."

"Okay. Theo it is… Emma, you know if we can find his owner, the best place for him is his home. I don't want you getting too attached."

She nodded, but he could see the mixed emotions play across her face. It was probably already too late for that caution.

Josh saw her out, and noted the efficiency and confidence of her stride as she walked away. That confidence seemed to be at odds with how ill-at-ease she was with him. Those contradictions made her that much more interesting.

Intrigued, he would look forward to seeing Emma again and hopefully would have the opportunity to do so on a more personal basis... Crystal be damned.

CHAPTER FIVE

THE GARDENS AND forest were ablaze with color as summer neared its end. Emma had finished the brand proposal and accepted two more assignments from Pinnacle Communications. With each assignment she completed, she got more of her self-confidence back. She was working on a media strategy for an initial public offering for a toy company. This was the first time since she'd been let go that she could say she was enjoying her work. If at times she still lamented how her life had unraveled, turning her mind to her assignments encouraged her. Each day she spent several hours working in her office, with Max sprawled on the rug next to her desk, more often than not sound asleep.

Afternoons, weather permitting, she spent outside. The cooler temperatures meant that she and Max could comfortably take long walks along the forest trails. They both loved the exercise and being outdoors. They'd hike across fern-edged, moss-covered paths in the shade of the high canopy of decades-old growth. They'd follow the gurgling, crystal-clear stream to the river, and the river to where it spilled over the rocks into the lake.

The juncture of stream and lake was a perfect spot to rest. Cattails and tall, wild grasses danced gracefully with the light breeze.

Emma would sit on a log or a boulder, while Max waded in the water. Eventually, they'd wander along the shoreline back to the cottage. Every few days, she'd take out a small kayak and paddle around the lake, occasionally pulling up on the opposite bank.

If the weather was inhospitable, Emma would curl up in one of the comfortable chairs near the fireplace in the great room and read.

For the most part, the only people she felt comfortable interacting with were the veterinarian and his assistant, Sherri. Once in a while, Emma's former assistant or one of her old colleagues would call, although as time passed, their contact became less frequent. She had to admit that it was mostly her doing, as they reminded her of the job she'd loved and lost.

Emma visited Theo regularly, but she avoided the clinic's closing time. Josh might have had a small-town practice, but she learned that it was a busy, thriving one. If she visited during the day, Josh was more than likely seeing patients, and odds were she'd manage to avoid him. He stirred up strange feelings in her that she wasn't comfortable with, and thinking about him caused insecurities of a different nature to emerge. Her relationship with Richard had apparently harmed more than her confidence in her professional capabilities. She didn't feel self-assured about her personal appeal, either.

Thus, Sherri became Emma's primary contact for Theo. But thinking of Theo invariably brought Josh to mind.

Emma stood in the kitchen and gazed out the window, trying *not* to think of him.

A sudden rustle of the brush at the edge of the forest helped her cause. A beautiful doe cautiously stepped into the clearing. Emma felt everything go soft inside her, as she watched the doe stop, its graceful legs slightly spread, and scent the air. Apparently satisfied that there was no immediate danger, she lowered her head, ears twitching, and began to graze.

Emma was enthralled. She placed her mug on the counter. Whether due to the muted sound or the motion that might have been visible through the glass, the doe's head whipped up, and she was immediately on alert. Emma remained motionless, not wanting to scare her away. A few moments passed and the doe continued to feed, until she finally decided she'd had enough and leaped back into the forest, her bright white tail held high.

The short vignette left Emma with a sense of contentment—even joy—she couldn't remember feeling for a while. Her spirits lifted, she felt eager to work on her current assignment and planned to keep at it until it was finished. Then she'd treat herself to a trip into town to visit Theo.

The work went better than she'd anticipated. Arriving at the veterinary clinic midafternoon, Emma walked into the empty waiting room. Sherri glanced up from behind the reception counter and grinned. "Hey! How's it going?"

Josh's assistant was compact in build, with short, spiky black hair, warm hazel eyes, a small, pert nose and a mouth that seemed to be turned upward in a perpetual smile. Sherri had a forthright, affable personality that Emma had felt drawn to right away.

Emma returned Sherri's smile and greeting.

"Theo's going to be happy to see you," Sherri noted. "He's definitely having a good day."

"Sill no luck finding his owner?"

Sherri shook her head, and Emma felt her

usual twinge of guilt for what she considered selfish relief each time Sherri told her no one had come forward to claim him.

"Just give me a minute to clear this stuff up," Sherri said, lifting a stack of papers, "and I'll take you back."

"No problem. Quiet day today," Emma observed.

"We had a couple of cancellations."

"Is Josh having work done to his house?" Emma inquired as she leaned casually on the reception counter and watched Sherri sort the documents.

"Work? Oh, you mean the ladder and the pressure washer beside his garage?"

Emma nodded.

"No. Not exactly work." The sparkle of humor that usually lit Sherri's eyes was distinctly absent when she rose and moved to the file cabinet. "More of a cleanup."

"A cleanup?"

"It's to get rid of a little farewell present that was left for him."

Emma arched an eyebrow. "Sorry, I don't understand."

Sherri shot a furtive glance at the closed examination room door. "Crazy ex-girlfriend. She wasn't happy about the relationship being over between her and Josh, and she likes to show her displeasure. Did some damage here a while back. Broke some exterior light fixtures, trampled some plants. The pièce de résistance was spray-painting exactly what she thought of Josh on the side of his garage."

"Oh, no. That's terrible…"

Sherri shrugged. "Josh can handle it. But thankfully she's been quiet for a couple of weeks now. He's hoping she's moved on. As for the graffiti, he's tried to scrub it off with soap and water, but it didn't work. He's finally gotten around to renting the proper equipment to do the job."

When Sherri was done, Emma followed her to the back. Listening to her friendly chatter, it occurred to Emma that she was starting to get a little tired of her self-imposed isolation. "Do you have any plans after work today?" she asked on impulse.

"No. Why?"

"Would you like to stop by my place for a drink?"

"I'd love to!" Sherri said with a grin as they entered the recovery room.

Upon seeing them, Theo stood and his tail thumped against the back of the cage. Emma noted happily that he was less awkward getting up. He came to her without hesitation. She ruffled his fur before snapping a leash to his collar. She took him for a slow walk around Josh's property. Theo still favored his injured leg, but as the weeks passed, the bone was healing and he was able to put more weight on it. Since Theo didn't seem to be in any discomfort or pain, Emma kept him out longer than usual, noting again how nicely he walked on a leash.

JOSH BACKED OUT of the examination room and held the door open for his last patient of the day. "There's no charge, for this visit, Mrs. Ross, since it's a follow-up."

After he escorted Mrs. Ross and her cat out, Josh joined Sherri by the window, where she was standing. Together they watched Emma exercise Theo.

"Good movement. Nice stride today," Sherri remarked.

Josh rubbed his chin and kept his eyes on Emma. "Hmm. I don't recall an occasion she didn't have good movement. Or a nice, ah... stride."

Sherri laughed and jabbed Josh lightly in the ribs with her elbow. "*I* was talking about Theo." She leaned against the sill and gave Josh a considering look. "If you're interested in Emma, why haven't you made a move?"

He folded his arms and shrugged. "I think

she needs some space. I also get the distinct impression she's trying to avoid me. So I've let her."

The phone rang and Sherri dashed over to answer it.

Still watching Emma, Josh murmured to himself, "It might be time to change that, though."

"No, I'm sorry but he's not here right now." Josh could hear Sherri behind him lie to the caller. He turned and gave her a questioning look. Sherri cast her eyes to the ceiling, and his smile faded. He had a feeling he knew who was on the other end of the line. His suspicion was confirmed when Sherri stated in a placating voice, "C'mon, Crystal. Calm down." For Josh's benefit, she moved her index finger in a circular motion next to her temple. "No. I'm sure your life isn't over simply because Josh isn't in it." There was a pause and Sherri dropped down into the chair. "Yes. I *know* he's a cad." She mouthed the word *cad* in an exaggerated manner, pointed at Josh and made a face that drew a reluctant smile from him. "No, I don't think he's changed his mind. No, definitely *not* a good idea for you to drive—"

Sherri held the phone away from her ear. Crystal was yelling loud enough for Josh to hear her clear across the room.

He'd had enough. He wasn't going to let Crystal be abusive with Sherri. He started across the room, but Sherri held her hand out and put the receiver back to her ear. "Crystal... *Crystal*!" The second time she'd said her name, she'd shouted. "Why don't you have a nice glass of wine and think about what a cad Josh is. I'm sure you'll realize he's just not good enough for you, and you're better off without him."

Josh raised both his brows.

"Yes. I know. That's right. I'm sure you'll feel better. A-ha. Okay. Good-bye." Sherri hung up the phone and exhaled. "Well, that was fun," she said sarcastically. "You really should tell the cops."

Josh regretted how things had ended, but his conscience was clear. He hadn't done anything wrong where his relationship with Crystal was concerned. It hadn't been all that serious and they just hadn't clicked. Regardless, he still felt responsible and didn't want to cause Crystal grief...even though that was exactly what she'd been doing for him. Also, the thought of going to the police about trouble with his ex-girlfriend was just too embarrassing to consider. Even though Sheriff Chad Atkins was a close friend—they'd grown up together, played some ball—and Josh trusted

Chad not to say anything, Sanctuary Cove was a small community and word would spread like wildfire. "She'll get over it," he stated dismissively. "I'm sorry you had to be on the receiving end of that. Why don't you head out now? I'll lock up."

"I will, as soon as Emma's back with Theo."

Josh was about to argue, but decided against it. Just as well, he thought as he retreated to his examination room. He wasn't in the mood to try to charm Emma after that call from Crystal.

As SOON AS Emma got home, she found a pair of pruning shears and took Max outside with her. She let him roam and sporadically chase chipmunks he had no hope of catching while she cut flowers. When she had a generous bouquet, she signaled for Max to follow her in. She placed the flowers in a vase and took the vase into the great room, setting it in the center of the coffee table. *Perfect*, she thought and grinned as she stepped back and surveyed the room.

She was arranging a variety of cheeses, crackers, fruits and sweets on platters when her phone rang. Glancing at the clock, she decided she'd let it go to voice mail so she could finish the preparations for Sherri's visit.

She was running late not only because she'd wanted fresh flowers, but she'd also spent more time than she'd planned on a quick cleanup. She couldn't help it. She wanted the house to look its best. Sherri would be her first visitor since she'd moved to Sanctuary Cove nearly four months ago.

She'd just finished the platters when Max's distinctive malamute "whoo, hoo" alerted her that Sherri had arrived. Emma wiped her hands on a dishtowel and followed Max to the front door to let Sherri in.

"This place is *marvelous*!" Sherri enthused. "The glimpses of it from the road don't do it justice." She bent down to ruffle Max's fur and scratch him behind his ears. The dog arched his back and leaned in toward her. "And what a gorgeous boy you are!" she said, continuing to delight him with affection.

"He's going to be plastered to your side now," Emma declared, as she handed Sherri a glass of wine.

Sherri took a sip and made a sound of approval before placing the glass on the coffee table. She leaned over to smell the flowers before sitting on the sofa. As soon as Sherri dropped her hand on her lap, Max nudged it until she gave him attention again.

"I told you," Emma said with a smile.

When Max finally stretched out by Sherri's feet, she reached for her glass. "I might as well be up front," she stated. "I'm wondering how many glasses of this excellent chardonnay we'll have to drink before you'll tell me who the real Emma Meadows is and why she's decided to leave the excitement of the big city in favor of admittedly quaint but nonetheless sleepy Sanctuary Cove?"

Emma's chuckle was spontaneous but her eyes darted away. "There's not much to tell."

"Let me be the judge of that. I emphasize the word *sleepy* as it relates to Sanctuary Cove. For those of us born and bred here, watching paint dry can be an event."

Sherri's comment surprised Emma. "If you're unhappy, why have you stayed?"

Sherri laughed. "Oh, I'm *not* unhappy! I was quite determined to leave when I was younger. I had a taste of city life while I was at college and I liked it—for the short term. But when it comes down to it, I'm not built for the city. Like most of us locals, I appreciate what I have right here. Family and friends. A job I love. And a pace of life I'm comfortable with." She swept an arm toward the windows. "How can you beat the beauty of nature all around us? I'm quite happy. So—" she smiled and swirled her wine "—back to you. What enticed you away from the bright lights?"

At Emma's sigh, Sherri reached forward and touched her knee. "I'm sorry. I don't mean to pry. Well, yes, I suppose I do, but I don't want to make you uncomfortable. I sense there's a story there, but we can leave it."

Emma glanced at the pale gold liquid in her glass. Took a small sip. She really liked Sherri and maybe it would help to talk about what had happened. At least some of it. She shrugged. "Things weren't working out for me in New York. Not on a personal level and not with my job. I thought a change of scenery would be good."

"Hmm…"

"Well, I've always loved spending time at my cottage. So, with no obligations, I decided to move here. I know that sounds cryptic…"

"You've been here for what, two months, maybe three?"

"Nearly four."

"For most city transplants, the novelty wears off in time, and they can't wait to get back to civilization." Sherri helped herself to a strawberry, then dipped it into the melted chocolate. "Something tells me you're different. That you might stay."

Emma smiled. "It's nice of you to say that. I would like to."

"If you don't mind me being honest, I think what drove you here was a lot harder on you than you're letting on. I remember the first time I met you. You had dark shadows under your eyes and there was an edginess to you." She returned Emma's smile. "Now the shadows are gone and I don't see the nerves, or at least not nearly as much."

"It's hard not to unwind in Sanctuary Cove," Emma said evasively and popped a candied almond into her mouth.

Sherri helped herself to a plateful of snacks and snuggled back in the chair, a distinct gleam in her eyes. "So, are you going to go out with the dreamy Dr. Whitmore?" she asked.

Emma choked on her wine. Grabbing a napkin, she held it to her mouth for a few moments until she could swallow. "Where did *that* question come from?"

"I've seen how the two of you look at each other. Not directly—but when you know the other isn't paying attention. You can't tell me you're not interested in Josh."

"Didn't you say he had a bad breakup recently?" Emma asked. She could feel the heat rise to her cheeks. "I'm sure you're reading us wrong."

"I know Josh, and he *is* interested in you." Sherri savored another strawberry. "Mmm. I might not know you that well, but I'd say you're attracted to him, too. Am I incorrect?"

When Emma stayed silent, Sherri continued. "So what's holding you back?"

"I don't want a relationship," Emma blurted out. "Besides, it's hard to imagine a guy like him wouldn't be with someone already."

Sherri shook her head, sending her dangly silver earrings dancing. "Nope. He hasn't seen anyone for months. Bad breakup, remember. And good-bye and good riddance to Crystal, if you ask me. Also, if he was with someone, he wouldn't be sending off those signals like he does with you. Josh isn't like that."

"Why aren't the two of you together, if you don't mind me asking?"

"Are you kidding? *Josh and me?* I haven't thought about him romantically since I was about ten. For his part, he's always considered me like a kid sister. I've known Josh a long time. His sister, Angie, is one of my closest friends. As kids, Angie and I were inseparable whenever their family was in Sanctuary Cove. I spent so much time at their place during the summers, Josh and I virtually grew up together. Over the years, he's become a good friend. I'd like to see him happy with someone. But that someone is definitely *not* me."

Loud cracking sounds from the direction of the forest caused Emma to jolt and she nearly toppled her wineglass. Max was instantly alert and up on all fours. "Was that what I think it was?" she asked.

Sherri frowned and nodded. "Yep. Gunshots."

Emma thought of the beautiful white-tailed doe she'd seen just that morning, and pushed out of her chair. The thought of a hunter trespassing on her property outraged her.

Sherri put down her glass and joined Emma and Max by the window.

At the sound of another series of shots, Emma winced. She'd check the regulations and, if warranted, report the occurrence to the authorities, she decided.

The incident left them in a more subdued mood. Regardless, when Sherri left hours later, Emma felt they had the beginning of a friendship. She cleared away the plates, glasses and empty bottle. She checked to see if the person who'd called earlier had left a message but there was no voice mail. Grabbing Max's leash, she took him for a long, brisk jog down the driveway and along Otter Creek Road. When they returned, her skin was flushed and damp with the exertion, despite the chill in the air.

Emma retrieved her laptop from her office, made herself a cup of tea and took both out to the back deck that overlooked the lake. The property dropped off steeply from the north end of the cottage, toward the shoreline. More gardens were visible from here, each boasting a dazzling array of colors of her late blooming perennials. Sipping her tea, she watched a great blue heron skim gracefully above the lake's mirrored surface to alight delicately in its marshy end. With keen eyesight, speed and agility, it plucked its dinner of fingerlings out of the shallow waters.

Emma heard the mournful call of a loon and its mate's answering cry, followed by the jarring ring of her phone inside the cottage.

Putting her mug aside, she went in with Max following.

"Emma, this is Daniel Leighton," the caller introduced himself as soon as she answered. "You'll remember—"

"Yes. I remember." Just hearing his voice caused Emma's palms to sweat. "But I don't think we have anything to talk about."

"I understand how you must feel, Emma, but I need to tell you something. Morgan knows about the information I have."

Exasperated, Emma strode across the room. "The *information*? I *believed* you. My fiancé didn't. But I believed you, and I tried to get Richard—Richard Peterson, he was my fiancé—to resign his contract, too. He wouldn't and our relationship consequently fell apart. And you've not used that so-called information in an article. At this point, do you really think I care what Morgan knows and whether you deceived me or not?"

There was a short pause. "I was entirely truthful with you." His voice was low and earnest.

"Then why didn't you run your story? It's been *months*."

"Morgan's attorney pressured the paper. Threatened, actually. That attorney was your ex-fiancé. Our lawyers were concerned about how I'd gotten the copies of those checks for the payments to Morgan. The *Advocate*'s editor refused to run my story."

Emma dragged her fingers through her hair and wished she hadn't answered the phone. "Then what do you want from me?" she asked, deflated.

"Morgan's aware I haven't dropped the story. He also knows I've been approached by other papers. Through some convoluted legal channels, he recently learned what I have on him, although they couldn't force us to turn over copies of our records.

"You're probably aware that Morgan has formally declared his interest in seeking the nomination to be the Democratic candidate in the next presidential election. If the story does break, it will be a huge hit to Morgan's chances, perhaps enough to derail his candidacy.

"I've given the police everything I'm able to, and they're investigating. Although I doubt Morgan realizes that yet."

Emma moved to the sofa and sat down. Max followed and settled next to her. "I'm sorry, but what does that have to do with me?"

"Up until now, Morgan and his people would only have suspected what I have on him, but now they're certain. Knowing I met with you and when, they more than likely deduced that I shared some, if not all, of the information with you. I suspect Richard would have corroborated it, if you told him."

Emma couldn't believe what she was hearing. "I don't have anything to do with any of that now."

"Granted, but they might also think *you* gave *me* information. I know you didn't, but they don't know that. Depending on how much they shared with you while you were under contract to Morgan, they might be worried about it. My understanding is you're not one of their favorite people. I also suspect I've been followed at times. Probably to keep an eye on me, to avoid surprises for them. All I'm saying is, be careful."

"I'm sorry to sound harsh, but aren't you overreacting, Daniel? What Morgan might or might not have done, wouldn't he be better off leaving matters alone? Especially since he was able to quash your article? If what you're suggesting is true and he gets caught, wouldn't it make matters worse for him?"

"A valid point, but there's more at stake here than even I suspected. I've reported it to the police, even though there's not much they can do about it. Just stay alert. If anything odd happens, call the police."

The police?

"And speaking of the police, they will probably want to talk to you."

"Me? Why?" She was horrified.

"Because you worked for Morgan at a crucial time. You were part of his inner circle."

"That's ridiculous and you know it! I didn't have any information. That was part of the problem. That he wasn't transparent with me."

"I just wanted to give you a heads-up so

you wouldn't be surprised if the police contact you."

Emma thanked Daniel for the call, although the last thing she was feeling was thankful.

It was late evening when Emma poured herself a glass of wine and took it out to the deck. Max stretched out at her feet as she sat at the table. The sun had dipped below the tree line on the opposite side of the lake, staining the lower sky a blazing crimson, and radiating streaks of vivid color above. The lake's surface shimmered iridescent red and orange.

The sorrowful call of a loon reverberated across the lake again, this time without response. Emma wondered where his mate was and sipped the last of her wine as the final smudges of color bled from the night sky.

Later still, with only the moon and stars to light her way, she gathered up her things and headed inside, Max trailing behind her.

After cleaning up the dishes, Emma climbed the stairs to the top floor. Her bedroom was a spacious room with a high, peaked ceiling and large, soaring windows overlooking the lake. There were smaller casement windows on each end wall, and she opened these to invite in the cool night air, along with the trilling of the cicadas.

She changed into a sleep shirt and climbed into bed. As she stared out a window, she realized that for the first time in weeks it wasn't regret, despair or anger she was feeling. Rather, a sense of calm and even hopefulness filled her—despite Daniel's warning—as she drifted into sleep.

Max's growl woke her. Groggy with sleep, she glanced at her bedside clock. It was nearing midnight. She spotted Max, his front paws braced on the windowsill, his body tense. She listened intently for what might have disturbed him, but heard only the usual nighttime noises.

"Come on, Max. Go lie down."

Max ceased his throaty growl and glanced back at her. "Off the windowsill," Emma instructed, and motioned toward his bed. Max pushed off and turned in a circle, but then rose up to rest his paws on the ledge again.

"Max, it was just an animal. Go back to sleep."

As Max wouldn't budge, with a sigh Emma got up and coaxed him back to his bed. Just as she was drifting off again, she thought she heard a car engine start but knew she was imagining it. She'd locked the gate at the foot of the drive and there was no possible reason for someone to have parked along Otter Creek Road in the middle of the night.

CHAPTER SIX

IT WAS A glorious fall day, with just a hint of a gentle breeze to flutter flower petals and blades of grass, and sunlight streaming down from a cloudless, clear-blue sky. It emboldened Emma and she took what she considered a daring move—visiting the clinic midday. She'd tried to rationalize it in a number of ways, but if she was honest with herself, it was because she'd hoped to see Josh. She felt an odd mixture of relief and disappointment to learn from Sherri that Josh had been called by another veterinary clinic to assist with a complicated surgery and wasn't expected back until late afternoon.

Wasn't that just her luck?

On the plus side, Theo was coming along nicely. Emma suspected, and Sherri agreed, that since they hadn't already found Theo's owner, it was unlikely they would.

After her visit with Theo, Emma spent much of the afternoon starting the fall cleanup of her gardens. In the evening, she finished off a speech she was working on for the CEO of a mining company.

The telephone had rung once while she'd been working, but she'd been on a roll and had ignored it. She felt a tremendous sense of accomplishment as she clicked on Save, satisfied with her first draft.

It was near bedtime, but her stomach reminded her that she'd skipped dinner...again. She ate leftovers while standing in the kitchen, her thoughts still on her assignment. When she finally remembered to retrieve the message from her voice mail, a pleasant male voice greeted her. She'd only spoken to Josh on the telephone a couple of times, weeks before, but she recognized his voice immediately.

"Sherri mentioned you asked about me when you visited the clinic today. I'm sorry I missed you. As you could see for yourself, Theo's recovery continues to progress well. So well, in fact," his message went on, "he's ready to leave here and go home. Emma..."

Home? Did they find his owner? Emma's heart started to beat painfully at the thought of not seeing Theo again.

Then Josh continued. "Why don't you give me a call and we can discuss your taking him, if you're still interested." There was another moment of silence. "Theo's been through a lot.

I want to make sure it's the right thing—for him and for you." Emma smiled.

If all went well, Theo could be home with her and Max by tomorrow afternoon. The thought of that made for a positive end to an already good day.

One day at a time, she reminded herself...

MIDMORNING THE NEXT DAY, Emma spread a blanket in the back of her X5. She and Josh had agreed she should bring Max with her to pick up Theo. Although Max got along well with all creatures—two- or four-legged—both she and Josh wanted to ensure the dogs' first meeting went smoothly. Neutral territory would help. Calling Max, she patted the back deck of the SUV. Max trotted over and leaped in effortlessly. She got him settled and rewarded him with a dog biscuit.

Emma drove to Josh's clinic with her window open, enjoying the sunshine and comfortable temperature. She hummed softly with a Tim McGraw song on the radio. She turned into the drive leading to Josh's house and clinic. A blur of motion to her left had her glancing toward the side yard. She stopped the vehicle and grinned as she watched Josh try to coax Theo into a game of fetch. A yellow Lab was with them, and he was clearly an old master at the game. Emma surmised that the Lab was Josh's dog rather than a patient, as he appeared to be in excellent health. The little guy did an energetic happy dance as Josh held the ball, bulleting after it when Josh sent it flying.

Theo, by comparison, wasn't quite certain what was expected. He sniffed the ball as Josh held it, but shied away from taking it. The Lab watched the interplay patiently and raced off as Josh sent the ball soaring once more.

Emma focused her attention on Josh. He wore a faded blue denim shirt, the sleeves rolled to his elbows, navy jeans and well-worn hiking boots. His movements were fluid and agile. A gust of wind swept his bangs forward, and he ran a hand through his hair, the thick, dark strands falling back in disarray. He paused, as if sensing she was there. He turned, his gaze settling on her, and he smiled and waved to her to join them. Emma's heart did a little skip and a jump.

She got out of her X5 and opened the back. Max hopped out and ran to greet the other two dogs. By the time Josh and Emma caught up with them, they were getting well acquainted.

Theo had been groomed and sported a new, bright-blue collar. All cleaned up, he looked very handsome and more dog than wolf,

Emma thought. He was only slightly bigger than Max. The larger dogs seemed to instinctively know to be gentle with the Lab.

With Theo distracted, his gait was steady and his limp nearly imperceptible. "He looks good," Emma observed.

Josh's gaze skimmed over her. "So do you. It's nice to see you."

She immediately felt self-conscious, but playful yips had both of them shifting their attention to the dogs.

Josh whistled and all three dogs bounded over. Reaching into his shirt pocket, he pulled out dog treats and offered one to each dog.

"Emma, I'd like you to meet Winston," he said, stroking the yellow Lab's head. "He's mine. Or I suppose it would be fair to say, we're each other's."

She crouched down in front of Winston and laughed when the dog licked her face exuberantly.

She rose and Josh sent the dogs off to play again. "Do you have time for coffee?" he asked.

Emma almost declined on instinct, but after a moment's hesitation, nodded. She *wanted* to get to know him. "Sure. Thanks. No appointments at the clinic this morning?" she asked as they walked toward his house.

"Not today. The clinic is closed." He flashed his heart-stopping grin. "Being the boss has its advantages."

As they reached the back deck, the dogs suddenly bolted in the direction they'd just come from. Josh and Emma followed to see what had captured their interest. All three dogs were running down the gravel drive chasing a cloud of dust.

Emma grabbed Josh's arm in alarm. "The road! They're heading for the road." There wasn't a lot of traffic, but the thought of one of the dogs getting hit terrified her. "Max, Theo, come!" she called, as Josh whistled.

It appeared the dogs had tired of the chase anyway, and headed back. "What was that all about?" she asked, once they were safely with them.

Josh shook his head. "I don't know. Could have been someone coming to the clinic, then realizing it was closed. Whoever it was apparently changed their mind and left in a hurry."

They walked to the back again, the dogs at their heels. Josh opened a gate to a fenced enclosure and let in the dogs. "They'll be fine there," he assured her.

Following Josh inside, Emma looked around the bright, airy kitchen. He motioned for her to make herself comfortable at one of the stools at the large center island, and he went about preparing the coffee. While the coffee brewed, Josh placed a basket of muffins on the island, along with plates and napkins. "They're fresh. Help yourself," he insisted.

"You *baked* these?"

"If my life depended on it, yeah, I could. But these are from Chadwick's," he said, referring to the local grocer. "I picked them up this morning."

They smelled delicious. She selected a blueberry muffin and placed it on her plate. Elbows on the counter, she rested her chin on her fists.

Josh was obviously at home in the kitchen. When she felt a flutter in her belly again, she looked for a distraction.

She was impressed with the open space, the big windows that allowed the sunlight to flood in and spill across the glistening hardwood floors.

"This is a wonderful space. It seems large for one person."

He chuckled. "Sometimes I forget just how large it is until I have to clean it. The house has been in my family since I was a kid. My parents first built it when I was a toddler and gradually expanded it, either because our family grew or simply on a whim." Turning, he smiled at her. "I'm responsible only for the final expansion. I added the clinic when I decided to set up my practice here."

"But you didn't grow up here?"

Josh shook his head. "We spent weekends and most of the summers here. It wasn't our family's primary residence, though. We lived in Westchester County. My father had his practice there." Josh placed two steaming mugs of coffee, sugar, milk and a spoon for her on the island counter.

"Your father is a veterinarian, too?" she asked as she mixed sugar and milk into her coffee.

Josh took a cautious sip of his own black coffee. "No. He was a surgeon. I disappointed him when I didn't follow in his footsteps."

"How could he be disappointed when you do such wonderful work?" she asked with a touch of defensiveness that surprised her.

"Oh, he never would have said so to me, but I expect he was for a short time, when he first realized my mind was made up. Fortunately, my sister stepped up to the plate so the pressure was off me."

Emma sensed there was no resentment and was happy for it. "What type of surgeon is he?"

"Was," Josh said, correcting her again. "He's

retired. He was a neurosurgeon. One of the best in his field. He was the head of neuroscience at the Westchester Medical Center up until his retirement a few years ago."

"Impressive. And your mother? What did she do?"

"She studied to be a nurse. That's how they met, though she had a short-lived career. She stayed home with us—me, my brother and sister—when we were young. The plan was she would work again when we were all in school. By the time Angie, the youngest of us, made it to that stage, my mother was heavily involved in charitable work and decided to keep with that rather than go back into nursing. She'd been away from it too long anyway. She ran a number of charities before my father retired."

Emma was intrigued. "Where are your parents now?"

Josh rose to retrieve the coffeepot and topped up their mugs. "Right now, Europe. In the summers they travel a lot. The winters they tend to spend in Palm Beach."

"Quite the lifestyle."

"It is, but they've earned it. My dad worked hard during his career. It's great they're able to enjoy themselves now."

"How often do you see them?"

"Not nearly enough," Josh said with a wistful smile.

His obvious closeness to his family touched Emma. She took a bite of her muffin and washed it down with coffee.

"What about you?"

Emma glanced up at Josh. "What about me?"

"Your parents. Where are they?"

"Oh…" The pain of loss could still overwhelm her all these years later. "They passed away when I was still in college."

He rested his hand on top of hers. "I'm sorry," he said softly. "So young. Do you mind me asking how?"

"My father had been ill for a while. A heart condition. Unable to keep working, his life became centered on my mother. When she died unexpectedly, I—I think he just gave up."

"I'm sorry," he repeated. "Do you have siblings?"

She shook her head. "My parents—"

The sudden barking outside caused Emma to jerk around, and she accidentally knocked over her coffee mug. Thankfully, it didn't break, but coffee spilled and dripped down to the floor. "I'm sorry. I'm so sorry," she said, quickly righting the mug. "I'll clean it up…

as soon as we make sure everything is okay outside."

"The dogs are fine. They're playing."

Despite Josh's assurance, she rushed to the window. Relieved that nothing was amiss, Emma turned. Seeing Josh mopping up her spill, her nerves jumped and she rushed back. "Oh, no. Please let me do that."

She reached for the dishtowel, but he pushed her hand away. "It's okay. I've got it." He gave her a long look. "There's no harm done."

"Good. I'm so—"

"Please don't say it again," he said, cutting her off. "You don't have to apologize, but even if you *had* something to be sorry for, you've done it enough already."

"I'm s—" She had almost apologized for apologizing so much, but caught herself. Instead, she chuckled awkwardly and glanced toward the window.

"You don't have to worry about those two getting along. They're doing fine and working out their hierarchy in a constructive way," he said as he tossed the dishtowel in the sink.

She placed her now empty mug next to it. "Speaking of the boys, I better get them home. I appreciate the coffee."

"Anytime." As they reached the back door, he placed a hand lightly on her shoulder. "It wasn't my intention to have made you sad. Before you leave, can I show you something that might lift your spirits?"

Uncertain of what it was all about, she followed him into the clinic. He pushed open the door to the recovery area and stepped aside to let her look in.

"Oh, gosh…!"

At the sound of her voice, the golden retriever lying on her side raised her head and the five tiny yellow balls of fur snuggled against her stirred with a chorus of yips and yawns. As soon as Emma squatted down, the pups scrambled to their feet and over to her. In their eagerness to get her attention, they climbed and tumbled over each other, and her, causing her to lose her balance and land on her backside. The pups wasted no time and piled into her lap.

"Aren't you guys the cutest?" she said, lifting one pup. He wiggled and slathered her face with lavish kisses before nibbling on her nose with his sharp puppy teeth. "Ouch!" Emma exclaimed, then hugged the pup to her and laughed.

"That's nice," Josh commented.

"What?"

"Hearing you laugh. It's a nice sound. You don't do it enough."

When she looked up at him, there was an odd light in his eyes.

"Have dinner with me, Emma. I'd like to get to know you." His smile was warm and encouraging. "How about it? Let me take you out one night this week."

Her mouth was suddenly dry. She wanted to say yes. She really did. But the flutter in her belly made her nervous and the word was stuck in her throat. "Umm, I…"

He arched a brow and held his hand out to help her up. When she was standing, he didn't let go but, rather, covered their joined hands with his. "I hope the word you're searching for is yes."

"Some communications professional I am," she said with a self-deprecating chuckle. "Yes," she finally said, and found herself drowning in his honey-flecked brown eyes. "I'd like that."

"Is Saturday good for you?"

"Sure."

"Terrific!" He nestled the puppies back with their mother, followed Emma out and helped her load Max and Theo into her X5. He waved to her as she pulled away.

As she drove home, she admitted to herself that she was looking forward to her meal with Josh. After all, he was intelligent, charming, funny and very appealing to the eyes. What did she have to lose?

Then she thought of Richard.

Josh was *not* Richard, she reminded herself again, and she had to stop making comparisons. Why shouldn't she enjoy the company of a good-looking, fascinating man who seemed to be interested in her? The possibility that he *was* interested in her sent a little thrill up her spine. It made her feel wanted, and she liked the sensation. Richard had hurt her and he'd shaken her self-confidence. It was nice to feel wanted again.

CHAPTER SEVEN

FOR EMMA, SATURDAY arrived in some ways much too soon and, in others, not soon enough. The day dawned clear and unseasonably warm. The trees were shrouded in their fall splendor, and the ground was carpeted in the russets and golds of the leaves they'd already shed.

Later, as she rummaged through her closet, she tried to convince herself it didn't really matter what she wore for her dinner with Josh. Then she berated herself for not having had the foresight to bring at least some of her dressier clothes from the city so she'd have more to choose from. It couldn't be helped, she resigned herself. She would just have to make do with what she had.

She pulled out a flowing silk dress in shades of blue on a white background and a simple gray jersey one, and took both into the bathroom. Holding first one, then the other before her in front of the mirror, she settled on the pretty, feminine silk. She had no idea where

Josh was taking her, but the silk dress would be suitable for a casual setting or something a little more formal. She was certain there were no restaurants in driving distance for which it wouldn't be appropriate.

Hanging the dress on the hook behind the door, she stood in front of the mirror and deliberated what to do with her hair. As Josh had only seen it loose or in a simple style, she decided she would do something different. She arranged it in a neat chignon high on the back of her head. She left some tendrils framing her face to soften the effect.

Brushing on pale blue eye shadow made her eyes more blue than gray. She added a couple of strokes of mascara, swept some blush along her cheekbones and finished with a light coating of natural lip gloss.

She removed the dress from its hanger and slipped it on. Walking back into the bedroom, she searched through the bottom of her closet. She considered blue pumps and white high-heeled sling-backs. Deciding it was warm enough, she settled on the sexier sling-backs. With shoes in hand, she headed downstairs.

The dogs were sprawled side by side across the tile hearth in the kitchen. She loved how well they got along, as if they'd known each other their entire lives.

"All right, guys. Let's go outside." She headed to the back door, the dogs scampering after her.

Barefooted, shoes dangling from one hand, the rich silk of the dress fluttering around her legs in the soft breeze, Emma strolled along the stone pathway beside the gardens still ripe with the dazzling colors of her fall-blooming perennials, and tried not to feel nervous about her date with Josh.

EMMA WALKING IN her gardens in a sexy dress, the dogs by her side, was the first thing Josh noticed as his Yukon crested her driveway. The very appealing sight made him think of an impressionistic painting—a Monet perhaps. It was a vision of a lovely woman and two playful dogs against the canvas of luminous fall colors. He laughed at himself for romanticizing things, yet he put his Yukon in Park halfway down the driveway and soaked in the view. He knew the instant she noticed the truck. She halted, then waved and strolled toward him.

As soon as Josh got out, the dogs dashed over and he squatted down to rub and scratch to their delight. When Emma reached them, he glanced at her and held up a hand to shade his eyes from the early evening sun that was haloing her.

Giving the dogs a couple of final rubs, he rose and walked with Emma toward the cottage, the dogs racing ahead of them. As he followed her up the porch steps, he couldn't help but notice her slender shape and long, graceful legs, and considered himself a lucky man. He hadn't seen her in a dress before and he liked what he saw. "You look...sensational," he declared. "You take my breath away."

She glanced over her shoulder, surprise registering on her face. Her smile wavered then firmed, and he wondered what had caused the look of uncertainty.

"Thank you," she said. Her gaze slid to the shoes she still carried in one hand. "I think it'll work better when the shoes are on my feet, not in my hand."

"It's part of the appeal," he assured her.

As they walked into the cottage together, he placed a hand on her elbow in a friendly gesture and felt her stiffen. The sensation was gone so quickly, he wondered if he'd imagined it.

Emma settled the dogs and slipped on her sandals as Josh brushed the fur from his clothes. He went to get his truck from where he'd left it on the driveway while she locked up. By the time Emma stepped outside, he was holding the passenger door open for her.

It was a short half-hour drive to Lake George. Josh had made reservations at the Charthouse, a historic boathouse converted into a casually elegant restaurant with stunning waterfront views. They were seated on the patio by the railing.

A waitress with a sleek cap of sable-brown hair and a bright smile took their orders and, after serving their drinks, discreetly left them alone.

Emma sipped her wine and gazed out over the water at the occasional passing boat. There was something wistful in her eyes that prompted him to ask "What's on your mind?"

She shifted her gaze to meet his. "Oh, I was just thinking how wonderful it is not to have to worry about my next appointment or listen to the blare of congested traffic. How much better to have no one to answer to for my time except myself and be lulled by the gentle sloshing of the water against the rocks and pylons as the waves roll ashore."

The corners of her mouth curved upward, but Josh sensed something melancholy about the gentle smile. He brushed his hand lightly along her forearm. "Despite your words, you don't seem happy."

The smile dimmed and she glanced back to the water. "I don't know if being unhappy would be possible here. There's something calming about this place. Not just the restaurant. I mean Sanctuary Cove." One side of her mouth quirked again. "So peaceful. There's so much beauty here." She gestured with her hands and her soft laugh stirred something inside Josh.

"That's why I set up my practice here," Josh responded. "I have no interest in living anywhere else. I'd suffocate in the city. It's not me."

Taking another sip of her wine, Emma placed the glass on the table and rested her hand next to it. "You don't miss the clubs, the restaurants, the activity...*the people*?" she inquired with a degree of skepticism.

He smiled. "What's there to miss?" He took her hand into his. It pleased him that she didn't pull it away. He stroked his thumb across the soft skin in the center of her palm, then the small ridge of calluses at the base of her fingers. He raised a brow inquiringly, but she didn't seem to notice, so he continued. "I was never much for clubs, although I went to my share of them while in university. As you can see, there are great restaurants here, and the views can't be beat. I find the people here warmer, more genuine, more community-minded than anywhere else I've been. Frankly, I've always found big cities too impersonal." He leaned forward and raised her hand to his lips. Placing a kiss on her palm, he curled her fingers over it.

When Emma drew her hand away, she kept her fist closed, as if trying to hold on to what he'd placed in it, and it pleased him.

As the waitress arrived to serve their appetizers, they lapsed into silence.

Once she left again, Josh asked, "What did you do in the city?"

Emma toyed with the food on her plate, then took a small bite of her stuffed mushrooms. "I worked in communications and media relations," she finally responded.

"That sounds interesting. What made you leave it?" He took a bite of his crab cakes and then reached for his wine.

"I—I found I wasn't as well suited to the job as I'd thought."

Josh glanced up. "What do you mean by not suited?"

The sun was drifting below the horizon, and streaks of crimson and gold shot into the darkening sky and across the midnight blue surface of the water. Emma shrugged her shoulder, popped another stuffed mushroom into her mouth and looked away. "I guess it just wasn't meant for me. I…in the end, I suppose I wasn't good enough to play in the big leagues."

He noted the look of hurt in the depth of her eyes again. "How long did you have your job?"

"Just over twelve years…but not the same job. I had a few promotions."

"Someone doesn't hold a job for a dozen years and get promoted if they're not good at what they do."

"Oh, well…"

She was clearly uncomfortable with the topic. Josh hadn't intended to push it, but he felt she was being much too hard on herself. He decided to let it go…for now.

They finished their appetizers and sat in companionable silence as their plates were cleared, their meals served and their wineglasses topped up.

Josh was struck again by how beautiful Emma was. Her eyes were a soft gray in the muted light, with just a hint of blue. Her cheekbones were strong slashes across her face, her nose straight and small. And her lips—her lips were full and wide, and glistened with warm color in the candlelight.

When the waitress left, Josh took Emma's hand in his again. "You're exquisite, Emma."

Her discomfort was immediate and palpable. She tried to pull her hand away but he held tight. She forced a smile but it didn't reach her eyes. Inadvertently, he'd already happened upon a number of hardships she'd had to endure, but he'd just hit on something else. She wasn't comfortable with compliments.

He released her hand so they could eat, but held her gaze a moment longer. "I like you, Emma," he said softly. "I want to understand what's hurt you."

She cut into her steak. "It's a long story."

"I'm in no hurry," he assured her. "And it might help to talk about it."

Emma poked the steak with her fork a few times, before tasting the piece she'd cut, then glanced up at him with guarded eyes. "Until six months ago, I was engaged to the man I'd believed I would spend my life with. And I had what I considered a successful career. My ex-fiancé, Richard..." She paused, and kept her head lowered. "I've always been a firm believer of leaving past relationships in the past." She took a sip of wine, and with a short laugh, she glanced up at Josh. "Are you sure you want to hear this?"

"I'm a good listener," he said." As he

watched her struggle, something inside him shifted and then seemed to settle in place. He was reminded again of a wounded bird, she looked so forlorn. Yet, what he was feeling wasn't sympathy for her pain, but something decidedly more.

"Richard, and I," she continued, "had collaborated professionally on occasion. I was with Tyson, Myers and Smith." She glanced at him and he shook his head, not recognizing the name.

"They're one of the top communications firms in the state, and Richard is a criminal defense attorney with a major law firm. Frequently, his corporate clients seeking legal defense also required advice from a communications or media relations perspective as their alleged acts were often a topic of shareholder or media scrutiny."

The waitress appeared to ask about their meals. When they were alone again, Emma gazed across the darkening water and continued. "Our last collaboration wasn't a successful one. We had a high-profile client who was attracting a great deal of media attention. In this person's line of work, reputation is crucial. When I learned more about the circumstances that led to the media interest… I couldn't do what my client wanted me to. Add to that, he wasn't forthcoming or truthful with us." Her gaze shifted back to Josh's and held. Her eyes were a deep gray, shadowed by regret and pain.

"I found that my fiancé didn't embrace the same set of...values as I did."

Her voice was steady, her expression calm, but he could see it was costing her. She paused to toy with the food on her plate once more.

"I wanted to resign the commission. Richard sided with the client, tried to pressure me into staying on and doing what he and the client wanted. When I refused, I discovered that...that Richard's career was more important to him than I was." The final words were said in a hushed whisper, so Josh had to strain to hear her.

"Richard thought it was a lifetime career opportunity for me. I just saw it as wrong. He considered me weak, lacking in some way, because I wasn't prepared to do what they wanted me to."

"Weak?" Josh said incredulously. "I'd call it principled!"

Emma stared at him for a long moment, and then slowly took another drink, nearly draining the contents of her glass. Josh refilled it. Their meals remained largely untouched for the time being.

"I suppose it's a matter of opinion," she said softly. "We separated. Actually, he left me. I resigned the contract, was fired from my job, packed my bags and here I am."

She'd tried to make light of it, but her hesitant smile seemed unbearably sad. She lifted her glass but just swirled the golden liquid within. "I know it sounds like running away, but it's not just that. There's nothing in the city for me any longer, and I've always loved it here."

"How long are you planning to stay?" he asked casually, yet it surprised him, as he thought about it, how much her answer mattered.

"Oh, I don't know." She continued to swirl the wine in her glass. "As much as I want to be here, the reality is I need to make a living. The question will be how long I can *afford* to stay. I've been fortunate that a small company has been giving me steady freelance work. My concern is that, although they need me to deal with their current workload, as they continue to grow, they'll hire someone full-time for their office. And I don't think there's much demand for my skills in Sanctuary Cove, particularly since I left my last job in disgrace."

"Based on what you said, I doubt that's true. You did what was right." He felt the tension build in her again and regretted probing further.

"*I* thought so. At least at the time, I did. The way the client and Richard portrayed it, either through intent or incompetence, I had harmed the client's reputation. Rather than managing the media in a manner that made the whole so-called 'inconsequential' matter go away, I exacerbated the situation by resigning the contract. Because of it, the senator was judged guilty…and so was I. The senator and Richard claimed that I caused the senator public embarrassment and reputational harm."

"I'm sure anyone with common sense would realize that wasn't true." It didn't make sense to Josh, but they'd spent enough time discussing weighty matters. "If all you need is a job to keep you here, Sherri's always pointing out that we could use some help at the clinic. How are you at cleaning out animal cages?"

She laughed—a genuine, natural sound this time. "It might well come to that, so don't offer something you aren't prepared to follow through on. But before I resort to that, I'll keep at my contract assignments. If I don't live extravagantly, it's enough to mostly pay the bills."

After dessert and coffee, Josh settled the bill. At Emma's cottage, with the silvery glow of the moon to guide them, they took Max and Theo for a walk together. Josh reached for Emma's hand. As they strolled along the edge of the lake, their presence silenced the chorus of the frogs. They cut across the field and took the driveway back.

On her front porch, Josh placed his hands loosely at Emma's waist. She didn't tense, as he'd feared she might. He nudged her a little closer and lowered his head slowly, giving her the opportunity—should she wish to take it—to back away. When her eyelids drifted closed, he brushed his lips across hers. The kiss was light, undemanding. After one more gentle kiss, he drew back. Although it tested his willpower not to take more, he now had some awareness of all that she'd been through and he didn't want to rush her.

His own head was swimming, an unexpected but pleasant sensation. When he loosened his hold on Emma, she wavered a little, making him think she wasn't unaffected by the kisses, either. He smiled. "Thank you for having dinner with me. I hope we can do it again…soon."

"I'd like that. I'm sorry to have gotten into all that—" She fluttered a hand.

"You don't have to apologize. You do too much of that. I think you're a remarkable woman with great integrity." When he framed her face with his hands and leaned in, her eyes closed again, but not before he saw the sheen of tears. He gently kissed both her eyelids, eliciting a surprised moan from her, then he gave her a final, lingering kiss. "Good night, Emma," he said as he turned to go.

He strode to his truck and climbed in, but he couldn't resist looking back at her. She stood on the porch, leaning on the rail, the dogs by her side. Bathed in moonshine, her blond hair appearing silver-white, she looked ethereal. In the light breeze, her dress molded against her slim frame. The urge to get out of his truck and run back to her was powerful. He was a strong man, he thought, to be able to resist the urge.

With a final wave, he drove off.

Back home, Josh let Winston out before going to his office and booting up his computer. Although he hadn't pressed Emma for the particulars, he was curious about the circumstances that had brought her to Sanctuary Cove. It was more than idle curiosity. He cared about her. Even his experience with Crystal couldn't dull the shine of the early stages of attraction he was experiencing with Emma.

After doing a couple of quick searches on the internet, he found what he was looking for. Senator Alan Morgan's pale blue eyes stared back at him from the screen. Morgan's alleged connection to an arms scandal was summarized succinctly below the picture. Scrolling through the web pages, he got a good sense of what had occurred, before a more recent article caught his interest.

It was written by Daniel Leighton from the *New York Advocate* and had run less than a week earlier. The other articles alleged government corruption and kickbacks, serious but certainly not unheard of. This article suggested a connection between the death of a soldier and Morgan's involvement in the arms scandal. It raised the stakes and took the claims to an entirely different level. This wasn't just about money. If the story proved true, a soldier had lost his life.

Glancing at the date again, Josh wondered if Emma was aware of this twist in the story. And if she wasn't, how would she take it...?

CHAPTER EIGHT

THE EARLY MORNING wind skimming across the lake carried with it the crisp bite of autumn despite the bright sunshine. Emma let the dogs out while she brewed a pot of coffee. Standing at the kitchen window with a steaming mug in her hand, she watched the dogs play outside.

Her lips curved as she thought of Josh, and how sweet and patient he'd been with her the evening before. He'd listened and simply accepted the matter of her failed engagement and the circumstances that had led up to it. He'd even jumped to her defense a couple of times. Had she ever known anyone so accepting, so nonjudgmental? she wondered.

And those kisses...

They'd left Emma a little dizzy and wanting more. He *was* interested in her as more than a friend. The last thing she probably needed right now was a relationship, but there was something appealing about Josh. And it ran deeper than the very attractive package he presented. She had to consider what it was—

exactly—that she wanted from him or, perhaps more accurately, was prepared and able to offer him. Although she'd have to think about it, she couldn't deny her feelings.

She placed her empty mug in the dishwasher and stepped outside. Standing on the back deck, with the rays of sunshine warming her skin, she called the dogs. Glancing at her watch, she wondered what time Josh got up on Sundays when the clinic was closed. She smiled, as she was about to find out.

JOSH WAS SPRAWLED FACEDOWN, diagonally across his bed when the ring of his cell phone dragged him from a pleasant dream. Opening one eye slightly, he glanced at his clock and groaned. He was tempted to pull a pillow over his head and ignore the ringing. He swore softly and dismissed the idea, knowing it could be a veterinary emergency.

Rolling onto his back, he reached for the phone. Half-asleep or not, he grinned when he saw the name on the phone's display. "Good morning," he answered.

"Umm… Josh?"

At the odd inflection in her voice, the vestiges of sleep faded, and he sat up abruptly. "Is there something wrong with one of the dogs?"

"No. They're fine," she assured him. "I'm sorry to have called so early."

"No problem." He was wide-awake now, so he propped a pillow behind him and leaned back against it. "It's nice to hear your voice. What's up?"

"Oh, I was thinking it's too nice a day to spend indoors."

Josh ran a hand through his sleep-tousled hair and glanced out the window. "I can't argue with that."

"I wondered if you'd like to go for a hike… or maybe canoeing? If you don't have any other plans," she added. "There might not be too many more days like this before the snow falls."

She was asking *him* on a date, and it wasn't just male pride that made him grin over it. After last evening, he appreciated why she'd want to take it slow. He'd expected that he would have to work on getting her to go out with him again.

That she'd called him and so soon was a good sign. "Either would work for me," he said. "Or how about both? There must be some terrific spots around your lake where we could have a picnic."

"A picnic?" she echoed with a laugh.

"Yeah. If you're willing to make sandwiches, I'll bring cheese and wine. How does that sound?"

"Terrific."

"Is it all right if I bring Winston, so he'll have some company?"

"Of course!"

"I'll see you in about an hour, if that works for you."

Josh showered and dressed in jeans, a long-sleeved T-shirt, a sweater and a windbreaker. He grabbed an insulated backpack, tossed in a blanket, napkins, paper plates, plastic utensils and cups, and took what he needed from the fridge, including a very fine bottle of pinot grigio. Almost forgetting the corkscrew, he rushed back into the kitchen before he whistled for Winston and they walked out the door.

Emma was outside with her dogs when he arrived. She'd dressed in layers, too. Her pale blonde hair was pulled back in a long, thick braid. She drew his gaze like a magnet. He just couldn't take his eyes off her.

Gathering his wits, he hopped out and released Winston. Snatching the backpack from the passenger seat, he joined Emma and the dogs.

Testing himself as much as her, he placed the backpack at his feet, cupped the back of her head and leaned in. Her eyelids closed just before he touched his lips to hers.

THE KISS WAS LIGHT. Yet Emma's heart skipped a few beats. With her eyes still closed, she ran her tongue across her upper lip and let out a soft, involuntary "hmm." Opening her eyes, she saw Josh's smile.

"Shall we get ready to go?" he asked, with laughter dancing in his eyes.

They let the dogs play while they carried Emma's canoe down to the dock and loaded it with their provisions. Well behaved or not, three dogs in one canoe with the two of them would have been a recipe for disaster, so they coaxed the dogs back in the cottage.

They put on life vests and, once on the water, they paddled leisurely around the lake. The colors of the trees edging the shoreline were a kaleidoscope of reds, ochers and oranges, reflected in mirrorlike perfection on the still surface of the water, until distorted by the ripples from the canoe.

Emma pulled out her oar and rested it across the hull. She motioned silently to Josh toward the shore. They floated without sound and watched a young white-tailed buck grazing on a sun-speckled, grassy patch by a small inlet. When he scented them, his head snapped up and his body tensed, but he remained motionless yet alert for any discernible threat. As the canoe floated closer, the buck turned abruptly, and with a flash of his snow-white tail, bounded off into the woods.

Emma was grinning as she twisted on her seat to look back at Josh. "Wasn't he beautiful?" There was an expression on Josh's face she couldn't read. It made her feel breathless, wanting to gulp air.

"Yes. Very beautiful," he murmured.

They resumed paddling and soon could hear the rush of water over rocks. The melodious sound became more distinct as they neared a curve in the shoreline. They navigated around an outcropping of rock, and caught sight of a fast-running stream plummeting over boulders into the lake. Emma signaled to a flat, grassy patch of shore close by and they paddled toward it. After beaching the canoe, they pulled it securely up on the grass and stowed their vests.

They made their way into the forest, following a trail that meandered along the edge of the stream, a crisp, colorful carpet of leaves crunching underfoot. Where the path was wide, they walked side by side. Where it narrowed, they hiked single file with Emma taking the lead. Occasionally, they heard the scurrying of a small animal in the underbrush or the cry of a bird overhead.

The musty scent of wet moss and water-logged wood blended with the spicy fragrance of wildflowers.

The sound of water rushing over rock crescendoed as they approached a sapphire-blue pool with a low waterfall plunging into it. The pool was edged with a profusion of tall grasses, butterfly weed and mountain phlox. The grassy area around the pond was soft as a pillow beneath their feet. Drops of water that clung to blades of grass sparkled like diamonds in the sunshine.

Delighted, Emma turned to Josh. Lowering his backpack to the ground, he gathered her into his arms for a kiss, while a whip-poor-will serenaded them.

They spread their blanket in a sunny spot near the edge of the pool. While Emma laid out the food, Josh uncorked the wine and poured some into plastic glasses.

Emma took a sip, then helped herself to a slice of cheese and a cracker, while Josh bit into a ham-and-cheese sandwich.

"This was a terrific idea. I'm glad you called," Josh said.

Taking it all in, the clear blue sky, the glittering rocks, masses of wildflowers, shimmering water and the gorgeous man next to her, she added, "I couldn't think of a more perfect way to spend the day."

As she was about to take a sip, the sound of a gunshot caused the cup to slip out of her hand, spilling wine on her jeans and the blanket. When another gunshot exploded, she scrabbled to her feet, glancing around with agitation.

"You won't see him. You might think he's close, but sound travels. He's likely deep in the forest."

"But...that's all my property. Right up to the protected land. And it isn't hunting season. I know, because I checked when I heard shots before, and reported it to the authorities."

"Unfortunately, it doesn't stop the hunters."

A third shot rang out.

"You can't tell me that wasn't on my property," she said, looking questioningly at Josh.

Josh rose, too. "I'd say that *was* close." he said with a somber expression. "I'll report it, too, when we get back."

The thought of someone hunting, especially on her property, made Emma queasy. She'd already filed a complaint with the state's Department of Environmental Conservation. For whatever good it did, she'd do it again.

They listened intently for several minutes, but there were no further gunshots.

The magic of the moment was broken and shortly after they packed up. They paddled back to her cottage in silence. It was after they'd carried the canoe up on shore and were standing outside letting the dogs get some exercise, that they heard several more shots.

In the silence that ensued, she heard another, faint sound. "Did you hear that?" she asked Josh.

"No."

"Listen... There it is again. It's like a screech... or a cry."

She didn't like the sound and the look on Josh's face did little to comfort her. Without a word, he strode over to his truck, unlocked a large metal box in the back and pulled out a shotgun.

Horrified, Emma ran over to him.

"Emma—" His voice was soft. "Take the dogs and *please* go inside."

He turned and headed for the forest. She hesitated only a moment before herding the dogs into the cottage and running after him.

He gave her a dark look when she caught up to him, but he must have realized that asking her again to go back would fall on deaf ears, so he continued into the forest and followed the trail.

Despite the crunching of leaves underfoot, Emma heard the sound again. This time it persisted. Her heart thudded heavily against her rib cage as she thought she now understood what the sound was and why Josh had the gun. Taking the next turn along the path confirmed her suspicion. She cried out and spun away as her stomach heaved and threatened to empty.

Gathering her courage, she went back to where Josh was now kneeling next to the beautiful elk that lay in a pool of his own blood. Eyes wild, the animal's screeching intensified. When Josh stood and raised his gun, Emma shouted, "No! You can't shoot him. You have to help him."

"Emma…" he said, his voice barely audible over the distressed cries of the elk. "There's nothing else I can do for him." His tone was cold and distant. She'd never heard him quite like that, not even the night they'd met.

"Please don't kill him," she pleaded, tears coursing down her face. Listening to the cries of the animal, she was beginning to grasp that it was too late. Sobbing, she lurched back down the path, her back to Josh and the animal. Hearing the gunshot, she crumpled to her knees and covered her face with her hands.

When she felt Josh's arms wrap around her from behind, she slapped at them. "Go away," she choked out. "You killed him!" On some level, she knew that Josh had done the necessary and humane thing—that the poor animal was badly injured and had been suffering. But emotionally? That was an entirely different matter. Too distraught, she couldn't think clearly.

Josh kneeled in front of her. "Emma, there wasn't anything else I could do."

Emma saw the pleading, and the pain, in his eyes, but she couldn't deal with it. She couldn't stop the tears and she couldn't stop shaking. She longed for the comfort of Josh's arms, but she wasn't capable of accepting what he'd done. She knew it was irrational to blame him, but she wasn't being rational.

"I'll take care of him," was the last thing she heard Josh say as she started to run blindly back toward her cottage.

CHAPTER NINE

LYING UNDER THE COVERS, staring up at the ceiling, Emma couldn't shake the horrific thoughts and images. That cry of the elk and the single, deadly blast from Josh's gun reverberated in her head.

A day that had started with so much potential had ended in a disastrous way. Her phone rang a couple of times. She'd ignored it, presuming it was Josh.

She'd reconciled herself with the fact that there was nothing Josh or anyone else could have done for the elk. Yes, she'd behaved badly toward him, but she couldn't bring herself to talk to him.

She wondered repeatedly if she'd come across the animal on her own, in the condition he'd been in, and if she'd had the means to end his pain and suffering, could she have done it?

Then the anger would take over. Anger at the hunter who might not have taken the kill shot, but was most definitely responsible for the elk's death.

She'd had enough of the hunters. This time, she'd report it to the sheriff, too, for trespassing, but it was time for her to send a message to the hunters, too.

It was with determination on her mind that Emma finally fell asleep.

The next morning, she drove into town shortly after Chadwick's opened for business. Chadwick's might have been a grocer, but they sold other supplies, as well.

Emma went directly to the hardware section and found what she was looking for. She grabbed a dozen large, stiff-backed black-and-yellow No Hunting signs. For good measure, she picked up five Private Property, No Trespassing signs, too. She didn't know how much of a deterrent posting signs would be, but she had to do *something*. Make a point; send a message. Returning to her cottage, she parked her SUV at the foot of the driveway. She'd loaded what she'd thought she'd need in the back before she'd left that morning. She grabbed one of the No Trespassing signs, slung her tool belt over her shoulder and carried the stepladder about twenty yards down the road. She set the ladder up next to a large oak and took the hammer and nails out of her belt. Balancing on the top step of the ladder, she held the sign in place and secured it with nails.

She was in the process of affixing another sign, when she heard a vehicle approaching. She'd just started to hammer in a nail when an ATV roared by her. The sudden, angry blare of a horn caused her to lose her footing. She tumbled to the ground, barely missing hitting her head on a rock.

When she heard the sound of a vehicle approaching again, she tried to stay out of sight. She had no idea who the men on the ATV were, but she wasn't taking any chances. With a modicum of relief, she noted that it was Josh's Yukon rather than another ATV. She rose and waved to him.

The Yukon screeched to a halt in a cloud of dust, and Josh was out of the vehicle and racing toward her. "What happened?"

"I fell. I was…" She paused, still more shaken that she wanted to admit.

He rubbed her chin with his thumb and showed her the blood on it.

"You cut yourself."

Emma wiped her chin with her own hand. She thought about how close she'd come to hitting her head and the small smear of blood on her palm was nothing. She must have scraped herself on a branch as she'd twisted away from the rock. "It's just a scratch. I fell off the ladder," she said, pointing toward the oak.

There were deep lines etched in Josh's brow. "Let's get you to the cottage." He glanced at the rock. "We should take you to the hospital. Make sure you don't have a concussion."

"I didn't hit my head. I'll be okay," Emma murmured, even as she wobbled a bit on rubbery legs as she tried to step out of the deep grass.

"Did you lose your footing?" Josh asked, as he helped her to his Yukon.

"No. Well, not of my own doing."

When he leveled a questioning look at her, she continued.

"I was posting signs," Emma said, and swept a hand toward the No Hunting sign she'd been securing to the tree. "An ATV went barreling by. As it passed me, it honked, loud and long."

Josh yanked open the passenger door with more force than was necessary. She started to climb in but she remembered her tools. "Um, would you mind getting my tool belt and the ladder? They're by the tree?"

"No problem." He helped her get in, then marched off to get her things. She had no idea what she'd done to anger him, but she decided to tread carefully.

After loading everything in the back of his truck, he climbed in and drove to her gate. She'd forgotten she'd left her SUV there. The occurrence must have shaken her more than she'd realized.

"I'll drive you to the cottage and come back for your vehicle," he stated.

"I'm okay to drive. It's only a half a mile and it's not as if I'm going to encounter traffic," she added, trying to ease the tension.

She was relieved to see that she'd teased a smile out of him. "You're sure you're okay to drive?"

"Yes."

She got out of the Yukon and climbed behind the wheel of her own vehicle and headed up the drive with Josh following her. Max and Theo greeted them excitedly as they entered the cottage.

When Emma moved in the direction of the kitchen to brew a pot of tea, Josh nudged her toward the great room. "Go sit down. I'll get it."

Emma was about to argue but thought better of it. She didn't feel quite steady yet, and was happy to settle on the sofa. She rested her head against the cushion and closed her eyes. It was just a fall and she was okay, but she didn't like the aggressiveness of the men on the ATV. She'd sensed rage. Hunters no doubt, reacting to her stance on hunting, as evidenced by the large sign she was posting.

She opened her eyes when she heard Josh enter the room.

"Sure you're all right?" he asked as he handed her the mug of tea. He held a damp cloth in his other hand, dabbed at her chin and took a closer look at her cut. "Do you have a first-aid kit?"

"Yeah," she replied and told him where he could find it.

He put disinfectant on the cut and a bandage over it. "It's not bad. Keep the bandage on it for today so it stays clean. I doubt it'll leave a scar."

"Thanks, Doctor," she said with a small smile. "I'm glad you're not angry with me anymore."

He gave her a baffled expression. "What made you think I was angry?"

His statement puzzled her. "You looked it. Sorry, I thought…"

Josh sat in the armchair next to her. "I was concerned about you. I was angry with whoever caused you to fall, but I certainly wasn't angry with you." Now he smiled, too. "And you just apologized again, without a need to do so."

She picked up her mug and sipped her tea. "What were you doing on Otter Creek Road?" she asked.

"I've tried calling to see how you were... after yesterday. There was no answer last night or today, so I thought you might've been outside. I wanted to make sure you were okay, so I decided to stop by."

Embarrassment crept up her cheeks. "I'm sorry about how I fell apart yesterday. When animals are involved like that..." She raised her hands, waved them around before letting them drop again. "I have a difficult time being rational."

He gave her a slight nod that she took as acceptance. "So you decided to put up signs?"

"I've reported the incident to the state authorities and, because of the trespassing, to the sheriff's office. He agreed with me posting signs. I don't know how much good the signs will do, but I wanted to make it clear that it was private property. I didn't expect that quick of an adverse reaction, though." She gave him a weak smile.

"Did you get a look at the ATV or who was on it?"

"It happened very fast. I just saw the back of the vehicle and it was in a cloud of dust."

He shook his head. "I wish I'd gotten here sooner." He leaned in and reached for her hand. "Finish your tea, and if you're feeling up to it, I'll help you put up the rest of the signs."

EMMA ACCEPTED ANOTHER assignment from Pinnacle Communications. This one had a tight deadline, so she spent most of her time working on it. Despite her preoccupation with the assignment, she found herself thinking of Josh frequently. When she did, invariably a warmth would spread through her, and she'd find herself grinning.

She and Josh spoke almost every day. Emma's feelings for Josh were getting progressively stronger, and she wasn't sure if she was ready to do anything about it. She completed the assignment midmorning. Rereading her work, even as her own worst critic, she had to admit it was quite good. With a sense of satisfaction, she clicked Send.

She lit a fire in the great room hearth and another in the kitchen's wood-burning stove to take the chill out of the air. As she gazed out the window at her lake, she thought about Josh. It astounded her how much she felt for him and so soon, but she couldn't say she was sorry. She was so deep in thought, she jumped when the telephone rang.

Rubbing at the knot forming at the back of her neck, she glanced over at the call display. She didn't recognize the number, and the name showed as private.

Hesitantly, she picked up the receiver.

"Emma, how *are* you?" the woman on the line greeted her. The voice sounded vaguely familiar, but Emma couldn't place it.

"Fine, thank you. Who am I speaking with?"

"Emma, really! It's Arlene. Arlene Greenberg!"

Now it clicked. Arlene was the CEO of Elite Consulting, a competitor to Tyson, Myers and Smith—an aggressive competitor, in fact. Emma knew Arlene from various industry functions, but the out-of-the-blue call surprised her.

"I've heard you've left Tyson, Myers and Smith—their loss, by the way—and that you've been taking on freelance assignments," Arlene said, quickly getting to the point.

"Correct on both counts."

"Would you consider doing freelance work for us? We don't mind sharing you, at first. Ultimately, I'd like the arrangement to be exclusive. I'm selfish that way," Arlene said with a laugh, and she went on to outline the details for Emma.

When Emma hung up the phone, she looked over at the two dogs sprawled out on the floor. "How about that, boys?" she murmured.

The more Emma thought about Arlene's offer, the more she wanted to discuss it with Josh.

When had she begun to rely on him so much? she wondered. Only now, when she wished she'd have someone close to her to talk about the offer, did she begin to realize the degree to which Richard had isolated her from her friends. Her circle of "friends" had been mostly the couples she and Richard knew and a few of her associates from work. Arlene's offer was definitely not something she would be prepared to discuss with her former colleagues, even if she was still in regular contact with them.

When she picked up the phone to call Josh, she found there was a message waiting. Hoping Josh had called while she'd been on the phone with Arlene, she retrieved the voice mail.

"It's Daniel Leighton from the *Advocate*. Emma, I'm sorry to bother you again. I imagine I'm the last person you want to hear from…"

You got that right, she thought to herself.

"But I need to speak with you. I'll meet you at your convenience, anywhere you like."

He left his cell phone number and, after a brief pause, added, "I wouldn't be bothering you if it wasn't important."

She replayed the message. This time she jotted down the phone number, although she wasn't certain she'd call. Her happy, buoyant mood gone, she stared out the window again at the fading fall colors.

Sensing her change in disposition, Max rose and walked over to her, resting his big head on her lap with a sigh. She stroked him as much to give comfort as to take it, yet the tension persisted.

"Let's go outside and burn off some energy," she suggested to the dogs. Tails wagging and tongues lolling, they followed her out of the cottage. She strolled toward a large outcropping of rock in the clearing and sat. Drawing her legs up against her, she rested her chin on her knees.

She concentrated on thoughts of Josh again and what was blossoming between them, and it lifted her spirits. She wondered if she could simply ignore the phone call—pretend it hadn't happened. Keep her focus on the positives in her life.

But Daniel had said it was important. She trusted that he wouldn't have said that lightly. It would probably mean that he'd keep trying until she spoke with him. Why, when she was just getting her life in order, did her past have to intrude again?

When they were back inside, she called Josh. There was no answer at the clinic and his cell phone went to voice mail, too. Sherri must have left for the day, and Josh was probably with his last patient, she concluded. If she hurried, she might catch him as he was finishing up.

Her hopes of seeing him alone were dashed when she pulled up in front of the clinic and saw a little blue convertible in the parking lot. She felt a mild sense of disappointment but was undeterred.

The sign on the clinic door was already flipped to Closed, but the door was unlocked, and the room was empty. She peered into the examination room. It was deserted, too. The sound of a playful bark had her looking out the window to the backyard.

Josh was strolling toward the clinic but he wasn't alone. Winston and a tall, slim, dark-haired woman were with him. With just a quick glance, Emma could see the woman was spectacular-looking, with flawless features and thick hair tumbling in rich waves well past her shoulders. She was dressed in loose-fitting jeans and an oversize sweatshirt. There was something familiar about her, but Emma couldn't recall seeing her around Sanctuary Cove.

She wondered if the woman was Josh's exgirlfriend, Crystal, but quickly dismissed the idea. Based on what she knew, she doubted Josh would be walking along companionably with her.

Just for a moment, the image of Richard with his arm around a woman not dissimilar to the one with Josh—that night so soon after he'd walked out on her—flashed through her mind.

She sucked in a huge breath.

She trusted Josh, and she wasn't going to jump to conclusions about who the woman was.

Josh said something, and the woman laughed. There was an easy closeness between the two of them. Before Emma could speculate further, they entered the clinic through the back door. Winston raced over to Emma, doing a full-body wag, and she obliged by bending down and scratching him behind his ears.

"Emma!" Josh's evident pleasure at seeing

her dispelled any feelings of doubt. "I'm glad you're here." He placed a light kiss on her mouth. "I'd like you to meet Angie. You remember me mentioning my sister, the doctor?"

Emma nodded.

"Angie, this is Emma. The woman I was telling you about."

Angie grinned disarmingly and extended a hand. "It's a pleasure to meet you." She spared a glance for her brother. "Josh has told me a great deal about you."

Emma now understood why she'd seemed familiar. It was the family resemblance. The hair, the eyes, the build and that captivating smile.

"I had a couple days off work and needed to recharge, so I decided to visit my big brother," Angie explained and patted Josh's cheek as they left the clinic and walked toward his house.

"She's interning at Westchester Medical Center," Josh stated with obvious pride.

"That can't be easy," Emma observed.

"The pace at the hospital's grueling, but I know my limit. When I'm nearing it, I try to take some time off. My favorite place to hide away is Sanctuary Cove. So I impose on Josh whenever I can."

"What brought *you* here?" Josh asked Emma. "Not that I'm complaining."

"Oh… I wanted to discuss something with you."

"Come join us," Josh responded. "And tell us what's on your mind."

Her glance at Angie must have shown her hesitation.

"I can make myself scarce, if you'd like," Angie offered.

"Oh, please don't leave on my account," Emma objected.

Josh took matters into his own hands, by guiding Emma into the kitchen and preparing coffee. "So, what's up?" he asked Emma when he sat down with them.

She could share the news about Arlene, Emma decided, but not about Daniel.

"I had a call this afternoon, completely unexpected, from the owner of a company that's one of my former employer's biggest competitors." To Angie, she said, "It's a communications and media relations firm. Anyway, Arlene Greenberg, the owner of Elite Consulting called me…" She let out a nervous laugh. "She wants me to do freelance work for her firm."

Josh was in the process of refreshing their coffees, but he lowered the pot. "That's great," he said enthusiastically.

"Oh, well, I haven't decided yet, if I should accept." She felt the heat rise to her face. "It's just nice to be asked."

Angie gave Emma a bright smile. "Whatever you decide, congratulations for being in demand."

After Emma briefly outlined her discussion with Arlene, they spoke about other matters.

"I'm pleased I decided to visit," Angie said when they reached a lull in the conversation. "As always, it's great to see Josh, but as an unexpected bonus, I got a chance to meet you, Emma!"

"It's nice to meet you, too," Emma responded. Checking her watch, she stood up. "I'd better get going."

Josh rose, too, and walked her out.

Once outside, he ran his palms along Emma's arms and took her hands into his. "Congratulations, again. That's great news about the offer."

"Um, there *was* something else I wanted to discuss with you."

"Would you like to do it over dinner? Get the dogs and bring them over?"

"No, Josh. This I'd like to discuss in private with you."

His eyes turned serious and he nodded. "Let me spend a little time with Angie and I'll come over to your place." Emma was about to protest, but he continued. "Give me an hour and a half. Angie will be fine on her own. She's here to rest anyway."

WHEN JOSH REENTERED the kitchen, he immediately noted the thoughtful look on his sister's face. Sitting back down, he topped up their mugs with coffee once more. "So, what do you think of Emma?" he asked in view of Angie's protracted silence.

Angie took a sip of coffee. "She's nice, beautiful…"

"I hear a but coming," Josh said and felt a pang of defensiveness.

"She's intelligent and articulate," Angie continued. "She has a sense of humor and has obviously done well professionally."

"But?"

Angie sighed. "I like her. I *really* do," she added with emphasis when Josh glowered at her. She shook her head. "She seems…uneasy. I can't think of a better word. She's reluctant to maintain eye contact, is too sensitive about not getting in the way or being a bother. I'd expect someone with her education, intelligence and accomplishments to be more confident… comfortable in her own skin."

Josh felt relief that the issue wasn't a matter

of Angie not liking Emma. It mattered to him what his sister thought, and what the rest of his family would think of Emma, too. "She's taken some hard hits recently," he said.

"Hmm, that might explain it. Are you comfortable telling me about it?"

Josh thought about it for a moment. He'd never betray Emma's trust, but he could generalize. He gave Angie a high-level summary of the failure of Emma's engagement and her job loss.

"Yikes. Those *are* some tough blows for her to take and in quick succession. Did she have support? Friends? Family?"

"No immediate family." He saw the immediate sympathy on Angie's face, as neither of them could imagine life without their close-knit clan. "From what I understand, her ex caused her to lose contact with most of her friends. With the loss of her job and how it happened, she's purposefully distanced herself from her former coworkers."

Angie nodded pensively. "Has she said anything about her ex being abusive?"

"*What*? No!" Josh was outraged at the thought that Emma might have been the victim of abuse. "She would never have tolerated it. She's too strong and smart for that."

Angie placed a hand on his arm. "First of

all, I don't mean physical abuse. I'm talking about emotional abuse."

Josh glared at her. "I think you took too many of those psych classes in university."

Angie linked her fingers together and leaned forward. "Hear me out. Abuse— whether physical or psychological—is very prevalent. It can manifest through constant criticism of a partner or even more subtle tactics, such as a refusal to be pleased by, or happy with, the partner. Blaming them for a variety of things fits the definition, too. Over a prolonged period, any of those behaviors can affect a victim emotionally. Erode the person's sense of self and self-confidence."

Josh opened his mouth to respond. Then closed it again.

"So the net effect," Angie continued, and squeezed Josh's arm supportively. "The victim's self-worth deteriorates to the point where he or she is no longer aware of what is happening to them. It's insidious in that it starts slowly and eats away at the person until they gradually fade away. Even the strongest, most intelligent people can fall prey to it."

Josh pushed out of the chair and stalked to the window. Shoving his hands in his pockets, he stared outside.

He didn't like what he was hearing. He

wanted to argue in Emma's defense, but he respected his sister's intelligence and he couldn't dismiss what Angie was saying. It would explain some of those contradictions he'd picked up on, not to mention Emma always feeling like she'd done something wrong and needing to apologize for it. And Angie touched on a point Josh hadn't been able to reconcile in his own mind—knowing what he did about Emma—as to why that would be the case.

He turned back to his sister. "So, Doctor Whitmore, what do you advise I do to corroborate your theory and, if you're correct, how do I help Emma get over it?"

CHAPTER TEN

ON THE DRIVE HOME, Emma was more preoccupied with what Daniel could want than the positive of Arlene's offer of work. By the time she arrived at the cottage, she'd decided to quit dwelling on the negative.

After letting the dogs out, she headed to the shed and gathered her gardening tools. The dogs, having tired each other out, stretched out on the cool grass in the shade of a massive oak tree.

Emma began with the garden that skirted the kitchen windows. She cut back perennials, pulled weeds and dug up spent annuals with single-minded determination.

The warmth of the sun felt good on her back, and gave her comfort. She paused to swipe at some loose strands of hair with her forearm, just as the dogs sprang up and raced toward the driveway. Soon after, she heard the sound of a vehicle approaching.

Josh's Yukon crested the driveway, and the dogs rushed forward to greet him. Emma rose and brushed most of the dirt from the knees of her jeans. Her lips curved into a smile as she watched him let Winston hop out. Perhaps Josh's company was all she needed to put things into perspective.

Having had their fill of hellos, the dogs headed to the shade to rest.

Josh turned to Emma. Placing his hands on her waist, he searched her face. "Whatever you're worried about, it'll be okay."

His comment startled her. Was she that transparent…or had he come to know her so well?

He placed a kiss on the tip of her nose. "Come walk with me."

He led her to the nearest entrance to the forest trails, the dogs bounding after them.

Soon they were on a path with the sun filtering through the denuded branches casting a mottled patchwork of light and dark on the ground. The dogs scrambled over or around brush, branches and rocks, eagerly exploring the undergrowth.

"So you said you wanted to talk about something in private." He glanced at the two large dogs racing ahead of them. "Let me guess. You want to start your own sled team."

Her own laugh surprised her. "No, that's definitely not it!"

He waited. When she didn't say more, he prompted her again. "What is it?"

"I had a phone call from a reporter today. He was one of the main reporters covering that whole mess I thought I had put behind me months ago."

An odd look came over Josh's face. "What did he want?"

"I don't know. I let the call go to voice mail. His message was cryptic. He only said he needed to speak with me."

They watched the dogs race off in hot pursuit of a chipmunk. It scurried up a tree, leaving them leaping and barking.

"Are you going to return the call?"

Emma sighed. "I don't know. I'd prefer not to and just let the past be the past, but Daniel—he's the reporter, Daniel Leighton with the *New York Advocate*. He's the one who gave me a heads-up about…" Emma caught herself before she blurted out what Daniel had told her. "What I should've known from my client. That being the case, I can't help but wonder what he wants now."

Josh remained silent for a time. "I read one of Leighton's articles," he said finally. "After the dinner we had in Lake George."

Emma shot him an uneasy look. "Daniel's

a relatively popular reporter," she said cautiously.

"I should confess that I did some research after our dinner about what you'd said. I know it sounds intrusive," he continued quickly. "But I was curious. I care."

Afraid to ask what the article was about, she started to walk again, and he fell in step. As the path widened toward the clearing, the dogs darted ahead and Josh swung an arm around Emma's shoulder. "There's no urgency calling him back, is there?"

"I don't think so."

"Then don't rush it. Take the time to decide what you think is best."

Suddenly, the dogs veered off the path. There was a distressed mew followed by the dogs' excited barking.

She and Josh rushed toward the sound and came upon a small fawn lying awkwardly on the ground. Emma pressed a hand over her mouth to keep from crying out. It was obvious that the fawn was injured. "What's wrong with her?" she asked in a strained voice.

Josh shook his head as he cautiously approached it. "I don't know. Take the dogs away with you, Emma, if you can."

All she could think of was the beautiful, injured elk that Josh had shot. She looked at the fawn, so defenseless and filled with terror, and froze. "You're—you're not going to…" Emma could feel the blood drain from her face.

Josh slanted a glance at her. "No, I'm not going to hurt her, Emma. The dogs' presence is doing more harm than anything I plan to do. Please take them back with you."

Emma was sure he hadn't intended to sound harsh, but his tone snapped her out of her paralysis. Inside the cottage, she tried to remain patient until she finally saw Josh emerge from the forest, carrying the fawn. Relief washed over her.

Leaving the dogs inside, she rushed out to meet him. She slowed her approach as she neared, not wanting to startle the fawn.

"How badly is she hurt?" she asked in a subdued voice.

"Probably a torn ligament."

"What are you going to do with her?" Emma knew the fawn wouldn't survive on her own in the forest.

"I'll examine and treat her, and then see if I can get her to an animal refuge." He made a sound of frustration. "I've been meaning to add on to the clinic to be able to accommodate wildlife, not just domestics. I'm not sure where to keep her, until I can get her to a reserve."

"How about here?" Emma asked.

They'd reached her cottage and he glanced around. "Where?"

She pointed to the stand-alone shed a couple of hundred feet away from her cottage. "I can fence off an area inside. She'll be safe in there. I can set up an outside enclosure for her, too."

"Emma, you can't save every wounded creature that comes your way," he said softly. "Let's get her checked over first. If I put her in the back of my truck, will you be able to ride with her, to keep her still? I don't want her injuring herself more on the drive to the clinic."

Emma nodded. "Of course. Let me lock up and I'll be right back."

She grabbed her keys, said goodbye to the dogs and rushed back out. Much as she did for Theo when they'd first found him, she opened the back of his truck and spread out the blanket he kept there, but then she hopped in first and he handed her the fawn.

At the clinic, she helped Josh get her inside.

A half an hour later, Josh emerged from the examination room and, to Emma's considerable relief, assured her that the fawn would be fine. Another hour passed by the time they'd settled the fawn, who Emma decided to name Daisy, in her newly constructed enclosure inside Emma's shed.

"Would you like to stay for dinner?" Emma asked when they entered the cottage.

"I was hoping you'd ask."

Emma pulled a bottle of chardonnay from the refrigerator and told Josh where to find the corkscrew and wineglasses.

He worked the cork loose, poured the wine and handed a glass to her.

Rummaging through the refrigerator, she pulled out ingredients. "How does orange chicken crepes sound?" Before he could respond, she added a bunch of asparagus spears to the ingredients she'd already set on the counter.

He raised a brow. "I wouldn't say no. How can I help?"

She glanced over her shoulder and smiled. "I have it covered. But thanks."

Josh perched on one of the stools at the center island and sipped his wine. "I never tire of watching you. Your movements are always efficient, but…graceful. You have, I don't know…a natural elegance."

It wasn't a compliment she'd heard before, but Josh wasn't an ordinary guy. It touched her, even as she became self-conscious of her movements. She laughed off her insecurity. "Thanks. Now I'll probably trip and fall, or drop the frying pan on my foot!"

"I doubt it," he said and took a drink, keeping his eyes on her as she prepared a marinade and placed the diced chicken in it. She sliced mushrooms, scraped a small amount of orange zest and mixed the batter for the crepes. She stir-fried the mix of chicken, mushrooms and marinade, while also preparing the crepes and asparagus spears.

As she was finishing, Josh set the table. When he returned for the bottle of wine and glasses, she already had the crepes and asparagus arranged on two serving platters and she followed him to the dining room.

They ate in the glow of the setting sun with the dogs contentedly snoozing at their feet. Josh topped off their glasses with the remainder of the wine.

Nudging her plate away, Emma took a deep breath. "I'm going to call the reporter back."

"Okay." He took her hand into his. "What made you decide?"

"I can't get my mind off it. It's better to know what he wants than to speculate and worry, isn't it?"

He squeezed her hand reassuringly. "When are you going to do it?"

Now that she'd made up her mind, she didn't want to procrastinate. She checked her watch. It was still early enough. "No time like the present. After we finish up here, if you don't mind. At least that way I'm unlikely to lose my nerve."

"Is it okay if I stay?"

She turned her hand palm up and linked her fingers with his. She understood and appreciated the support, and it fortified her more than she would have expected. The fact that she didn't have to *ask* made it all that much more meaningful.

They cleaned up together and he made them each a cup of her favored Earl Grey tea before she went to her office to make the call.

The line rang several times without going to voice mail. She was just about to hang up when Daniel answered.

"This is Emma Meadows returning your call."

"Emma, thanks for getting back to me. Sorry for being out of breath. I just finished a workout."

"No problem. You said there was something important you had to tell me."

"By the tone of your voice, I get the impression you're still not keeping up with the New York papers."

Emma felt a trickle of dread. "No." Her voice wavered slightly. "Why?"

"First off, we've got Morgan on the kickbacks, but the prosecution wants to charge the senator with criminal negligence."

"Beyond being glad he's being held accountable, why should I care?"

"Let me finish. The charges would be criminal negligence *causing death*."

"Death?" The trickle intensified. "I don't understand. The senator might be unscrupulous but you're suggesting he did physical harm?"

"The charge would be in relation to the recent death of a young soldier. Although I sincerely hope I'm wrong, more incidents might follow."

Death? Emma tried to put the pieces together in her mind but they just wouldn't fit. "While the senator's greed is deplorable, how can he be responsible for a soldier's death?"

"The defense contract he forced through had certain service-level stipulations, including specific delivery dates. If the dates were not met, significant financial penalties would apply. The first three of those dates had already come and gone, and the rifles had been delivered to Kabul before the scandal broke.

"But the deadlines were too tight for a company the size of American Freedom Munitions, and the rifles that have been distributed to the soldiers had not been properly manufactured and tested. They might have a significant material defect that can result in failure."

Emma placed a hand over her mouth.

"Private First Class Benjamin Laurence was only twenty-one and eager to serve his country. He was deployed to Afghanistan a couple of months ago for his first tour of duty. He never saw action. The first shot he took in training with his new rifle caused the chamber to explode. The shrapnel killed him instantly.

"At first the military thought it was misadventure—an unfortunate accident associated with that specific rifle. Upon further investigation, they determined that it was a material defect that could affect more rifles in the shipment. The nature of the flaw, the way I understand it, is that in the case of Private Laurence, the failure happened upon initial discharge, but that won't be the case with all the defective rifles. It could occur upon initial discharge or after considerable use. Our soldiers could be walking around with time bombs in their hands. That means other men and women are at risk—not from the enemy, but from the greed of their own countrymen."

"But if that's the case, surely the rifles have been recalled."

"They have been, yes. The military has also

put a hold on further shipments, but the logistics associated with getting all the rifles back is complex."

"I can't believe this could happen. Isn't there more that they can do?"

"With the death of a soldier, the military is all over this. They're conducting a full investigation. The key players at AFM and Morgan have already been charged with respect to influencing the award of contract. But if what I suspect is true, that they were aware of the faulty manufacturing, they must be held accountable for that, as well. Especially Morgan. To date, the fatality hasn't been linked to him yet, other than through an article I wrote."

Emma wondered if that was the article Josh had seen. But how could Daniel know more than the military, if they were doing a full investigation? She was beginning to wonder if he was just on a vendetta against the senator. "Daniel, I'm having a hard time accepting what you're suggesting."

"Look—" His voice had taken on a sharp edge. "I'm convinced it was more than negligence. That Morgan and the AFM executives knew about the defects and the potential consequences. My editor gave me some latitude with my last article because I had been right about Morgan's role in influencing the award of contract. And because I was careful not to make specific accusations. Even so, it's caused some backlash, but I had to get the matter out into the open."

"But if you can't prove that Morgan was aware of the manufacturing issue, it's supposition…"

"I can't prove it, *yet*. But the prosecutor assigned to the case agrees that I'm on to something. However, we need something concrete for the criminal negligence charges to be laid, and then be able to back it up in a court of law. That's why I'm asking for your help."

"The loss of Private Laurence's life is very tragic, but even if I accept everything you're saying, I'm sorry, but I have no knowledge of any of this. I don't see how I can help."

"Listen, Emma. The outcome of all this should no longer be a bit of embarrassment for the senator and a slap on his wrist for the public record because of the wrongdoing related to the award of contract. Not only should he never be considered for the presidency, he should go to jail for a long time, along with the chairman, and the CEO of AFM, both of whom should also be charged. I have no doubt Morgan is complicit. I believe all three of them knew precisely what they were doing and were aware of the consequences."

"If you're right about this, it's horrific. As I said, I don't know what I could do to assist."

"You spent time in Morgan's office. You were in his inner circle. You might have some knowledge that could connect the dots for us with Morgan and the faulty rifles. Or at least point us in the right direction. I'm appealing to you, Emma. You have to try."

There was a long pause, as she mulled over what she'd heard. "You might have seen me as being in Morgan's 'inner circle,' as you put it, but I learned the hard way that Morgan had never taken me into his confidence. I'm really not sure there's anything I can do, but I'll think about it."

"I appreciate it, Emma, but please don't take too long."

JOSH HAD GONE out to check on the fawn while Emma was on the phone. Now he was on the sofa in the great room, waiting. When he glanced up and saw Emma, he immediately noticed how pale she was. He rose and went to her.

Up close, he also saw the redness of her eyes and tension in her features. He enfolded her in his arms. "Tell me," he said simply.

She shared with him what she'd learned, most of which was no great surprise to him, since he'd read Leighton's article about the incident. As he'd suspected, she'd had no prior knowledge of the death of the solider. The guilt ate at him that he hadn't tried to talk her out of calling the reporter to shield her. Then again, what he knew about her—and one of the many things he admired—was that she wouldn't want to be shielded. She'd want to know.

They sat together long after they'd finished discussing the matter. Once or twice he'd suspected she might have fallen asleep, but when he moved to check, she stirred, and he knew she was turning things over in her mind. Shortly before ten, they took the dogs for a long walk, before he finally said good-night.

At his home, Josh hung his keys on the hook by the door and pulled a dog biscuit out of his pocket for Winston.

He didn't like what he'd heard about the Morgan situation from Emma. He might have been a small-town boy at heart, but he knew enough to understand that things could easily get out of hand under such circumstances. He decided it was time he had a beer with his friend Chad Atkins. It wouldn't hurt to let the sheriff know what Emma had been involved in and what the reporter from New York suspected.

Josh was shrugging out of his jacket when the phone started to ring. Thinking it was Emma, he grabbed it.

"Josh, I miss you so much..." He couldn't mistake the whiny, high-pitched voice. Damn, why hadn't he taken the time to check the call display. He couldn't hold back the sigh. "What do you want, Crystal?"

"You, baby. Just you. I need to see you."

"Crystal, we've been through this." Countless times. "I'm sorry you're having a hard time, but you *have* to accept it's over between us."

"Come on, Joshy. You can't mean that."

"Yeah. I do mean it." His patience was wearing thin. He and Crystal had only dated a few months, and he'd never pretended it was anything more than casual. When he'd started to see her true nature, he'd ended it as quickly and considerately as he could. But she'd convinced herself there had been more to their relationship than there had been, and the lady didn't like not being the one to call things off. "And I would appreciate it if you would stop playing your little games," he added, thinking of how much time and effort it had taken him to clean up the graffiti she'd left for him on the side of his garage.

"What games?" She drew out the words, made her voice sound almost childlike.

Josh rolled his eyes heavenward. "Oh, let's see. Vandalizing my truck. Damaging my property. Painting obscenities on my garage—"

"Okay. I'm sorry. All right? I just couldn't bear the thought of losing you." Now she sounded pouty. "I went a little crazy."

That was an understatement. "Fine. Apology accepted." Then he remembered the car that had driven in and out of his driveway one of the days Emma had visited, and wondered again if that glimpse of red had been Crystal's car. If it was, he didn't want her causing problems for Emma. "The day Emma was here—"

"Who?" The word exploded from her. "Who's Emma?" she demanded.

"The blonde who was here the day you came—"

"Are you seeing someone else?" she shrieked. Josh's head began to pound.

"Calm down, Crystal. She's just—"

"Who is she?"

"Crystal, please don't get worked up. The point is—"

"If you're seeing someone, she should worry!"

After calling him several choice words, she hung up.

Josh tossed the phone down and rubbed his hands over his face. He'd messed that up big-time. He knew Crystal was an accomplished liar, but her reaction suggested she hadn't known about Emma. And now—thanks to him—she undeniably did.

"Great. Just great." Now he had a whole new issue on his hands with Crystal. And he hoped it wouldn't become one for Emma, too.

CHAPTER ELEVEN

JOSH ENDED UP grabbing that beer with Chad
Atkins sooner than he'd expected. Chad had
Thursday off and they met at The Lookout,
the small waterfront restaurant in downtown
Sanctuary Cove, shortly after Josh's last pa-
tient for the day.

The patio had closed for the season a couple of months ago, so they sat inside by the
floor-to-ceiling window. Chad was dressed
in jeans and a sweater, an outfit Josh didn't
see him in often enough these days, as he was
mostly in uniform. Even without the inch or so
added by the cowboy boots he wore, he was a
tall man, nearly the same height as Josh. But
that was where the resemblance ended. Chad
had sandy-blond hair, blue eyes and a stockier
build. It was one of the reasons Chad had been
defensive tackle and Josh a quarterback.

Chad leaned back in the chair, stretched his
long legs out and crossed his feet. "We don't
do this nearly enough, if you ask me."

"And whose fault is that?" Josh retorted

good-naturedly. "You're the one with the seventy-hours-on-average work week."

"Perhaps, but I hear you might not have as much spare time these days as you once did," he joked with a cocky grin, before lifting his beer bottle and taking a long swig.

"And where did you hear that?"

"C'mon, Whitmore. I'm the sheriff around here. Do you really expect me not to know what's going on in our small town?"

"I didn't realize it was part of the job description to keep track of my personal life."

Chad arched an eyebrow. "It must be serious if you're this sensitive about it. And, no, it's not part of the job description as the sheriff, but it is as your best friend."

Josh took a drink of his own beer and shook his head. "Yeah, I've got it bad for her. I've never felt this way about anyone else I've dated."

"She must be a special woman. I look forward to meeting her."

"Hopefully you'll get to meet her soon, and not in an official capacity."

That had Chad sitting up straight. "What are you saying? Has she had more trouble with hunters trespassing on her property? I've been told we've gotten a couple of calls from her about it."

"She has had trouble with hunters, but that's not what I'm referring to." Josh told Chad as much as he thought he needed to know about Morgan, the reporter and Emma's ex.

Chad let out a short whistle. "I've read about some of it. Morgan has serious political clout. Thanks for telling me."

"Do you think she's in danger?" Josh felt his insides turn at the thought.

"No. No, I don't. But I'd rather know and keep an eye out, just to be on the safe side."

Josh relaxed, as that's exactly what he had hoped for. "Thanks for that."

"By the way, since we're speaking of your private life, is that woman you dated a few months back still upset with you?"

"Crystal? To be honest, she hasn't given up entirely yet."

Chad shook his head. "I knew she was trouble from the get-go."

"You did say that. I wish I would have listened. And since I don't have the highly refined investigative skills you do, I must ask, are you seeing anyone?"

Chad's response was a loud crack of laughter. "You should know better than that! Who'd put up with me, my job and the hours you yourself noted I work."

EMMA AND JOSH discussed Emma's upcoming meeting with Daniel Leighton at some length. Although Josh didn't like it—and it warmed Emma's heart that it was out of concern for her—he seemed to understand that she needed to become involved again.

The morning of the meeting dawned dull and gray with the low-hanging clouds heavily pregnant with either rain or snow, depending on which way the thermometer settled. Emma showered, dressed and was on her way downstairs when the dogs alerted her that there was someone at the door before the knock sounded.

When she swung the door open, she was surprised to see Josh there. "What are you doing here? Don't you have appointments at the clinic?"

"I asked Sherri to push them back. I wanted to see you before you left."

She felt the flutter in her belly at his words...because of his caring. "I'll be fine," she assured him.

"I know because I have all the faith in the world in you." He stroked a finger gently under her lower lids. "But your eyes tell a different story. They're hollow and shadowed."

When she was about to protest, he slipped his arms around her. "I never realized I could feel so protective of someone outside my family…or an injured animal," he murmured into her hair. "Let me go with you."

"We discussed this last night." She'd been adamant about it. "It's something I have to do on my own."

He placed a kiss on her forehead. "I thought I'd try one more time."

"I appreciate the offer." She stepped away from him and placed a soft, cool palm on his cheek. "We both know it's for me to do."

"Emma…"

"No, Josh. I can't—won't—bring you into this."

He gently grasped her shoulders. "Too late. I already am."

She sighed and let him fold her into his arms again.

"I'll be here, waiting."

"Thank you for understanding." She spoke so softly, she wasn't sure if he'd heard her. "It makes the burden lighter."

Emma took comfort in that thought as she drove to meet Daniel. She pulled into the parking lot of the diner off Interstate 87, where she and Daniel had arranged to meet. She was there well before ten, the appointed time. She parked, turned off the engine and sat motionless for long minutes, trying to steady her nerves.

She had to acknowledge that her anxiety wasn't just about the meeting with Daniel. The situation was bringing back all the bad memories of what she'd already lived through.

Checking her watch, she took a deep breath. *Showtime*, she thought, and bolstered herself with the knowledge that, if at the end of their meeting, she asked Daniel not to contact her again, she believed he'd honor her request.

As she walked in, she noticed that Daniel had arrived early, too. He sat in a corner booth, removed from where most of the patrons were seated, but with a clear view of the entrance. One glance at him reminded her that he was relatively young for his position and the considerable influence he held. With his slim build and medium height, smooth skin, tousled blond hair and sparkling blue eyes, he looked even younger than his years. She knew that his clean-shaven, boy-next-door good looks masked a keen intelligence, a relentless tenacity, a sharp wit and—surprising to those who didn't know him—a strong moral fiber and sense of fair play. She was trusting in the latter.

She noted he was nursing a cup of coffee, which had probably gone cold. There was no notepad or recorder on the table. Emma surmised that he wanted to put her at ease as much as he was able.

She walked toward him and he rose. She offered him a ghost of a smile as she proffered her hand in greeting.

"Thank you for agreeing to meet, Emma."

"I didn't see I had much choice," she responded as she slid onto the bench seat opposite him. "I'm sorry. I didn't mean to be rude."

"It's okay. What would you like?" he asked as the waitress approached. "Coffee? Something to eat?"

"A coffee would be fine. Thanks."

He ordered a pot. When they both had mugs full of coffee, he began.

"Emma, let me say again how sorry I am to intrude on you. I can fully appreciate your reluctance, and why you'd want to forget about all this."

A sardonic smile flitted across her face as she glanced down at her coffee. "That was the plan."

"The stakes have increased substantially with Private Laurence's death."

She didn't blink. She kept her eyes steady on his, but various emotions—sympathy and outrage—were swirling within her at the mention of the young soldier.

"All the kid wanted to do was make a difference. According to his family, he wasn't afraid of dying, if it meant that others could live in peace and freedom." Daniel topped up their coffees but left his untouched on the table. "The kid never saw action. His chance to make a difference was denied him. How can his family accept that this brave and selfless young man died in vain, and because of the greed of a handful of powerful individuals?"

"What do you expect from me?" Her voice was strained, as she struggled to keep it together. "You already have your story. You know more than I ever did. I can't see how I can help."

"For me it's gone beyond the story." He leaned forward. "I have a younger brother who serves. He's not in Afghanistan. But what's happening there with AFM and those rifles could happen anywhere. I don't want another soldier to die like that. I don't want it to be my kid brother. The truth should be out in the open. Then, perhaps, Private Laurence's family can find, if not comfort, at least closure. And the private's death will have, in an indirect way, saved other lives." Daniel's voice hardened and he frowned. "Morgan and the executives at AFM should be held accountable. I'm convinced they knew the rifles were defective. Charges will be brought against the AFM executives, but it's only right that if Morgan knew, he's charged and has to face a trial, and a jury of his peers. He and others like him shouldn't think they're above the law."

Emma shook her head and lowered her gaze. "This is all very disturbing, but I still don't understand what I can do. I wasn't aware of any of this when I worked for Morgan."

"I don't know if you'll be able to help or not, but I can't leave any stone unturned. You had access to documents when you worked for Morgan that I don't. You might have information or have seen things that could help us prove the connection. Prove Morgan *knew* the shipment was rushed and the rifles might have been unsafe. We need that proof."

Daniel placed a hand on her wrist to still her fidgeting. His touch drew her gaze back up to his. "As to why you should do it? You didn't deserve to lose everything...including your fiancé."

Emma jolted at being reminded of what had caused her the most pain.

"It had to do with your sense of right and wrong," Daniel continued. "I don't see how someone with such a strong moral compass can put this behind her, knowing now what's at stake."

She stared out the window. "I wish I'd never been involved to begin with. As I can't change the past..." Her voice trailed off. At length, she glanced back at Daniel. "Even if I might have come across information that could help you, I didn't hold onto much when I left. I took my personal notes, which I had a right to keep. But I'm still bound by the confidentiality provisions of my employment agreement and the contract with Morgan's office. If I did have any information that could be useful, I might not be at liberty to disclose it. Unless I'm legally compelled to do so."

Daniel nodded. "I sought a legal opinion from one of the *Advocate*'s lawyers. We expect there are some caveats and exclusions, such as you said, if required by law, if it relates to unlawful activities, if it's in violation of a morals clause that might have been included in the agreement, or if the information has already made its way into the public domain through other means. What would help us would likely be covered by one of the exemptions. I could have one of our lawyers review your contracts and offer an opinion."

Emma narrowed her eyes. What he said made sense, but if it came to that, she didn't think she'd rely on a lawyer working for the paper.

"Or, to satisfy yourself of the independence of the opinion," Daniel continued, as if he'd read her thoughts. "If you would prefer to use your own lawyer, the *Advocate* will reimburse you for your expense."

"I appreciate the offer. I'll consider it."

"You should also know Private Laurence's body has been repatriated. There's a funeral planned for next Thursday."

A short while later, they walked out together. Shaking hands, they said goodbye.

Emma promised to think things through and get back to Daniel. It was the most she could give him for now, but she suspected there was only one decision she could ultimately come to. She didn't see how it would be possible, but Daniel seemed to believe that she might be able to provide the missing piece to the puzzle. As she pulled out of the parking lot, she noticed in her rearview mirror a dark sedan following her. She kept an eye on it until it slowed and took a right turn a few blocks away from the diner.

She hissed out a breath. She hadn't even agreed yet to try to help Daniel, and she was already jumpy and imagining things.

CHAPTER TWELVE

EMMA FELT AS if a jackhammer was in full throttle at the base of her head as she merged onto the highway. She called Josh on his cell phone to let him know she was on her way and would discuss her meeting with Daniel with him when she got home. The drive passed quickly. As she parked in front of her cottage, she'd already resolved what she had to do for her own peace of mind.

She and Josh spent a quiet evening together, taking the dogs for a walk and checking on the progress of the fawn.

The next morning, Emma advised Daniel of her decision.

The following day, a large box of files arrived at the cottage by special delivery. Daniel provided Emma with copies of all his research notes and other relevant information he had been able to gather, for her to go through to see if anything jumped out at her that might be useful to their cause.

Emma sat cross-legged on the carpet in

front of the fireplace in the great room with the files Daniel sent spread out in front of her. Next to her were two legal pads—one blank, and the other with her own personal notes from her previous work with Senator Morgan. She tried to decide where to start and what to look for, when Theo gave a friendly woof and scrambled to his feet to run to the front door. Max, lying on the floor close to Emma, opened one eye before deciding sleep was more important than greeting whoever had arrived. When Emma opened the door, Sherri stood on the porch, a large cloth tote in one hand. She gave Emma a one-armed hug.

"Aren't you supposed to be working today?" Emma asked.

"Hey, I'm entitled to a day off now and then."

Emma stepped back and let her friend in, but gave her a skeptical look. She knew how much Josh relied on Sherri.

"Okay, the truth is, my mother and I were scheduled to have a spa day today, but she had an emergency at work and couldn't take the day off. Since Josh had already arranged for Jenny—the girl who fills in for me when I'm off—to cover for me, I thought I'd take the day anyway and do the next best thing to having a spa day with my mom. I brought what we need," she said, hoisting the tote. "You and I are going to have a spa day right here! What's all this?" she asked, gesturing to the files on the floor as they walked into the great room.

"It's a long story," Emma said as she gathered the folders into a pile and placed them on a side table.

Sherri eyed the stack of folders. "If I'm disturbing you, just say so and I'll go."

"Oh, no. I'm glad you're here." Emma checked her watch. "I had to stop anyway to feed Daisy."

Sherri placed her tote on the table and rubbed both dogs. "Who's Daisy?"

"Didn't Josh tell you about her?"

"No."

"Come with me and I'll introduce you. It's her feeding time."

Emma filled a baby bottle with the milk mixture she'd prepared from the recipe Josh had given her, and led Sherri out to the shed. Letting Daisy into the outside enclosure, she observed happily that she was moving much better and no longer seemed lame.

"You have a fawn?" Sherri asked in surprise.

"For now." Emma crouched down and held the bottle out for Daisy. She walked over cautiously, but then eagerly accepted her meal.

"You really do have a soft spot for animals, don't you?" Sherri observed and squatted down beside Emma. "You know, Josh and I have talked about setting up some sort of facility to be able to accommodate injured wildlife." She glanced over to the shed and around the temporary fenced area that Emma had erected with Josh's help. "This sort of setup is ideal."

"Then why hasn't he done it? He's got the space at his property."

"We always have domestic animals coming, going and staying at the clinic. Josh is concerned about the impact all those animals and associated noise would have on wildlife. If the goal is to release them back into the wilderness once they're healed, having them become too comfortable with domesticated animals—and, for that matter, people—could be problematic. Max and Theo don't bother with the fawn, when she's outside in the pen?"

Since Daisy finished her bottle, Emma rose. "No. They showed some interest when they first saw her in the enclosure, but not much since." Daisy bent her head and tested some of the grass. "She's cautious around them, which is a good thing. The plan is to release her once she can fend for herself, and I don't want her to consider wolves as playmates."

Sherri wandered over to the shed and stepped inside. "What do you use this space for normally?"

"I use it mostly for gardening tools and equipment. The canoe and kayak are in there over the winter months. I don't park my vehicle inside, which is what it was built for by the original owners."

"Hmm. Josh would need inside pens and a more securely fenced outside area to accommodate multiple patients. I'll have to speak to him about it again."

The rest of the afternoon passed with pampering and girl talk, something that Emma wasn't accustomed to, but found she enjoyed with Sherri.

After Sherri left, Emma felt relaxed and mellow, and she had to admit that her skin had a nice glow from the facial.

She had a light dinner, then checked on Daisy, and inspected the shed with a more critical eye. It was spacious and open, with lots of natural light flooding in through the large windows at either end. She had no idea how often Josh had to deal with injured wildlife, but if he needed someplace to keep them—and someone to look after them—she suspected it would be fairly easy to convert the space.

In the evening, Emma resumed her review of the files. A soldier was dead, and she had to see what she could do to make sure that if Morgan had knowledge of the issue with the rifles, he would be held accountable.

How could he live with himself, she wondered, if he *had* known?

Emma turned to the next page and sighed. Some aspects of the information were harder to grasp than others. The file she was reviewing was technical in nature. It included the results of the independent testing of a sample of the rifles. She didn't understand all the details related to the properties of the metals, weld thicknesses or the manufacturing process.

Absently, she rubbed at the stiffness at the base of her neck and flipped to another page. With some relief, she noted it was the final page of the report commissioned by American Freedom Munitions. She scanned the remaining technical information but reviewed the conclusions section more carefully. She knew that when the military had commissioned additional tests, and that they were conclusive. There was an inherent problem with the rifles that could result in catastrophic failure upon discharge. The two sets of test results—those done by the military and those conducted by AFM before the shipments were released—were contradictory. Did that mean that not all the rifles were flawed, or could the AFM tests have been wrong or falsified? At least the military was, naturally, taking matters very seriously and were doing everything they could to get all the rifles back. Certainly no others from AFM were being issued to soldiers.

And if Morgan knew about the problems with the rifles before they were shipped, how could they prove it? Her gaze dropped to the date below the signatory line on the final page of the report. She squeezed her eyes shut in horror at the realization that the tests had been completed nearly a month before the first shipment of rifles left for Kabul. Had they known?

If they had known, *had* the test results been falsified, and the rifles still shipped?

She turned back to the front of the AFM report. It was authored by Grant Stewart, a materials engineer who'd been retained to undertake the testing. The transmittal letter indicated it had been provided to Jack Hughes, the CEO of AFM.

Daniel had suggested that the chair of the board of AFM, Chuck Innes, and Hughes were both aware of the flaws, which made sense. But what about Morgan? Would Morgan have known as well? Daniel seemed to think so. To her, it wasn't a given.

The contract was awarded to AFM. Morgan was paid for his involvement in making it happen. Why wouldn't it have stopped there? Could Innes or Hughes let Morgan know that they were having trouble? Maybe they asked for more time, and Morgan wouldn't allow it?

Emma reread the summary of findings. When she got to the end once more, she focused on the name of the engineer typed below the large, scribbled signature. Grant Stewart.

She stared at the name a few moments longer, but it didn't jog any memories. With a shake of her head, she closed the file and rose from her chair, taking her empty mug with her and placing it in the dishwasher.

She'd known AFM had tested the rifles. Senator Morgan had gone on at some length to tell her and Richard about it when they'd first been retained. He'd given her a copy of the test results, in case the media asked any questions. As she thought back to the conversation, Morgan had encouraged her to provide copies to the media if she considered it in his best interest. In hindsight, she questioned why he would've been so insistent about her having the report. He'd shown no reservations about the test report making its way into the public domain.

It *was* in the public domain already, he had assured her. As such, she hadn't needed to return her copy to Morgan's office when she'd terminated her contract. Her boss at Tyson, Myers and Smith had been so furious with her when he couldn't talk her out of dropping Morgan as a client, he'd fired her in such haste, the company never bothered to get the documents she had at her home office back.

She searched her memory. Did she keep the copy or did Richard have it? She hurried into her office and rummaged through her old files.

Before she had a chance to determine if she had it or not, the dogs alerted her once more that someone had arrived. She dropped the file on the coffee table on her way to the door.

This time, it was Josh…holding a bakery box from Chadwick's, Winston by his side.

Emma accepted the box from him. The scent of fresh pastries made her mouth water. "They smell delicious." With her free hand on his chest, she rose up on her tiptoes and brushed her lips across his. "Thank you."

He leaned in and sniffed playfully at her neck. "Mmm, you smell nice. Not that you don't always, but this is something different."

He ran a finger along her cheek. "Smooth. Again, not that that's not usually the case, but there's something extra today."

Emma chuckled. "You can thank Sherri."

"Sherri? I thought she had a spa date with her mother."

"She did. When that fell through, she brought the spa to me." She led him into the kitchen, where she arranged the pastries on a plate. She snagged a chocolate éclair and held the plate out to him. "Would you like one?"

"No. I'm fine. Thanks. I had an early dinner after my last appointment. Other than the spa treatment, how was your day?"

She placed the plate on the counter and covered it. "I got the files from Daniel today," she responded.

Josh followed her into the great room. "I can see that. Your rug is barely visible under all of it. Have you found anything?"

She shook her head as she swallowed a bite of the pastry. "Mmm. This is delicious. As for the files, I'm just getting started."

"Can I help? With the files?"

She shrugged. "I appreciate the offer, but I'm not sure what I'm looking for, so I don't know what you could do."

"A fresh pair of eyes might do some good."

"It's worth a try," she said as she brushed

the crumbs off her fingers with a napkin. She settled cross-legged in the midst of all the files. Smiling up at him, she handed him a folder, while placing another on her lap. "Good point. Personally, I'm going to work through the files chronologically. See if anything jumps out at me."

"Sounds like a plan." With the file folder in his hand, he opted for comfort and sprawled on the sofa.

Josh paged through, looking more for impressions or something out of the ordinary. He paused to stretch, then turned to a series of photographs that he surmised had been taken by a high-powered zoom lens from a considerable distance. He recognized Senator Morgan immediately, as well as Mark Lemus, his aide, from the various media segments he'd seen.

He leafed through the pictures once, then started over. On closer scrutiny, he recognized several other leading political and business figures as well. There were a series of pictures that appeared to have been taken at someone's summer home on a lake. The senator and his aide were featured prominently in the photos, both dressed casually in khakis and golf shirts. One shot showed a group of people on a large deck leading to a dock with an impressive boat tethered to it. The senator stood on the bow with his aide and another man. The senator was smiling broadly, a drink in one hand and his other on the back of the diminutive gentleman beside him, giving the impression that the photographer captured him in action as he was jovially slapping his companion on the back. Josh scanned the other faces in the picture, some distinct, others blurry due to their distance from the camera's focal point.

When nothing struck him as being of relevance, his gaze shifted to examine the boat. Having a personal fondness for fast boats, he appreciated its graceful styling and what he knew would be a powerful engine. Inspecting the picture more closely, it looked to him that the boat had been customized, probably at considerable expense. As he gave the boat one final appreciative glance and was about to flip to the next photo, something caught his eye. He focused on the boat again. Its cabin, to be precise.

He could distinguish two men standing by the window inside the cabin, one taller and heavier set than the other. They both held drinks in their hands and, based on their posture—tense and leaning in toward each other—they appeared to be in deep conversation.

Josh's eyes narrowed as he examined the

image of the two men. He couldn't put his finger on it, but he thought he recognized the taller man.

At Emma's sigh, he glanced down at her. She'd placed the file she'd been reviewing on the floor and was rubbing her temples with her fingertips. He knew the frustration of not finding anything helpful despite the hours invested was taking its toll on her. He set aside the file with the photos and rose.

Lowering himself down behind her, he started to massage the knotted muscles of her shoulders.

"That feels wonderful," she murmured. She closed her eyes, as he continued kneading her tense muscles.

"It seems it might be long overdue."

"Better late than never." She rolled her shoulders. "I can almost feel the stiffness melting away."

As he started to work on the base of her neck, she let her head drop forward, giving him better access.

"Mmm, my headache's nearly gone, too." She twisted to look at him. "That was nice. Thank you."

He brushed his thumb under her eyes. "You look tired."

"I haven't been sleeping well, knowing what

happened and being unable to do anything about it."

"You're trying. That's all anyone can ask."

"I suppose," she said, but she didn't sound convincing.

They decided to call it a night and took the dogs out for their evening walk. A myriad of brilliant stars twinkled overhead and the moon was nearly full, guiding their path along the driveway. On their way back, Emma paused on top of the large granite boulder that afforded a panoramic view of the forest, cottage and lake. Josh wrapped his arms around Emma from behind, and she leaned back against him. Gazing out over the water, she asked, "Have you ever had a place that just felt right to you—calming, comfortable?"

He glanced down at her. "In your arms?"

She laughed. "Thanks, but I'm serious. You know, a place where you could sit and think, and feel all was right with the world?"

He smiled as he considered. "I suppose the closest thing would've been the tree fort I built in my family's backyard as a kid. When the weight of the world was on my skinny eight-year-old shoulders, I would climb into the tree fort, read my comic books, play with the games I had hidden there, or simply sit with my feet dangling over the edge and look out over our backyard. Whatever had been bothering me—my parents grounding me for some transgression, a kid at school bullying me, whatever—would simply melt away. Is that the sort of place you mean?"

"Yeah. That's exactly it. I was just thinking that this place, this rock under us, is that type of place for me. Since I've owned the cottage, whether I have something on my mind that I need to work through or I'm happy, this is where I like to sit and deal with it. I find it impossible to look over the field, the gardens, the cottage and the lake, and be in a bad mood. If there's nothing specific on my mind, I can just as easily sit here and let my mind wander, absorb the beauty around me."

Josh glanced toward the forest line, readily visible in the silvery glow of the moon. "It's amazing to think some of those trees have been around a hundred years or more."

"It is. I own the cottage and the property, but I look at these trees and the concept of ownership just doesn't make sense. Many were here long before I was born and most will be here long after I'm gone."

He gathered her close to him as they made their way back to the cottage.

That night, with her thoughts on Josh, she had no trouble drifting into sleep.

In the morning, she dressed for comfort in a pair of black leggings, thick wool socks and an oversize white shirt. She spent the morning on an assignment. This time it wasn't for Pinnacle Communications—the assignments from them were dwindling, which concerned her greatly. This one was from Arlene Greenberg's company. With Josh's encouragement, she was giving freelancing for Elite Consulting a shot. She was glad to have the income opportunity but was nervous about proving herself. She wanted to do a good job for Arlene, and she wanted to complete the assignment ahead of schedule. When she finished, she'd get back to Daniel's files.

Midmorning, the telephone rang and she considered not answering as she didn't want to interrupt the flow of what she was doing but ended up reaching for the receiver.

"What do you think you're doing?" The voice on the phone was harsh and accusatory. The caller needed no introduction, though. It was Richard. While Emma's heart rate spiked and her palms turned clammy, she forced a tone of cool nonchalance.

"Richard, we don't have anything to discuss. Did you misdial?"

Her sarcastic response, no doubt unexpected,

fueled his ire. "Don't joke around, Emma," he said, his voice raised.

She held the phone away from her ear for a moment and took three long, calming breaths before responding. She would *not* let Richard know the effect he was having on her. "If you're going to yell at me, I'll hang up."

Richard's anger flared, and a series of abrasive words spewed forth.

"Richard. I'm hanging up."

"Okay. Wait..." He continued in a more controlled voice. "I'm calling because we're aware you're working with Leighton from the *Advocate*."

How would he know that? She took another deep breath and switched the phone to her other ear. She wouldn't let him intimidate her despite all her insecurities rearing up. She wouldn't admit anything to Richard, but she wondered if, instead, she would be able to get some information that might be helpful for Daniel. Thinking quickly, she turned on a small tape recorder that she had on her desk for capturing her creative ideas for her assignments. "What makes you say that?"

"Don't play games." The anger simmered in his voice, but she could tell he was trying to curb it. "We know you met with Leighton."

Who was he referring to by *we*? He and

Morgan? "Why would it have anything to do with Morgan?"

"Don't be obtuse."

Emma squeezed her eyes shut. Richard's caustic words could still cut her to the bone.

"We know you have his files," he continued.

How was that possible? The person watching Daniel? She felt an adrenaline rush. Was she being watched, too?

"But that's not the point," Richard continued. "The point is you're still bound by the confidentiality provisions of the agreement you signed. If you breach the agreement, we *will* take legal action." He paused. She could hear his ragged breathing. "I *will* go after you, Emma. Don't delude yourself. What we had together won't shield you. You have no idea what you're getting involved in. You sacrificed our relationship and your job because you didn't want to be involved. Stay uninvolved."

Is *that* how he remembered it? That *she* was the one to walk away from him and her job? The bitterness she felt surprised her, but she had no doubt he meant what he said about taking action against her. Thinking of the brunette she'd seen him with that last night in NYC, she wanted to ask what exactly they'd had together, but caught herself. "Trust me, Richard. I wouldn't expect 'our time together'

to influence you in any way." Having brought
to mind what they'd once shared, when she'd
seen some decency in him, Emma decided to
challenge him. "Richard, how can *you* stay involved? If the ethics don't concern you, what
about the loss of a soldier's life? You must
know about that, since it's been in the papers."

She could hear his breathing again and the
sound of a glass being slapped down on wood.

"You don't know what you're talking about,
Emma. You wanted out? *Stay* out. If you don't,
I'll be the least of your worries."

She felt her own annoyance mount, and
glanced at her recorder to make sure it was
still capturing their discussion. "Is that a
threat, Richard?"

"Stay out of it, Emma," he repeated before
the line went dead. She placed the receiver
back in its cradle with exaggerated care before shutting off the recorder, her hands not
quite steady.

CHAPTER THIRTEEN

Josh paced Emma's office that evening as he listened to the recording of Emma's telephone conversation with her ex. He didn't like what he was hearing. The threat was loud and clear. Josh tended to take most things in stride, but he had fury in him over the ex-fiancé's treatment of Emma. Richard had caused enough harm to her in the past, and he obviously could still affect her. Emma seemed meeker than he'd seen her in a while. Her ex had no right to treat her the way he had.

After Emma switched off the recorder, Josh pulled a chair up close to face her. Taking her hands into his, he felt the chilled dampness of her palms. "I'm tempted to say ignore him, because it's you I'm worried about, Emma. Morgan will already be facing the consequences for the wrongdoing and the company executives will, no doubt, be held accountable for the defective rifles. Maybe that's enough."

She glanced down at their joined hands. "I'm grateful for your concern...and support.

But I made a commitment and I need to follow through." She lifted her gaze to his. "If it was only about money, I'd probably stop." Her voice softened. "But it's not. It's about the soldier who lost his life. As for Richard..." She sucked in a huge gulp of air. "He's pushed me around enough. I'm not going to let him do it again."

Josh searched her face, the depth of her stormy gray eyes and knew there was nothing he could or should say to deter her. He was proud of her for taking a stand against her ex. Isn't that what he'd been hoping to help her do? Get back her self-confidence and strength?

He drew her toward him and kissed her. There was no gentleness in the kiss this time, borne of the frustration and anger he felt over all that she'd had to endure.

JOSH ACCOMPANIED EMMA to Private Laurence's funeral. Emma wore a simple black dress with a black coat over it. Her hair was pulled back into a ponytail. Josh was also dressed in black out of respect for the deceased. They arrived a half an hour before the service was scheduled to begin and took seats at the back of the church.

By the time the service started, the church

was filled to capacity, and the crowd overflowed to the parking lot. The media remained respectfully outside.

It was obvious that Private Laurence was well liked and respected. And, of course, the military turned out in full force. A good portion of those present were in uniform. There were many moving eulogies, but none more poignant than the one delivered by the soldier's father. Mr. Laurence spoke haltingly, pausing often to dab at his eyes with a handkerchief. He talked about a young man who was the light of his and his wife's lives. A selfless young man who would do anything for a friend, a stranger or the country he loved so much.

Mr. Laurence was perhaps in his mid-fifties, but his grief made him look considerably older than his years. He had to be escorted off the podium when he ultimately fell apart.

By the conclusion of the service, Emma's cheeks were moist, like everyone else's. "He was so young," she murmured to Josh. "He didn't deserve what happened to him."

They filed out of the church and were heading to the parking lot when someone called Emma's name. Josh recognized the reporter, Daniel Leighton, from the photo accompanying his articles. He was with a pretty redhead.

Emma tensed and Josh draped his arm protectively around her shoulders as they waited for the couple to reach them.

"Josh, this is Daniel Leighton, from the *New York Advocate*," she said.

Josh shook Daniel's hand. Daniel introduced his fiancée, Jenna Walsh.

"Emma, I'd like you to meet someone." At the hesitant look on her face, he added, "Trust me, please?"

She nodded and Daniel excused himself. He returned a few minutes later with a young man in a wheelchair, a black Labrador retriever by his side.

"Emma, Josh, this is Specialist Samuel Reading. He was injured a couple of weeks ago. He has nerve damage, which has caused paralysis in his left leg, but it's hoped that that can be fixed. He also lost sight in one eye and mostly in the other. This is Sailor," he said, pointing to the dog. "He's a seeing-eye dog, trained and provided to Specialist Reading through the Operation Pawsitive Change Foundation. The organization provides service dogs, therapy dogs and companion dogs to veterans. Sailor will be Specialist Reading's eyes from now on."

Specialist Reading reached out and groped around until he touched Sailor's head and gave them a weak smile. "It's hard to imagine that I'm the lucky one...but under the circumstances, I have to remind myself that I am."

"Emma," Daniel continued slowly. "We believe Specialist Reading's injury was a result of the failure of another one of American Freedom Munition's rifles. Before the recall was complete."

"I understand from Daniel that you refused to work for Senator Morgan when you'd learned about what he'd done with respect to the contract award," Specialist Reading said. "I want to thank you for that."

"I couldn't have done anything else," Emma murmured.

"Well, a lot of people wouldn't have done what you did, and I appreciate it."

"I'm—"

Whatever Emma was about to say, a sudden commotion distracted her.

Private Laurence's family was being escorted from the church by police in an attempt to hold the media scrum at bay. They were moving at a quick pace through the crowd gathered outside the church and were headed in their direction. Daniel was about to step back to clear a path but wasn't quick enough. To shift out of the way of another reporter, Mr. Laurence bumped into Daniel.

Nearly losing his balance, he reached out and grabbed Daniel to steady himself. "I'm sorry," he mumbled apologetically and turned devastated eyes to Daniel. Those eyes narrowed, his body straightened and Josh could tell from the whitening of his knuckles that he'd tightened his grip on Daniel's arm.

"It's you," he hissed. "You wrote that article about my son."

"Yes, sir. I'm Daniel Leighton. I'm very sorry for your—"

"You're *sorry*?" Mr. Laurence's voice grew in strength and intensity. "You *knew* about this before my son lost his life."

The media scrum had stopped its forward progress when Laurence had, and now surrounded not only Laurence, but also Daniel, Jenna, Emma, Josh and Specialist Reading and his dog.

One of the police officers placed his hand lightly on Laurence's back. "Let's go, sir. This way, please."

The tired, defeated man they'd watched on the podium was now filled with raw emotion. "Hold on," he snapped and turned his attention back to Daniel. "If you would have made public what you knew sooner, you could have prevented it. My son's death was avoidable. It's on your head."

Daniel's complexion turned ashy white and his eyes were huge and round with shock. "I'm very sorry for your loss, Mr. Laurence," Daniel stammered, ineffectually. "I promise you, I will continue to do what I can to get the truth out and I will cooperate fully with the—"

"You will *cooperate*?" Laurence exploded in a rage. Neither the police officer nor Laurence's wife could get him to calm down. He brushed them away. "My son is dead! My only child. You could've gone to the authorities with what you had sooner instead of being concerned about your story."

Another police officer stepped forward and tried to help his colleague steer Laurence away. The media was recording it all. Laurence's wife was in the arms of another family member, quietly crying.

"I'll remember this. I'll never forgive you." He stared hard at Daniel before taking a long, measured look at the others. He glanced down at Specialist Reading. His anger dissipated and grief resurfaced as the officers finally led him away.

"Parents should never have to bury their children," were his final words, spoken in a weak, broken voice.

Josh glanced at Daniel, who stood pale

and dazed as the media continued to swarm around them.

Josh took charge. After saying goodbye to Specialist Reading, whose father had stepped up behind him when the commotion had started, he herded them all toward the parking lot. He had no idea where Daniel's car was, but he didn't care. Under the circumstances, he thought it best if he and Emma took them home. He didn't think Daniel was up to driving. They could make arrangements to pick up their car some other time.

Josh led Daniel by the arm, and Emma followed, helping Jenna as they weaved between the parked cars.

As they skirted a van, Emma nearly collided with a man about to get into his vehicle. She gasped and Josh turned just as the man reached for Emma. Josh's arm snaked out lightning-fast, and he yanked the man back by the collar of his coat.

"What the hell?" the man exclaimed and swung out at Josh, but Josh had longer arms and held tight.

"Josh, let him go."

He looked at her, perplexed.

"It's Richard," she whispered. "My ex-fiancé."

Josh gave Richard a hard look before releasing him.

Richard tugged his coat into place and combed his hair back with his fingers. Slim and disheveled, he certainly didn't look the way Emma had described him.

Josh started to lead Emma away but Richard clasped her arm again. "Can't you just stay out of it?" he hissed at her.

Josh could smell the alcohol on his breath.

"What's happened to you, Richard?" Emma murmured. She gestured with her hand. "You look... You don't look like you used to."

He waved away that comment. "I won't lose this opportunity because of you."

"What opportunity? The partnership with your firm?"

Before he could answer, Josh stepped closer and Richard glared at him. "Keep your hands off me," he said to Josh, letting go of Emma's arm and pushing past them. "Don't ask for trouble, Emma," he warned, before stalking away.

CHAPTER FOURTEEN

EMMA STARED AT Daniel's files lackadaisically.
She'd spent very little time with them in the
two weeks since Private Laurence's funeral.
She wished she could think of something useful, but she'd resolved there was likely very
little she could do. Leafing through the files
just brought an ache to her heart.

She hadn't accepted any new assignments
to work on, either. Not from Pinnacle or from
Arlene Greenberg's company. On the bright
side, she and Josh had taken Daisy to a nature
reserve, where she could be monitored for a
period of time before being released. Report-
edly, she was doing well and she was where
she belonged.

Emma prowled around the cottage listlessly.
She had begun to question the wisdom of what
she was doing. How foolish was it for her to
think she could be of any help to Daniel? And
even more so to think she could earn sufficient income doing freelance work. Was she
destined to fail at everything she tried?

And living in Sanctuary Cove? How realistic was that? If she couldn't earn enough, she wouldn't be able to stay. She should seriously consider moving back to New York City and finding a full-time job with a salary, she told herself. Something that she could do competently. If her savings were depleted too much, she might not even be able to afford to keep the cottage for the weekends.

Maybe Richard had been right about her all along.

The one thing that had brought her some pleasure was researching the Operation Pawsitive Change Foundation. She'd been touched by the little black Lab, Sailor, who would be Samuel Reading's eyes for the rest of the dog's life. She read about the wonderful work that the foundation did, and how they acquired and trained their dogs. She'd wondered if that might be something she could do at some point.

Dressed in loose-fitting yoga pants and an old college sweatshirt, her hair down and disheveled, she stood at a window watching a great blue heron glide just above the surface of the water. She didn't know why the graceful beauty of the heron made her want to cry.

It was an unusually beautiful late November day. The sky was clear and cerulean blue, the air crisp and still. While a few tenacious leaves still clung to branches, most now formed a thick, brown tapestry on the ground. A thin sheen of moisture glistened on their surface, a remnant from the early morning frost.

Emma knew there were going to be few more—if any—days like this before the snow fell. Her mood might not have matched the weather, but she considered it a shame not to take advantage of it.

She wanted both dogs accompanying her for the walk in the woods, but she'd noted that morning that the change in weather was affecting Theo. He was favoring his leg that had the plate in it. Although she generally stayed on the forest trails, they were uneven and arduous. She hated to leave Theo, but she decided it was best for him to stay indoors to avoid aggravating the discomfort or possibly reinjuring his leg.

Not above bribery, Emma offered Theo a new chew toy to gnaw on while she and Max were gone. With a world-weary sigh, Theo took it to the great room and settled down on the rug with his prize.

Emma put on a bright yellow jacket to keep her warm and to alert any hunters who might've chosen to trespass on her property.

For the latter reason, and especially since Max could easily be mistaken for a wolf at a quick glance, Max sported a bright red-and-yellow bandana.

Although there were the occasional rounds of fire, she hadn't heard any close enough recently to suspect that hunters were trespassing on her land. Maybe the combination of her signage and the notifications to the Department of Environmental Conservation was finally working. She still wasn't prepared to take chances with herself or her dogs.

She and Max entered the forest near the crest of the driveway through one of the trails that crisscrossed her property.

They weren't too far into the woods when Max tensed and emitted a deep throaty growl. Emma grabbed his collar and held tight as he strained against it. Clearly Max sensed something that Emma didn't. Max was neither aggressive nor territorial, so his reaction was abnormal and disconcerting.

On full alert, Emma scanned her surroundings for movement and listened for any unusual sounds. She heard a rustle ahead and to their left. Her eyes trained on the spot, she noticed the swaying of the brush.

Through the trees and shrubs, she saw a form, black and large. Her breath clogged in her throat. She felt the adrenaline rush and her heart hammered against her rib cage.

It had to be a black bear.

She knew black bears were present in abundance in the woods, but she'd never encountered one before. They weren't usually aggressive and would generally flee if they had a choice. They were only truly dangerous if they were protecting a cub, if they felt cornered or, in rare instances, if they became predatory. She'd heard of isolated cases of the latter, and the outcome was, more often than not, tragic. And she was standing no more than fifty feet from a black bear that was *not* retreating.

Max continued to growl and strain against her hold. With the dog nearly a hundred pounds, most of it muscle, Emma was uncertain how much longer she could restrain him, and she was terrified of the consequences if he pulled free. For the time being, whether due to Max or his own reasons, the bear was holding his position and not advancing.

Although Emma's distress left a metallic taste in her mouth, her mind was working frantically. The bear was still concealed by the brush, but Emma sensed this bear was not protecting a cub and it definitely wasn't cornered. A bear's sense of smell was extraordinary, as was his speed, remarkably so for a creature of its size. If he wanted to avoid them, he could've easily done so before they'd even become aware of him.

This bear was intentionally staying where it was despite the aggressive stance taken by Max. That terrified her.

For the moment, they seemed to be at a standoff. The bear didn't leave, but thankfully, he wasn't charging, either. On the other hand, Max's hostility was escalating. He was more than likely feeding off her anxiety and was fueled by his instinct to protect. He tried repeatedly to lunge forward, letting out a series of menacing barks. Desperately, Emma continued to hold onto him with both hands and all her strength. Her shoulders were screaming from the effort, her hands were numb, the skin raw where the leather collar rubbed against her palms.

Unless the bear retreated, Emma couldn't see the confrontation ending well for her and Max.

Yet the bear still didn't advance. Emma started to think they might have a chance, if she could control Max and they could cautiously back away.

The next instant, it was all out of her control.

A silver-gray blur streaked past Emma and

toward the spot where the bear was. It was Theo, snarling and barking, fur standing on end, and ready to do battle. With the moment's loss of her concentration, Max tore loose from her grasp and joined Theo behind the shrubs, the two of them forming a protective barrier between the bear and Emma.

Emma was panicked now for Max and Theo, but all she could do was add her voice to the clamor of the dogs, yelling at the top of her lungs in as deep a voice as she could manage, hoping the bear would have enough and leave.

Then she saw through the shrubs the black form lunge and she heard the yelp of one of the dogs. An anguished "no" tore from her throat, her fear and anger at a peak.

Without logical thought, she grabbed a large branch from the ground and rushed forward to where the dogs were. To her immense relief, when she pushed through the brush, she saw the bear some distance away, retreating deeper into the woods. The form appeared smaller than she would've expected and moved awkwardly, perhaps an indication that one of the dogs might have injured it.

The adrenaline rush abating, Emma called the dogs. Despite not entirely taking their attention away from the direction the bear had gone, they obeyed.

Tears of relief welled in her eyes and she hugged the dogs to her. She gave silent thanks that they appeared unharmed and had not given chase. Their bodies were still tense and quivering, and she tried to mollify them with soft words and gentle strokes.

Running her palm along Max's side, to her horror it came away wet. Lifting her hand, she saw blood. She scrambled to her knees to examine Max. She couldn't see clearly through his thick fur, which was matted with blood. She prayed the cut wasn't too deep. Regardless, she knew he needed attention as soon as possible. She led the dogs back to the cottage at a moderate pace, fearing if they went quicker, the exertion could cause Max to lose more blood.

Inside the cottage, she got Max settled and formed a compress with a towel, before she rushed to the phone to call Josh's cell number.

No answer.

She tried his office number next. When Sherri answered cheerfully, she felt a modicum of relief. "Sherri, I need to speak with Josh. It's urgent."

"He's with a patient right now. What's wrong?"

At the sound of a soft whimper, Emma

glanced over at the dogs. Max had dislodged the towel covering his wound aside and was licking it. Theo was beside him, nuzzling him reassuringly. Watching the dogs, Emma leaned against the wall behind her and slid down to the ground. With a strangled cry, she cradled her head in her free hand.

"Take a deep breath, Emma. What's wrong?" Sherri mollified on the other end of the line.

"Tell Josh it's an emergency. See if he'll take my call. Please," she implored.

In moments, Josh was on the line. "Emma, are you okay?"

"No. I mean yes. It's Max." She was struggling not to cry. "He…he's hurt. He was attacked by a bear."

"How bad is it and where is he?" Josh's voice sounded calm and authoritative. It helped steady Emma.

"He's here. At home with me. The bear must have swiped his side with his claws. Max is bleeding." Her words hitched on a sob. "Can you see him right away if I bring him in?"

"Stay where you are, Emma. I'll come to you. Try to keep him from moving too much. Place a compress on the wound and see if you can stop or at least slow the bleeding. I'll be there as soon as I can."

"Please hurry." The final words were said in a whisper and likely lost to Josh as she heard the line disconnect before she'd finished.

Josh pulled into Emma's driveway no more than fifteen minutes after they'd spoken. He must have driven above the speed limit the entire way, to make it in such a short time. Having been watching for him, Emma opened the door before he could knock.

Max was still lying on his side, the white towel, now stained red, covering his wound. Theo remained near him as Max's self-appointed protector.

Josh asked for warm water and more towels. With soft words, he reassured Theo that his friend would be fine and gently nudged him out of the way. When Emma returned, he was kneeling beside Max. She sat cross-legged on the floor and gently stroked the dog's head.

"Explain to me what happened," Josh asked as he worked efficiently and competently to clean Max's wound.

"I told you on the phone—"

"No," he interrupted. "Sorry. I didn't mean to snap at you," he added quickly. "Tell me *exactly* what you saw."

"Well, I'm not entirely sure," she began, her voice faltering. "I left Theo in the cottage. Max and I were walking in the forest when

Max must've heard or scented the bear. We're lucky the bear didn't attack us. I tried to hold Max back. He was growling like crazy. As aggressive as I've ever seen him." The terror washed over her again at the recollection, and she struggled to steady her breathing. "Oh, God..." She dragged her fingers through her hair.

Josh glanced up. "Emma. Emma," he called to her tenderly. "As much as I want to, I can't help you now. I need to concentrate on Max." His tone was soothing. "All three of you are safe and Max'll be fine. You don't have to finish it now, if you don't want to, but I'd like to understand what happened."

Scraping her teeth over her lower lip, she nodded. "Before I knew what was going on, Theo was there and Max broke free. Theo and Max rushed into the brush where the bear was and scared him off, but not before the bear took a swipe at Max." As her gaze shifted to Max and then Theo, standing alert a few paces away, her vision blurred and she felt the tears finally spill over. Recounting the events, she realized the dogs had probably saved her life. But Max was injured as a result and she sought reassurance. "He'll be okay, as you said?"

"Yes. I promise. The wound isn't deep." He

glanced up at her briefly as he finished cleaning and disinfecting it. "How did Theo get out?"

"I don't know. As I said, I'd left him in the cottage."

"Were there any windows open?"

She considered for a moment. "Yes, a couple slightly in the great room. The weather was too nice not to let the fresh air in." Before Josh could ask, she was up and rushing to the great room. The screen of the window closest to the forest had been knocked out, the casement frame was cracked and open. "Theo forced the window open."

Josh nodded. "He must've heard Max and known the two of you were in trouble and came to your rescue. With his size, a partially open window wouldn't be an obstacle if he was determined to get out."

Emma sank down on the floor across from Josh again and stroked Max while he stitched up the gash.

When he was finished, he raised his eyes to meet Emma's. "Did you actually *see* the bear?"

"Yes. He was right there. In the bush. I could see him rustling around. And also when he was running away."

Josh wiped his hands with a disinfectant

towel and touched Emma's knee. "But did you actually see him?"

"I don't know what you mean." She shook her head in confusion. "He was there, in front of us. He clawed Max…"

"Max wasn't clawed."

Emma's gaze dropped to her dog, the cleaned and stitched cut on his side, as she struggled to make sense of what Josh was saying.

Josh pointed to the dog's flank. "See how straight and narrow the cut is?" Emma nodded. "And it's a single cut. That wasn't done by a bear. Max was cut with a knife."

CHAPTER FIFTEEN

"OH, GOD. OH, MY GOD. What are you saying?" Emma's eyes were huge. "It *was* a bear. I *saw* him."

"Did you?" Josh's voice was quiet, gentle.

"Yes. He was right there. Behind the bushes." She gestured with her hand, as if seeing it in her mind's eye.

Josh finished bandaging Max and stayed silent, letting Emma work things through.

"All black...but I didn't actually see him. He—he was mostly concealed by the brush. When he was running away, I saw him..."

Josh could see from her expression that something was troubling her. "I remember thinking he was smaller than I'd expected."

Finished with Max, Josh wiped his hands again and reached out to link his fingers with Emma's. "We'll have to call the sheriff to report this."

Josh called Chad Atkins from Emma's office for privacy. Their friendship gave him easy access to the lawman. He wanted to explain the situation to Chad, and what he suspected.

Josh knew that Chad was a shrewd and fair man, who valued law and integrity above all else. He'd been sheriff of Sanctuary Cove for six years now and took his job very seriously. In fact, Josh understood that Chad considered it as more than a job. He saw it as a grave responsibility, a true calling to serve and protect. He was both thorough and pragmatic in discharging his responsibilities. He also had well-honed instincts that were right far more than wrong.

He listened to Josh explain what had transpired. "My intuition tells me you're correct, and it wasn't a bear that Emma Meadows and her dogs happened upon in the forest. It just doesn't sound like customary bear behavior to me."

"Then what do you think happened?"

"Could have been a hunter trespassing again. She's reported them a couple of times. Because of the consequences, they might do something like this to avoid being caught. Odds are that's what it was."

Josh thought back to when Emma took the tumble off the stepladder because of the ATV and whether the driver had intentionally startled her. "Do you think this guy in the forest would have hurt Emma?"

"I doubt it. That would be going too far, but I don't like what I'm hearing. I've got some time right now. Mind if I stop by to talk to her?"

"I'd appreciate it. We'll be here."

Josh joined Emma in the kitchen again. "Chad'll be here shortly," he advised her. She was still sitting with Max, Theo stretched out next to them.

She stayed there until Chad knocked on the door.

Josh made the introductions. Chad declined the offer of coffee and requested a glass of water instead as he settled in a chair in the great room. He took notes and asked the occasional question as Emma explained exactly what had happened. He covered much the same territory as Josh had, but in more detail.

"But you didn't actually see the bear?"

"That's correct."

"Is it all right if I have a look at your dog's injury?"

Emma had put Max and Theo in her office when the sheriff had arrived, to keep Max from getting excited. She rose to take the sheriff to him, and Josh followed them.

As Chad crouched down beside Max, Josh

lifted the bandage for him. When Chad was satisfied, Josh reapplied the bandage and they walked back to the great room.

"I have to agree with you, Josh. That's a knife wound, but the cut doesn't look like it was done with a hunting knife." He turned his attention back to Emma. "And from what you told me, if it was a hunter you startled in the woods, he would've had ample opportunity to retreat into the forest while you still had a grip on Max, isn't that right?"

Emma nodded.

Chad shifted his gaze to Josh. "You still having trouble with that, ah..." He gave Josh an apologetic look. "The woman you were seeing for a while a few months ago?"

Josh glared at Chad. "C'mon, Chad. You can't be serious. She might be unstable but she's not crazy enough to skulk through the woods carrying a knife and cut a dog."

Emma shifted her focus from one man to the other.

Chad spread his hands. "Just saying, Josh. We have to consider all possibilities."

"Okay." Josh combed his hair back with his fingers. "Not so much in the last few weeks. But this is beyond mischief. I couldn't see her using a knife."

"You know the saying—desperate people,

desperate measures. Though I agree it's unlikely," he conceded. "Emma, can you say for certain it was a man?"

She let out a short, nervous laugh. "I didn't even know it was a *person*. The form was large enough that I believed it was a bear. That would make me think it was a man rather than a woman, but I can't be sure."

"There's something else you should know," Josh interjected. "Tell Chad about what happened at the funeral for Private Laurence," he said to Emma. "Both with the soldier's father and with your ex."

Emma paled. "You don't think this has anything to do with that?"

Josh lifted a shoulder and let it drop again. "As Chad said, we have to consider all possibilities. You should give him the full picture."

She held Josh's gaze for a long moment.

"Might as well tell me what that's all about," Chad said, drawing their attention to him.

Emma outlined the run-ins they had with Mr. Laurence and with Richard. "In addition, Daniel Leighton, the reporter I told you about?" At Chad's nod of acknowledgement, she continued. "He believes he's been followed, and he believes Senator Morgan is responsible for it."

Chad leaned closer, his interest apparently piqued.

Emma succinctly repeated what Daniel had told her before concluding, "They filed a report with the NYPD. If you would like the contact information, I can get it for you."

"That would be helpful." Chad exchanged a meaningful glance with Josh, and Josh was glad he'd given Chad a heads-up about it. "If anything else happens that you consider suspicious or relevant, call me. Now, would you mind taking me to where it happened?"

They left the dogs in the cottage, and Josh and Chad followed Emma along the trail. When she indicated the spot where she believed the person had been, Chad searched the area carefully. Bending down and examining the ground, he found something of interest and picked it up. He showed Josh and Emma a couple of spent bullet casings.

"Did you hear any gunshots either before or during your walk?" he asked Emma.

Emma shook her head.

Chad looked toward the cottage. "At this distance, if you were inside, I'd think you'd hear a shot, but you never know. If you had the water running, or music playing, maybe not."

As they walked back to the cottage, Chad assured Emma that she shouldn't get overly concerned. His take was that she happened to be at the wrong place at the wrong time, and caught a hunter on her land. Finding the casings had reinforced what he'd already suspected. He handed her a business card. "Call me if you have any trouble. We'll examine the casings. I'll spread the word around that we're looking into this and that might be enough of a deterrent to keep whoever it was off your property in the future. Still, keep your eyes open and don't take any unnecessary chances for the time being," he said before climbing back into his cruiser.

EMMA PUSHED HER chair back and rolled her shoulders, trying to ease the tension from having been sitting at her computer most of the morning working on an assignment. The chair's legs scraping over the floorboards woke Max. He was stretched out on his good side beside the desk. She was glad his wound was healing well. When she glanced over at him, he rolled partially onto his back and raised a front paw into the air to invite a belly rub. With a quick laugh, she dropped down next to him to oblige.

She soon had the large dog purring almost like a cat. When she stood up, she pressed her hands to the small of her back and stretched to loosen the kinks.

Although she'd continued to be nervous about working for Arlene Greenberg, with Josh's encouragement, she'd finally accepted another assignment from her. Yes, she worried about not doing a good job, but Pinnacle had hired a full-time staffer, so Elite Consulting was her only source of income for the time being. She tried to remain positive.

Checking her watch, she decided to take the dogs out and then spend some time going through Daniel's files. "How about a walk?" she asked Max. He was immediately up on all fours. With an affectionate rub of his head, she left her office, Max close beside her.

Theo was sprawled on the floor in the kitchen. He came to attention as Emma and Max entered. Grabbing her coat, she led them out the back, and they had a leisurely walk around the property.

Back inside, she took Daniel's files into the great room. Josh had said he'd be over that evening after dinner to help, but she wasn't sure there was much either of them could do.

Emma had been through all the files at least once and most of them a few times. She was more convinced than ever that she wouldn't be of any use to Daniel, although this time it wasn't for lack of trying. She opened the file that contained the results of the tests of the rifles. Suddenly, she remembered that she'd never gotten around to comparing the report she'd gotten from Morgan to the one Daniel had tracked down.

She retrieved the copy of the testing report Morgan had given her. Turning from one page to the next, her attention was caught and she examined a page more carefully.

"That's odd," she said out loud. The font size for the paragraphs outlining the test results appeared to be slightly larger than for the rest of the document. Then she noticed something else. In the left margin of the page, there was an imprint, a scoring of the paper. Although illegible, it seemed to be handwriting.

She took the report with her to her office and rummaged through a drawer until she found a soft-leaded pencil. With the point sideways, she gently rubbed the tip over the scoring until the entire area was lightly shaded. The writing was now clear in reverse contrast. There were two lines of script angled across the margin. The beginning of the lines flowed off the paper. What was visible read:

ll Grant. Let him
ow this version is acceptable.

Emma huffed out a breath and leaned back in her chair. Someone must have placed a piece of note paper on top of the report and jotted a message. But what were the missing letters?

She copied the truncated message on her own notepad and started writing down words that ended in *ll* and *ow* that might fit. She tried various combinations until she had it narrowed down to what she considered most likely.

The first word could be *call* or *tell*. Either made sense. She was almost certain the letters missing from the second line were *kn* for *know*. Although she couldn't be positive, she acknowledged that it wasn't that important. The message was clear.

Grant had to be Grant Stewart, the scientist who did the testing of the rifles for American Freedom Munitions. It would be too much of a coincidence to be anyone else. And the *version* being *acceptable* seemed to imply what Daniel and she had suspected. The report had been altered—falsified. The difference in font size also pointed to that possibility.

But whose writing was it?

Then a thought occurred to her. She still had the handwritten note Morgan had given her with all his contact numbers. She scrambled up, startling the dogs in her rush to get her address book from her office. Finding the note, she compared the reverse image on the testing report and Morgan's handwriting.

She was no expert, but the angle of the script, the showy flourishes for the capital letters and the unusual way the letter *a* was written—more like a type font than handwriting—caused her to conclude the writing on the margin of the report was Morgan's. A handwriting expert would be able to verify it.

She pushed out of the chair and with a self-satisfied smirk on her face, she paced to the window and back. She'd done it! She found something that could show that Morgan *had* been aware of the defects with the rifles.

She thought about calling Josh. Checking the time, she realized he would be arriving shortly anyway. She did, however, leave a message for Daniel.

She fed the dogs and had a quick bite to eat, then retrieved the copy of Grant Stewart's bio that she'd printed from the internet. His credentials were solid, his educational background impressive. The awards and recognitions bestowed on him considerable. There was nothing in his background to suggest he wasn't competent or would be anything less than scrupulous, but if she was right about what the scribbled note meant, he was complicit, too. Someone else to be held accountable.

She examined his photo at the top left corner of the bio. It was a professional head shot of an unsmiling narrow face, with pale blue, watery eyes behind wire-framed glasses. He had short blond hair, showing the early stages of a receding hairline. There was something vaguely familiar about him.

When the dogs clambered up, she knew Josh had arrived. She followed them out, placing the file folder on the coffee table, and tossed the bio on top.

As soon as Josh walked in, he took Emma in his arms and held tight for a few moments. "Mmm, this is what I needed."

She smiled up at him. "Bad day?"

He rubbed his palms over his face. "It started with an emergency call early this morning and it didn't let up."

"Would you like a glass of wine?" she asked as she led him into the kitchen.

"Thanks. It can't hurt," he responded.

She poured them each a glass and he followed her into the great room. Taking a sip, he placed his glass on the table. "What's this?" he asked, picking up the sheet of paper with the photo on its top left corner.

"Oh, it's the bio of the scientist who did the testing on the rifles."

Josh frowned at it. "I don't remember seeing it in any of the files."

"You wouldn't have. I printed it today from the web. I was curious about his credentials. But wait until you see what I found!"

"Mmm-hmm," he responded distractedly as he continued to stare at the picture.

She could see he was trying to sort something out in his mind. "What's up?"

"This guy looks familiar." Josh continued to scrutinize the picture. "I just can't place him."

"So, about my news…" She opened the file and pulled out the report with the writing in the margin and the slip of note paper with Morgan's handwriting on it.

Josh scanned both and glanced back up at Emma. "The writing looks to be the same person's. Whose is it?"

She grinned. "The one on the note paper is Morgan's. Which makes it likely that the one in the margin of the report is his, too!"

He looked at the truncated words. "What do you think it says?"

She explained what she thought.

"Have you told Daniel?" he inquired.

"Not yet. I tried his cell but it went direct to voice mail. If he really is under surveillance, it might not be a huge leap to think they're monitoring his cell phone, too. I didn't want to leave the details in a message, so I asked that he call me."

THE NEXT MORNING, Josh was still thinking about the testing of the rifles and the scientist who did it. He was giving Toby, a charcoal-gray standard poodle, his annual physical, when an idea sprang to mind. His thoughts were racing while outwardly he remained focused on the examination, finishing up as quickly as possible without appearing to be rushing.

"Toby looks to be in excellent health, Mrs. Burton. He's a beautiful dog and very well behaved."

Lisa Burton beamed at him. "Thank you, Dr. Whitmore. Phil and I love our Toby. With our kids now off at college, we do dote on him. It's a good thing he likes all the attention."

"I'm sure he does," Josh agreed as he ruffled the wiry fur on Toby's head, and walked dog and owner out of the examination room.

He checked his watch. Two more patients and at least forty-five minutes before he could follow up on his supposition.

When Josh finally finished with his last patient of the day, he grabbed his coat, stopped in front of the reception counter and smiled at Sherri. "Turned out to be an okay day, huh?"

"Not bad. We've had worse," she replied as she filed the records of their last patient.

"Sherri, I'm in a bit of a hurry. Would you mind locking up?"

"Not at all." She grinned. "Hot date with Emma tonight?"

"You never know. But first there's something else we need to deal with. Thanks for taking care of things," he said. Whistling for Winston, he waved goodbye and rushed out the door with his dog.

He drove to Emma's through lightly falling snow.

"You're here earlier than I expected," Emma said when he arrived.

He brushed his lips over hers. "Have you heard from Daniel?"

"Not yet, and it's unusual for him to take so long to return a call."

"Don't worry about it. I had a thought today I want to check out. Where are the files?"

"In my office." She tilted her head slightly. "I'll go get them. Any particular file you want?"

She looked so darn endearing he almost forgot what had prompted him to rush over.

"The one with all the photos in it. The pictures of the senator and his associates by that boat. Bring the bio of the scientist who did the testing and last year's American Freedom Munitions annual report, too, would you please?"

While Emma headed to her office, Josh added some logs to the fire in the great room and poured them each a glass of soda. When she returned, he handed her a glass, and accepted the file and documents. He took a close look at the photograph on the bio first. He then turned to the third page of the annual report, AFM's president and CEO Jack Hughes's message, and studied the photo.

Placing the bio inside the annual report to mark the page, he put the documents aside. Next, he found in the file folder the photo of the senator on the bow of the boat with a drink in his hand, slapping his companion on the back with the other.

Josh's gaze shifted to the cabin of the boat. Holding the picture closer, he narrowed his eyes and focused on the two men visible through the cabin window.

"I knew it!" he exclaimed, startling Winston, who'd been in a deep sleep at his feet. "Sorry, pal." He patted Winston's head to reassure him.

Emma scooted forward to the edge of her chair. "What is it?"

"Hold on a second," he said, pulling the photo out of its plastic sleeve and turning it over. Other than a number on the bottom right, the back was blank. He handed the photo to Emma. "Do you know when this was taken?"

"Yes," she said, gesturing toward the file with her glass. "The log of the file contents inside the front gives the date and location for each photo." She flipped over the photograph, as Josh had done. "This number should be on the list."

He scanned the entries. "July 2015. At the senator's summer house." When he leveled his gaze on her, his smile was feral. "Independent testing, is it? Do you have a scanner?"

"Yes, in my office, but…"

He took the photo, the bio and the annual report with him. After scanning the photo, he sat down at her desk to manipulate the image. He zoomed in on the two men inside the cabin. He played with the resolution to clarify the image the best he could while Emma stood behind him, peering at the screen.

"This is as good an image as I'm going to get." He glanced at her over his shoulder. "What do you see?"

She shook her head. "Two men on a boat," she said, stating the obvious.

"How about with this?" He opened the annual report to the president and CEO's message, where he'd placed the bio. He held up the two pages for Emma to examine, one displaying Hughes's image, the other Stewart's.

Her eyes widened and her lips parted slightly as she let out a soft "Ohhh. It's them, in the senator's boat at his summer home."

He smiled. "And that photo was taken over a year before the award of the contract."

"And a year and a half before the so-called independent testing of the rifles," she added, understanding. "So the senator had entertained not only the CEO of AFM at his summer home, establishing a clear connection before the tender, but they both knew Stewart, too, well before he was commissioned for the testing."

Josh nodded. "Wait a minute!" he said suddenly. "There might be more to it than that." He grabbed the AFM annual report again and leafed through it. "Well, what do you know," he exclaimed again.

Emma inched closer to be able to see what he'd been reading.

"You said that the picture was taken in July 2015?" he asked.

"Yes. Why?"

In answer, he pointed to a paragraph a third of the way down the page.

She scanned it and shifted her gaze to hold Josh's. "Hughes hadn't been appointed as CEO at that time. Robert Ferguson held the position until the end of January 2016."

"Isn't that a cozy bit of coincidence that the man who facilitates the contract award, the man who would later run the company and the man who presumably falsified his own test report to allow the sale to go through all knew each other before the process even began."

"It might be circumstantial, but it can't be ignored." She glanced down, her eyes resting on Hughes's picture. She examined the photo more closely. "I've seen Stewart before."

"There might have been another picture of him in the files."

"No. That's not what I mean. I've seen him in person. In Morgan's office."

Josh swiveled around in the chair and looked at her intently.

"I was waiting for an appointment with Morgan. My meeting before had been canceled, and since I was already in the area, I went directly to his office. I was there very early. He—Stewart, that is—was just leaving," she added. "It had struck me as odd that when Morgan saw me waiting, he seemed to block my view of the man going out of his office."

Josh drew her down on his lap and rubbed her back gently. "I'd say we have some information of substance for Daniel."

"Yes." She checked her watch. "I'm going to call him again."

When her call went to voice mail again, she kept her message brief. "Daniel, it's Emma. Please call when you get this message. Don't worry about the time."

She huffed out a breath and turned back to Josh. Now that they'd found something that could link Morgan with the faulty firearms, she was impatient to pass it on to Daniel. She gathered up the file and other documents, and placed them together in a single new red file folder and slipped it into her desk drawer. It seemed she might be able to help Daniel bring the senator to justice after all.

CHAPTER SIXTEEN

EMMA, JOSH, DANIEL and Daniel's fiancé, Jenna, sat around Emma's dining room table, file folders and papers piled in front of them. Jenna had accompanied Daniel, because she'd been helping him with his research. Although Daniel had a pad of paper and a pen, Jenna had her laptop in front of her.

As none of them had had time for dinner, Emma put out a variety of snacks in serving bowls in the center of the table along with two bottles of wine, one white, the other red. Emma munched on a pretzel as she opened the red file folder in front of her. She glanced around the table, her gaze settling on Daniel. "Would you like me to start?"

At Daniel's nod, Jenna positioned her hands over the keyboard.

Emma showed them the copy of the testing report she'd received from Morgan. Daniel and Jenna read the two lines of script:

ll Grant. Let him
ow this version is acceptable.

They filled in the missing letters as easily as Emma had. "Call Grant. Let him know this version is acceptable," Daniel guessed. "If we only knew whose writing it was."

"I think we do." Emma showed them the sample of Morgan's handwriting.

Daniel and Jenna agreed that it appeared that both notes had been written by the same hand. In response to Daniel's question, Emma explained the report's origin. With a little guidance, it didn't take long for Daniel to notice the discrepancy in font size as well.

"Emma, this is very helpful. Each piece of the puzzle makes our case stronger, and this does point to Morgan."

She took a sip of her wine. "Just wait. There's more."

Emma handed Daniel the photo of the senator on the boat. "This photograph was taken in July 2015—over a year before the award of the contract, and a year and a half before the testing of the rifles. It was a fund-raising event for Morgan at the senator's summer home." She tapped a fingertip on the image of the senator. "Our guest of honor." She moved her finger to the faintly visible figures in the boat's cabin. "Some guests, you will note, preferred to stay out of the glare of the sun…and cameras."

She pulled a second photograph from her

folder and placed it next to the first. "This is an enlarged version of the first photograph, zoomed in on the cabin. Josh digitally enhanced it to make the image of the two men inside clearer."

Emma placed the American Freedom Munitions annual report, open to the page of Hughes's picture, next to the enlarged photo.

"So Morgan knew Hughes before he became CEO of AFM," Daniel concluded.

"So it would seem."

"How convenient." Daniel reached for a chip and munched on it as he made a notation on his pad.

"It gets better." Emma shifted her gaze to Josh. He had kicked back in his chair, and was swirling the red wine in his glass. When her eyes connected with his, he gave her an encouraging smile. It gave her the confidence to continue. Knowing Daniel would have recognized Hughes, she wasn't so sure about Stewart. "Do you know who the other man is?" she asked him.

Daniel lifted the print to take a closer look. "No. Should I?"

"Let's see if this helps." Emma handed Stewart's bio to Daniel.

Jenna reached for some pretzels and leaned in toward Daniel to take a look as well. The smile that spread across Daniel's face was a little predatory. "Small world, isn't it?"

Emma couldn't help but feel self-satisfied at Daniel's reaction. She reached for Josh's hand as she summarized their findings. "So the senator knew the CEO of AFM before he actually became the CEO, entertaining him at his summer home. We presume Hughes had made a donation to the senator, and had done so well before the tender for the contract was even issued. They both knew Stewart, too, well before he was engaged to provide *independent* testing of the rifles."

Daniel started to lift his glass in a toast but Emma raised a hand to forestall him.

"The final piece of information I have is that I personally saw Morgan and Stewart together at Morgan's office. That was after the contract had been awarded and already had the media's attention. Because of Morgan's odd behavior at the time, it made me wonder who he was, although I had completely forgotten until Josh made the connection. Now I wonder what business they'd have had after the award of the contract." Emma frowned. "Could his presence further support the allegation that Morgan knew about the manufacturing defects associated with the rifles? If so, why meet so openly?"

"Arrogance," Daniel stated with a shrug. "Morgan has been in the game for a long time. I expect this isn't the first time he's stepped over the line. He likely believes he can outsmart everyone and that being a long-serving, all-powerful senator, he's above the law...untouchable. I've seen it before."

Emma nodded thoughtfully. "He wouldn't be the first politician to think that."

"Nor the first to be proven wrong. This will all be very helpful to us. We'll have to prove the authenticity of the photo. Try to find the photographer, if we can, and get the original file and maybe have him testify, but we have no idea if he's a friend of Morgan's. The defense might argue that it was a major gathering—a political fund-raiser—and there were bound to be a lot of people there, not necessarily all of them connected. You testifying that you *had* seen Morgan and Stewart together would solidify the personal connection." He watched her face intently. "Will you be prepared to testify, Emma?"

Emma had been so pleased about what she and Josh had discovered, she hadn't considered that possibility. To take her involvement back to a public level, and the thought of facing Morgan, and more than likely, Richard, in a court of law disconcerted her. Her palms were getting clammy just thinking about it.

She slid her hand into Josh's under the table, and he gave her hand a reassuring squeeze.

With a resigned sigh, she responded, "Yes. If I have to, I will."

"Good. Now, let me bring you up-to-date on what I learned," Daniel said. As he shuffled some of the papers in front of him, Emma topped up everyone's wineglasses.

"Most of the background you already know, so I'll summarize briefly for context. You're aware of the connections between Morgan and Chuck Innes, the chairman of AFM. Those connections date back as far as twenty years, by the way. You are also aware that Innes's appointment to AFM was a major coup for him. He was, and is, an ambitious, driven individual. Yet the first time he appears to have truly excelled has been in his role as chairman of AFM. Over the course of his tenure as chairman, share value for the company has nearly doubled. Not a bad return on five years' investment, and much stronger performance than their competitors.

"The CEO before Hughes, Robert Ferguson, had been hired by Innes shortly after he became chair. A solid enough individual, but, like Innes, not someone who was reputed to be an exceptional leader. Nor was he seen as strong-willed. Yet together, Innes and Ferguson had, as I noted, steadily been creating shareholder value. It was believed that Ferguson was more of a figurehead and that Innes essentially ran the business.

Daniel took a moment to grab a pretzel. "When Ferguson announced his intention to retire in January 2016, being only in his mid-fifties, it came as a surprise to everyone. He stated that it was for personal reasons. Not soon after, he was said to have left the country. Despite my best efforts, I hadn't been able to find anything on him in terms of business ventures since then. It seems he really did retire." Daniel glanced around the table. "Odd but not unheard of. He did leave the country. But not for long. Ferguson had some contact with the media before he left; however, he was guarded. He would not go into details about his retirement. After those initial contacts, there has been no communication with Ferguson, and no one could find him. At least until now. I located him."

This *was* news to Emma.

"He's living in Arizona. He was resistant to talking. He'd only recently returned from overseas, and he wasn't aware of the fatality." Daniel's gaze met Emma's and held. "Much like you, he had purposefully avoided following the media. I caught him unaware. He was greatly disturbed by the turn of events. Eventually, he agreed to meet with me. I flew to Phoenix to see him on Sunday."

Emma placed her glass down. Resting her arms on the table, she laced her fingers together. "And? Did he shed any light on what happened?"

Daniel's lips formed a hard, straight line, as he nodded. "Yes, he did. He was willing to talk, but was cautious enough to have his lawyer with him."

"If Ferguson had legal representation, it would suggest he knows something he's worried about, but I doubt you could get much out of him that would be of use," Josh interjected.

Daniel tilted his head in acknowledgment. "True. To a point. But what I *was* able to get is crucial. And he can and will be subpoenaed to testify."

"What did he say?" Emma asked.

Daniel shifted his gaze back to her. "Most of it we've suspected. But here's the key. He's corroborated our suppositions. And because of his direct knowledge of the circumstances leading up to the events, his testimony will carry more weight in a court of law.

"AFM was already considering putting a

bid in for the tender. Preparing a bid for such a substantial government contract is a long and onerous process. Although appreciating the upside potential—huge for a company of their size—Ferguson had advised his board of directors they shouldn't pursue it. In conducting an assessment of the selection criteria and resultant probabilities of success, Ferguson believed that unless they partnered with another, larger firm, their chance of being shortlisted, let alone for winning the contract, was negligible."

"Interesting that his view is consistent with what everyone generally believed," Josh noted.

"Yeah. He was being realistic in his assessment. Ferguson's position was that the time, effort and expense they would have needed to invest in preparing the qualification document and financial bid would have been a wasted effort, and not insignificant in terms of the drain on the company's resources. Resources he believed could have been better utilized. I agree he had a compelling argument. After Ferguson made his recommendation to the board, they met in-camera without Ferguson—according to Ferguson, a couple of times, in fact. He believes that with Innes being the driving force, they decided to overrule him."

"Is that unusual?" Josh inquired.

"Not necessarily, however, in a matter as significant as this contract, and with the company having so much at stake, win or lose, it's not a good sign if a board completely rejects the recommendation of its CEO. It can be interpreted as a vote of no confidence."

"That would explain why Ferguson left?" Emma mused.

"It could, yes, but that wasn't what happened, according to Ferguson. Ferguson was told to prepare the bid. In addition, he was advised not to seek a partner, but have AFM's bid stand on its own merits. Ferguson wasn't happy about it, as he still believed it was wasted effort. But, unless he chose to resign—which he didn't at that time—he had no alternative but to comply with the board's directive. In Ferguson's opinion, he and his team did the best they could.

"It was a two-stage selection process. A two-envelope system, whereby the proponent firms had to demonstrate their qualifications and compliance with the terms of the bidding process in the first envelope. The firms meeting the criteria would advance to the second stage and the second envelope, which would be the financial bid. If they qualified in the first stage, the selection at the second stage was based on lowest bid.

"Ferguson felt that the financial bid they prepared was solid and, as ultimately demonstrated through the selection process, their bid was the lowest. The assumption is that there was no manipulation of the financial bids. A relatively small firm, they had considerably lower overhead than the major players. His concern was that they would never make it to the second stage, as they wouldn't meet the mandatory qualifying criteria."

"What did he say about how they qualified, then, and Morgan's role in it?" Josh asked.

"First of all, it was during the qualification process, while the submissions were being assessed, that he decided to step down as CEO."

"If he didn't resign when the board overturned his recommendation, why would he have done so in the midst of the selection process?"

"That's the key. Ferguson left, Innes stepped into the role of CEO on an interim basis and Jack Hughes was hired, all while the government was evaluating the submissions."

"You would think that such a substantial change in control of the company would hurt them in the evaluation process, and they would've wanted to avoid it," Josh noted.

Daniel gestured toward Josh with his glass of wine in acknowledgement. "One would think. It certainly had an impact on share value in the short term."

"I'd thought the same thing," Jenna added. "That if there was already some concern about the company's ability to deliver, would a change in leadership not make it worse?"

"Yes. It would make sense, as it could hurt stability and continuity of operations, especially when they were already seen as a long shot, at best. I asked Ferguson about that and this is where he became more guarded. Although Innes had always been hands-on, more so than is good governance practice for a nonexecutive chair—and most CEOs would like—Ferguson acknowledged that this was Innes's style. He'd accepted it over the years for the most part."

"So Innes had been essentially in control as had been suggested in the media," Emma reflected.

"Yes. And according to Ferguson, he was becoming progressively more controlling through the bidding process. Innes, according to Ferguson, chose to attend bid clarification meetings on his own, without Ferguson, which was highly unorthodox, and he chose to be involved in every aspect of the process. When

Ferguson became aware that Innes was in fact having private meetings with certain key decision makers, including Morgan, his concerns were exacerbated. Questioning Innes led nowhere, not until Innes came to him to suggest that to win the bid, AFM would need to make certain strategic investments."

"Investments in the business? To increase their production capacity?" Emma asked.

"That's what Ferguson first believed. It would've made sense. But no. Apparently that's not what Innes had in mind. Ferguson asked his lawyer to step out at this point."

Emma edged forward.

"Innes wanted Ferguson to make the payments to Morgan in exchange for an assurance that they would win the contract."

"The kickback…"

"That's right." Daniel paused and took a drink of his wine. "In two installments. Half for short-listing and the other half for winning the contract."

Josh interjected, "But you already knew that. You have copies of the canceled checks. Morgan has been charged."

"But there was the whole question of admissibility because of the way I got the checks. The prosecution has also obtained them through the appropriate channels, and we have Ferguson to testify to it."

"So what happened? Why did Ferguson quit?"

Daniel let out a mirthless laugh. "It seems Ferguson had some scruples after all."

"He balked at paying the senator," Emma declared, understanding what had happened.

"That's right. He claims he might have been willing to stretch the line but was not prepared to step completely over it. That was the deal-breaker for him."

"So Innes fired him," Josh concluded.

"More or less. Ferguson claims he was given a choice. Pay the bribe or resign. Applying his own code of ethics, he chose to resign."

"But why wouldn't he have gone public with what was going on? Why not go to the authorities?" Emma asked.

"Probably had to do with the severance that they would've payed him. He also had shares in the company. If he went public, share value would have dropped dramatically. He had a lot to lose."

Emma made a snorting sound. "And his departure cleared the way for Innes to step in."

"And to negotiate the deal with Morgan. Ferguson said it was Morgan who recommended Hughes for the job. Innes hired him,

Hughes paid the bribe and Morgan manipulated the short-listing process. From that point, AFM's bid was the lowest and won the contract. Ferguson believes they had a contingency plan in place in case their bid wasn't the lowest, but it never had to be exercised. That was the purpose of the second payment, whether needed or not. Hughes made the final payment to Morgan, and the contract was awarded."

"Hughes was hired to carry out the dirty work?" Emma concluded.

"Yes. That's why Morgan had recommended him. Innes and Hughes were on common ground to do what needed to be done to win the bid. We have proof of the payments and the rest—the connections between the key players and the prior knowledge of the defects with the rifles—you provided. To state the obvious, Innes and Hughes both had a lot at stake financially."

Daniel looked around the table and raised his glass in a toast. "I believe we have what we need. The prosecutors will definitely be in touch with you, Emma, and thank you," he said, before taking a long drink.

EMMA PACKED UP all the files that Daniel had provided in a cardboard box. She made copies of her own personal notes and included them as well. Daniel took everything with him when he and Jenna left. They agreed that other than testifying in court, Emma had now done all she could. The rest was up to the legal team. Daniel and Jenna drove off with a final wave to Emma and Josh, and a promise to keep them updated.

FROM A HIDDEN driveway a short distance down the road, a dark sedan pulled out behind Daniel's car and followed him until he reached Interstate 87 to New York City. It then turned and headed back in the direction it had come from.

Toward Emma's cottage.

CHAPTER SEVENTEEN

EMMA FELT AS if a huge weight had been lifted off her shoulders. She knew the whole Morgan situation wasn't over yet, but she'd spoken at length with the prosecuting attorneys and they felt that they had enough to charge not just Hughes and Innes, but also Morgan and Stewart with one count each of criminal negligence causing death and another of causing injury. Specialist Samuel Reading's injury had been verified to also have resulted from a defective AFM firearm.

Emma checked her watch again. Josh had said he would be there for dinner. Usually that was six or seven, by the time he closed the clinic. That meant she had time to relax with a cold glass of wine. She took the wineglass with her to the great room, lit a couple of scented candles and grabbed the book she was currently reading. She got the dogs settled, and with a long sigh stretched out on the sofa and started reading.

WHEN THERE WAS no answer at the front door, Josh let himself and Winston into Emma's cottage. She'd given him a key a few weeks back. After greeting Max and Theo, and offering each dog one of the treats he regularly carried in his jacket pockets, he went in search of Emma.

The scent of something soothing and floral led him to the great room. Leaning against the wall by the steps leading down, he indulged in watching Emma for a few moments.

She lay on the sofa, her lips slightly parted and curved into a soft smile, her skin glowing with the flickering candlelight. A few strands of hair had escaped from the clip on top of her head, and were curling around her face.

Emma must have sensed his presence, as she opened her eyes and looked directly into his. With only a moment's hesitation to shake off the vestiges of a light sleep, her smile spread and her eyes sparkled. "Hi," she said in a dreamy, sleepy voice.

She pushed up into a sitting position and he joined her on the sofa. He settled her against him, her head resting against his chest, and placed a kiss on the top of her head. "How was your day?"

"Productive—for the most part. I completed another assignment for Arlene. Then I hit a wall and here I am sleeping the evening away. How was your day?"

"Busy. I had several unscheduled visits, including a delivery. A healthy litter of seven German shepherd pups." Lowering his head so they were cheek-to-cheek, he inquired, "You wouldn't be interested in another dog, would you?"

She laughed. "Not likely. Don't you think I have enough with a total combined canine weight well over two hundred pounds, and their joint mission to eat me out of house and home?"

"Point taken. All right. I'll tell Mrs. Shaw to look elsewhere."

He turned her slightly and tipped her chin up with a finger so that he could see her face.

"Wait a minute!" She scrambled up and looked at him, her eyes glowing. She'd moved so quickly, she'd startled the dogs. "Just since I've known you, you've delivered three litters that I know of, and somehow have taken it upon yourself to find the pups good homes. Have you ever considered getting some of those pups into the service-and-therapy dog program, so they can help disabled people? Maybe even former military personnel specifically?"

He arched a brow. "What made you think of that?"

"Meeting Samuel Reading at Private Laurence's funeral. I've been thinking about it on and off. How wonderful it is that he has Sailor, and how important and special those dogs are. I did some research on it. I looked up the organization that trained Sailor."

"It's a great thought. Labs and German shepherds are especially well-suited for that type of work…"

She nudged his knee. "I can see the *but* written all over your face."

"As I said, it's a terrific idea, but someone has to train the dogs, and it takes a lot of time and commitment."

Her eyes lit up again. "I'll do it! I'll take one of the pups and train him or her! I'm sure someone at the Operation Pawsitive Change Foundation could teach me how."

Josh chuckled. "Yeah, I expect they could." But he was still skeptical.

"Look, Josh…" She turned serious and the sparkle in her eyes dimmed. "I doubt I'm going to get any more assignments from Pinnacle Communications, at least not in the foreseeable future. Yes, I've taken a couple of assignments from Arlene, but I don't know how long that'll last."

He was about to respond to her last statement but she rushed on.

"I know I'll have to find a job, probably sooner rather than later, but in the meantime, this would give me something to do that I believe in. A way for me to make a difference..." she said, the words trailing off.

Yeah, maybe it was what she needed. Another step in her healing process, Josh thought. If she wanted to do it, he'd support her. "Go for it, if it's what you want to do."

And what a remarkable woman she was to think of it.

Although he'd known his feelings for her had been growing and there was no question he was falling in love with her, watching her now—relaxed and unguarded—he realized the fall was complete and he'd fallen hard.

He loved Emma.

EMMA WAS EXCITED. Why hadn't she thought of training service-and-therapy dogs before? She could do it! She had the time, at least for now. And Josh was willing to stand by her again in this, as he had been with just about anything she'd done since she'd arrived in Sanctuary Cove.

She looked up at him and was about to thank him...

But in Josh's eyes, Emma saw what was in his heart.

Her own heart skipped a beat at the discovery, in the dreamy glow of candlelight and swirling fragrance. But the memory of Richard intruded. Suddenly, what she saw terrified her.

Of course she had feelings for Josh. She knew and understood that he had feelings for her, too. But she was afraid he would say the words. Those three words that she didn't think she could trust and believe in. She didn't want their relationship to change. He'd come to mean so much to her, and she didn't want to lose him. But if he said those words, it would shift everything to a different level.

She could almost see the words forming on his lips so she blurted out the first thing that came to mind. "What would you like for dinner? Never mind. I'll take care of it. All you have to do is select the wine and uncork it."

He ran his finger gently along the side of her face. "Emma…"

"After dinner I'd like to take the dogs for a long walk and watch the sun set from the granite rock. How does that sound to you?" she continued, in near desperation.

"Emma…" he began again.

She knew she was jabbering on, but couldn't

seem to control it. "If I'm going to make dinner, I should get started."

"Emma, listen to me—"

She was ready to interrupt again, but he forestalled her by closing his mouth over hers in a long and achingly tender kiss. The kiss drew her back into the dreamy world she'd inhabited before it had been overshadowed by the fear of what she'd seen in his eyes.

When he sat back, her breathing was uneven and she couldn't manage a smile.

He cupped her chin in his palm, keeping her from turning away. She placed her hand on his chest to keep him at a distance, but he continued to gaze steadily at her, his feelings evident in his eyes.

"Emma, you're caring, intelligent and beautiful. I'm fortunate to have found you. You make me feel happier than I've ever been." He brushed his lips over hers, gently. "Emma... I love you."

She could feel her heart thunder, could almost measure time passing by counting the beats.

She was certain Josh was waiting for her to say something, but she had no words.

Her emotions were muddled and conflicting. A part of her was stunned and elated that Josh loved her.

But mostly she was terrified.

Her wounds from the relationship with Richard were—apparently—still raw.

How could she trust in love again? How could she trust her own judgment when she had erred so fundamentally before?

She closed her eyes for a moment and felt Josh's heartbeat, strong and steady, under her hand. Intellectually, she knew Josh wasn't Richard. She *knew* he was so much more, but her heart trembled. She was hurting Josh—she could see it in his eyes—and was very sorry for it. He didn't deserve it. The flaw was in her, not him, but she wasn't sure what she could do about it.

A voice inside her urged her to back away from Josh, yet she felt so right—so protected—in his arms, sheltered by him, the feel of his heartbeat solid and true. She squeezed her eyes closed again, forcing back the tears.

She dropped her head to rest her forehead on his chest "Oh, Josh…" Even to her own ears, the two words sounded regretful, not pleased.

JOSH LET HIS head fall back against the sofa and tried to make sense out of what just happened. He'd never said those three words to another woman outside of his family before. Emma might not like it, he thought. But there it was.

I love her. It's how I feel and she's just going to have to accept it and deal with it.

If she didn't or couldn't, he wondered if he could.

He knew she had been badly hurt and her confidence had been shaken, but he'd hoped she wouldn't allow her past to rule her present forever. He'd hoped that over the months they'd known each other, he'd earned her trust.

They spent a quiet evening together. Neither one of them broached the matter that loomed between them, driving them apart.

Josh left shortly after dinner. Although on the surface all seemed well, the undercurrents from earlier in the evening remained.

THE PASSAGE OF days hadn't helped to resolve matters between Emma and Josh, and Emma was as conflicted as ever about her emotions, which she knew were at the root of it.

She bundled up in a heavy sweater and jacket, and headed outside. For once, she left the dogs inside. She craved solitude. It felt as if her world was falling apart again, just when she'd thought she was on level ground.

She wasn't surprised to find herself walking toward the large outcropping of granite on the elevated tract of land roughly midway between the cottage and the forest line. She settled down with her knees drawn up, forearms resting on them. The light breeze blew her hair away from her face. She inhaled deeply, enjoying the clean, crisp air.

From her vantage point, Emma could see the forest, the gardens, the lake and the cottage. The trees were denuded and the perennials in the gardens cut back. The surface of the lake was a deep, unrelieved midnight blue. Yet even with the late fall starkness of the landscape, it held a tremendous appeal for Emma. It calmed her, just sitting there.

She cared about Josh a great deal. He treated her wonderfully, with consideration. He made her happy. She should be elated to have him want her and love her. But instead, she'd felt fear when he'd told her. She knew her reaction was irrational and entirely due to what had happened with Richard. But knowing it didn't help to dispel it. She didn't think she could handle being hurt like that again. She let out a long breath, and dropped her chin on top of her arms.

Instead, *she'd* hurt *Josh*. She hated that it had happened. She had no answers by the time she rose to walk back to the cottage.

As the days passed, the distance grew between her and Josh. Regret meant nothing, if she wasn't prepared to do anything about it. She missed Josh, and she finally acknowledged she'd have to be the one to take that step to try to make things right again.

Emma walked into the clinic shortly before closing. Sherri was behind the counter organizing files. She glanced up when she heard the door open and smiled warmly at Emma.

"Am I ever glad it's you!"

"Bad day?"

"Oh, yeah. When I heard the door open, I realized I'd neglected to flip the sign over to Closed. All we needed was another emergency!"

Emma turned the sign over herself and locked the door.

"Thanks." At the sound of a mournful whimper, Sherri glanced toward the examination room. "If Josh was expecting you, I'm afraid he's going to keep you waiting for a while."

With concern furrowing her brow, Emma asked, "Problem?"

Sherri smiled and rolled her eyes. "Not really. Unless you're concerned about the canine population exploding. The Hansons' dog is having puppies again. Every time she does, we try to convince them to have her spayed, and every time they say they'll think about it. Yet here we are again."

"Oh, no. More pups to find homes for?" It reminded her of her idea of training a service dog, something else that had fallen by the wayside, as the distance had grown between her and Josh.

"Don't worry about them. The Hansons always find loving homes for the pups, and there's no question they take good care of both Mom and the litter."

"That's good." Emma wondered if she could take one of those pups for training, if there was one that seemed like a good candidate. She'd have to do some more research on training service dogs, she decided. "Will Josh be long?"

"He'll be a while yet."

"Oh, well. Could you let him know I stopped by and he can give me a call when he gets a chance?"

"Why don't you stay? I'm sure he'd love to unwind with you after the day we've had." Sherri nudged a file. "These can wait. If you want to go into the kitchen and give me a moment, I'll join you for a cup of coffee."

"Are you sure it's no trouble?"

"None whatsoever. It'll give me a well-deserved break." She flashed another grin at

Emma. "Help yourself to a cup of coffee—it's reasonably fresh, at least by our standards."

Emma was sitting at the small kitchen table, her hands wrapped around a mug, when Sherri strode in a few minutes later. Pouring coffee for herself, she sat down opposite Emma and toed off her shoes with a sigh of relief. "Gosh, that feels good. I envy you, working at home and being able to stay in sweats and bare feet all day if you want. So, how're things going?"

"I've hit a rough patch." She frowned as she thought about it. She hadn't really gotten into the swing of things since the day she and Josh had... *Had what?* She couldn't call it a fight. If anything, they'd been painfully polite with each other since.

"Is that what's causing the problem between the two of you?"

Emma looked up, wanting to deny that she and Josh were having problems, but if Sherri could read her so easily, there was no point. "Is it that obvious?"

"Only to someone who knows you and cares about you both."

Emma remained silent, staring into her coffee mug, considering.

Sherri touched her hand in encouragement. "C'mon, Emma. What is it?"

Emma pressed a hand over her stomach in

an effort to quell the churning and raised her eyes to meet Sherri's. "I'm terrified," she admitted in a barely audible voice.

"Of what?"

"Of being hurt."

"By Josh?"

"Yes." The word was a whisper.

"Of course you'll be hurt," Sherri said cheerfully. At Emma's shocked look, Sherri patted her hand. "I don't mean he'll do it intentionally. It's just the nature of the beast. If you care about him, at some point you'll hurt." She said it matter-of-factly. "But that shouldn't stop you from enjoying what the two of you have."

Emma lowered her gaze again. She knew what Sherri meant. That was not what she was afraid of at all. It was the type of hurt she already had to endure once with Richard that scared her. That slice-you-right-down-to-the-bone hurt.

Sherri smiled in reassurance. "Josh's a great guy. He's one of the most decent, loyal, even-tempered, positive people I know. I like you, Emma, and you're good for him. He cares about you. Not like other women he's dated. I can see it because I've known him practically forever. There is something deeper there for him with you."

Emma blushed a little and took a sip of her cooling coffee. "I, ah, I care about him, too."

"So, problem solved?"

Emma could see that Sherri was confused. She wasn't used to sharing her feelings, her most personal thoughts, with anyone. It astonished her that she felt compelled to do so with Sherri. She sensed a genuine concern and interest. Maybe talking about what had been weighing so heavily on her mind for days might help. "Oh, Sherri, he said he loves me," she admitted softly.

"That's *wonderful*! What's wrong with that?"

"There *shouldn't* be anything wrong." Trying to ward off the ache that was forming behind her brow, she rubbed her forehead with her thumb and forefinger.

"Do you love him?" Sherri asked.

"I have *feelings* for him…but I don't know." Emma hesitated. Was she being honest, if not with Sherri, with herself? "Well, yes. I think I do."

"Okay, I'm trying to understand the issue here, so I can figure out how to help. If you ask me, you two belong together." Propping her elbows on the table, Sherri leaned forward. "What's the real problem?"

"It's me…"

Sherri cocked her head to the side. "How so?"

Emma watched the coffee in her cup form little eddies as she swirled it. "My last relationship—engagement, in fact—didn't go so well. Oh, I know it's foolish making comparisons. Josh isn't Richard—my ex. I understand that. But I'm not sure I could handle being hurt like that again." With a sardonic smile, she added, "I suppose you could say I have trust issues."

Sherri squeezed Emma's hand reassuringly. "I'm sorry for whatever went on with your ex, Emma. I expect whatever happened, you didn't deserve it. But let me say this again about Josh. He *is* a great guy. He has a heart of gold and a deep-rooted core of decency. In all the years I've known him, he has never hurt anyone, at least not knowingly." She paused. "You *can* trust him. You're a lucky woman to have his affection and not just his attention."

Emma knew it was true and appreciated Sherri's affirmation. It was her bruised and battered heart that she needed to convince.

"Emma, I hope you consider me a friend. If you ever want some company or to talk, give me a call."

"I appreciate it, Sherri. I will."

They were finishing their second cup of coffee when Josh walked into the kitchen, wiping his hands on a towel. He raised an eyebrow in amusement. "Am I interrupting?"

When Emma and Sherri glanced at each other, but neither of them said anything, he continued, "Should I leave?"

Sherri checked her watch. "Oh, my gosh. I didn't realize it was so late." Rising, she took the two empty mugs. She shot a brief, conspiratorial glance at Emma. "I better get going." She turned her attention to Josh as she placed the mugs into the dishwasher. "How did the delivery go?"

"Mother and pups—all nine of them—are doing well."

"Oh, my lord! Nine more pups?"

"Yes. And the Hansons have assured me yet again they'll get Misty spayed."

Sherri let out an unladylike snort. "That'll be the day. Bye, Emma." As she walked by Josh, she gave his cheek a friendly pat. "See you tomorrow, Doc."

CHAPTER EIGHTEEN

JOSH HAD BEEN trying hard to keep things light, to forget about the night he'd told Emma he loved her. He could rationalize—he could *understand*—that she needed more time, but his head and his heart were a considerable distance apart on the matter.

Emma had made the effort to come see him, and that said something.

He swung his arm around her shoulder as they strolled to his house. Winston greeted Emma enthusiastically when she walked in, but his tail drooped and he gave her a mournful expression when he realized that his pals didn't accompany her. With a humanlike sigh, he trudged off into the kitchen.

Josh watched him go and shook his head. "I might have to adopt one of the Hansons' pups, if this keeps up."

"As you've said, they're pack animals. I know Max is a lot happier since Theo's come into our lives."

"You, Theo and Max could just move in

here… Sorry," he added hurriedly when he saw the pained expression on her face.

"Speaking of the Hansons' pups," she said, changing the subject, "do you think one would make a good service dog?"

"I don't know that much about it," he said, as they walked into his living room. He gave her a considering look. "You're serious about this?"

"I'm thinking about it. I can't get it out of my mind." She glanced away. "I want to do something that's meaningful. Worthwhile." She linked and unlinked her fingers in a nervous gesture. "I feel useless, not doing anything."

He moved to sit next to her. "Don't think that." He heard the anger in his own voice and saw her cringe. Slight but there. He tamped down his frustration. "What about the work you're doing for Elite Consulting?" he asked. "That's going well, isn't it?"

"Yes. I suppose. I like working for Arlene… but I've noticed a change in her. Something is different, and I've been afraid to ask her what it is. I wonder if I've made a mistake on something, or she's just not happy with the quality of my work."

The exasperation reared up again. To vent it, Josh rose and paced away. "I don't like hearing you talk like that. Emma, you can do whatever you want to do. Richard was wrong. Morgan was wrong. Your former boss was wrong."

When he turned back to her, there was a sad little smile playing at her lips. "Really? All those people were wrong and I was right?"

He shoved his hands into his pants pockets to keep from throwing them into the air. "Yeah. They were. If anyone hears negatives and criticism long enough, they'll start to believe it. It's time you started hearing the positives and believed in yourself again."

Emma laced her fingers together again, and he noticed her hands were trembling. She rose, her eyes glistening. "I—I better go."

Josh cursed himself silently for upsetting her, but he didn't know what else he could do to get through to her. He took three long strides to stand in front of her and gently rested his hands on her shoulders. "Let's not talk about that anymore, okay?" He stroked a thumb along the side of her neck. "Please stay."

She nodded mutely, and lowered to the sofa again, perching on the edge, her back straight and stiff. "Can't we just go back to the way things were? I don't want there to be problems between us. I—I care about you a great deal. I've missed you…and how we were before."

Josh reached for her hand and squeezed it. He understood what that admission meant, coming from her. Leaning in, he rested his forehead against hers.

"Can that be enough for now, Josh?" she continued. "Can—"

A loud knock interrupted her. Josh rose to answer it and returned shortly with the sheriff by his side.

Chad Atkins slid off his hat and nodded in greeting toward Emma. "Sorry to interrupt. When I saw your SUV out front, Emma, I thought it would be easier to catch you together."

Josh gestured for him to sit.

Chad chose an armchair, crossed his legs at the ankles and rested his hat in his lap.

"What's up, Chad?" Josh sat down beside Emma. "This obviously isn't a social call."

"No, it isn't." Turning his attention to Emma, he asked, "Have you had any further problems since the incident in the forest?"

She shook her head.

"All right. That's good."

"C'mon, Chad. What aren't you telling us?"

Chad's gaze met Josh's. "Those shell casings I found in the forest?" Josh nodded.

"They weren't recent. They're weathered. They had to have been there for a couple of months, probably since the start of the hunting season."

Emma's hand tensed in Josh's.

Chad looked back at her. "Unfortunately, they don't help us move forward to determine who injured your dog. One of my deputies and I have questioned a number of the local hunters, and we've come up empty there, too."

"Where does that leave us?" Josh inquired.

"Back at square one, I'm afraid. I went out there with one of my deputies. I wanted to check with you, but your gate was locked. I hope you don't mind, Emma, but we wanted to have a look."

"No, that's fine."

"Well, we found reasonably fresh footprints leading off the path." He turned to Emma again. "Do you stay on the trails when you go through the woods or wander off them?"

"I stay on them mostly," she confirmed. "Especially when I have the dogs with me."

Chad nodded. "The reason I ask is the footprints were relatively small. It could be a man who wears a small shoe, or a woman who wears a large one. Josh, tell me again about, ah…that former friend of yours."

"It wasn't her," Josh said curtly.

"How can you be sure?" Chad asked.

Josh glanced at Emma. "Because she called me this week."

Her lips firmed into a straight line. He understood what she might be thinking. He would have told her, if they'd been talking the way they used to.

He gave her a grim smile. "So *she* could tell *me* it's over. If it means no more contact, I don't care how she rationalizes it in her mind." He turned back to Chad. "She couldn't have cut Max. She was out of the country. The reason she said it's over between us is she's met someone. A Wall Street investment banker. She said he took her to Mustique for the week. You can check it out and confirm easy enough."

Chad nodded.

"She did admit she came to my house the day Emma picked up Theo, but she said when she sped off she headed straight back to New York City."

"So what now?" Emma interjected, her eyes darting back and forth between the two men.

"I'm still inclined to think it was a hunter you encountered in the forest, but just to be on the safe side…" Chad let the words hang for a few moments. "I'm going to have a chat with the guys from the NYPD. I've got to get going. "Remember, we're due to have a couple of beers again soon," he said to Josh as he rose and put his hat back on.

"Looking forward to it," Josh said and walked Chad out.

EMMA TRIED HARD not to dwell on three things. She and Josh didn't seem to be able to get the equilibrium back in their relationship, and it bothered her. On the surface, everything seemed normal, but there was something missing. She thought of it almost like a light dimming. It still shone, but not as bright. And she knew it was her fault.

Secondly, since the assignments from Pinnacle Communications had dried up completely, she wondered how long Arlene Greenberg would keep giving her work. That shift in their relationship had persisted and she wasn't sure what had caused it or what it meant.

Finally, the sheriff had continued to inquire about the incident in the woods, but the local hunters either didn't know anything or weren't forthcoming. There were still no leads as to who was responsible. To the best of her knowledge, the NYPD hadn't given him anything that he could go on, either. The matter concerned her sufficiently that she and the dogs stayed out of the forest.

Without assignments to occupy her, to keep herself from dwelling on the negatives she did some more in-depth research on service-and-therapy dogs, and their training. She reached out to a member of the Operation Pawsitive Change team, and started a discussion about the qualification process of becoming a service-dog trainer. The more she thought about it, the more serious she became about adopting one of the Hansons' puppies for that purpose.

She was making a sandwich for lunch, although she wasn't feeling very hungry, when the phone rang. It was a blocked call, but with the mood she was in, she didn't care who it might be.

"You've done it, haven't you? Wasn't enough what you'd already done, was it?" It was Richard but it had taken her a few moments to realize it, since his speech was slurred. She glanced at her watch. It was barely noon.

"Richard, are you drunk?" she asked, incredulous. He'd always enjoyed a drink or two, but she'd never known him to drink during a workday or get sloppy drunk.

"S'nothing. It's not like I have anything important to do. Thanks to you."

"What are you talking about?"

"I've been pulled off the defense team. Morgan's furious about the new charges that have been laid against him. He knows you were involved in making it happen, and he didn't think it would be good to have me defending him 'cause of my relationship with you."

Emma was stunned. She knew how much Richard's career meant to him—it had cost them their relationship, after all. "Richard, I'm *so* sorry."

"S'rry? You kidding? If you'd listened when I told you to leave things alone, just stay out of it? I'd still be leading the defense team. Now? I'm just a witness. The partnership is gone for me. Poof! Just like that! Gone, because of you," he added bitterly.

He was definitely drunk. "Why are you calling me? What do you want?"

"Watch y'self, Emma. That's all. It might not just be that damn dog that's hurt next time."

Emma froze. "Richard…what are you saying?"

"Nothin'. Just watch yourself."

After Emma hung up the phone, she wondered how Richard had known about Max's injury. Who had she told? She couldn't remember. Could Richard or someone from

Morgan's defense team be watching her? Regardless, she heard the threat loud and clear and wondered if she should tell the sheriff.

She dismissed the thought. Despite how it had ended between them, she was certain that Richard wouldn't physically hurt her or Max. The last thing she wanted to do was further antagonize Richard. That could only lead to more trouble for her.

CHAPTER NINETEEN

JOSH HAD ALREADY ordered a beer and was sipping it slowly when Chad entered The Lookout, wearing jeans, a sweatshirt and their university's bomber jacket. Josh rose and shook his friend's hand as he walked up to the table.

"I have to say, I prefer seeing you in plain clothes, even if the haircut still shouts cop."

Chuckling, Chad signaled to the waitress to bring him a beer, too. "Never got over your healthy respect of the law, huh?"

"Hard to believe we're those guys who used to sneak beers out of our homes when we were fourteen and drink them behind the school."

"Not to mention our attempt at forging IDs so we could get into a bar and check out the women when we were seventeen."

"Yeah, fun times! We're getting old, Chad, and what have we got to show for it?"

Chad's face sobered and he took a long drink from his bottle. "That didn't sound like idle banter."

Josh glanced up in surprise. He hadn't intended to let his melancholy show.

"Does it have something to do with our newest resident?"

As usual, Chad got right to the heart of the matter. Josh shouldn't have been surprised. Other than his family, no one had known him longer or knew him better than Chad. He let out an exasperated sigh.

"I'll take that as a yes. You want to talk about it?"

Josh considered how to best broach the subject. Directness was always his preference. "I'm in love with her."

Chad's eyebrows shot up and he leaned back in his chair. "Well, well, well," he said, grinning. "That's a first for you, isn't it?"

"Yeah, it is."

Chad had another drink of beer, but kept his gaze leveled on Josh. "I don't have to be an expert investigator to figure out you're not happy about it. Hey, pal, we're all destined to take the fall…sooner or later."

Josh gave Chad a half smile. "You've managed to avoid it, at least since Janie Miller in university."

Chad rubbed a fist over his heart. "Yeah, she broke my heart pretty good. But we're not talking about me. Emma seems like a great lady, and she's a looker, too. What's wrong with being in love with her?"

"It's not that I don't want to be in love with her. It's the complications."

"I'm listening."

It couldn't hurt to get Chad's perspective, Josh decided, so he gave his friend the gist of it. "So I've been trying to subtly help her rebuild her self-esteem. If that works, and she starts to believe in her professional capabilities again—and understanding she needs to work—will she just pick up where she left off with her career, and move back to New York City? And I lose her? Add to that, when I told her I loved her, I scared the heck out of her and it hasn't been the same between us since." He finished his beer. "Why can't love be easy?"

"Nothing that's worth having is. Let's take it one problem at a time, shall we? First, she doesn't look like the skittish sort to me. She's handling the problems she's experienced like a trooper."

"Oh, she's got backbone, I have no doubt about that. It's only where her own abilities are involved that she's fragile."

Chad shrugged. "Okay, you're working on that. I believe with time—and distance from her ex—her resilience will be restored. If you love her, as you say, investing time should not be a problem."

Josh didn't have to think about it. "Of course not."

"Then let's take her regaining her confidence and resuming her career in the city. That's a tougher one. If she wants to continue where she left off, and you believe it's the right thing for her, you need to support and encourage her. Otherwise, you'd be selfish and that's not what love's about."

"And therein lies my dilemma. I don't know if I'd survive in the city, let alone have a viable veterinary practice there," Josh said with a scowl. "And when did you get so smart about love?" he added with a shake of his head.

"I understand it enough. You know, there's an old saying—'if you love something, set it free. If it returns, it will always be yours. If it doesn't, it never was.'"

Josh nodded again. "Yeah, that about sums it up, doesn't it? I do love her, so I'll have to back her...no matter what."

EMMA FINALLY DECIDED to call Arlene. Much as she'd concluded when Daniel had first left a message for her wanting to talk, knowing—however hard it might be—was better than fearing the unknown. If Arlene didn't want her to keep working for her, she'd rather be aware of it now, so she could deal with it.

The call only took fifteen minutes and now she knew where she stood with Arlene. Arlene had explained that the assignments had been a test of Emma's capabilities, to make sure she was as good as Arlene had surmised.

According to Arlene, Emma had exceeded her expectations. What Arlene had been leading up to was deciding how best to get Emma to work for her exclusively. She obviously hadn't known that Emma was no longer freelancing for Pinnacle.

Arlene asked to meet with Emma as soon as possible to discuss her proposal.

Putting her insecurities aside, Emma was thrilled. If Arlene sent more assignments her way, she'd have a bit of breathing space from a cash-flow perspective. And she was relieved that Arlene liked her work, when she'd begun to suspect it might just be the opposite.

Emma wanted to see Josh and tell him in person. He'd been so kind and understanding. She decided to surprise him at the clinic. Going into town would also give her the opportunity to stop by the post office to pick up her mail.

Emma hopped out of her X5 in front of the post office. The young man behind the counter turned toward the door at the sound of the chimes. His cheeks flushed a bright red.

Emma smiled as she greeted him.

"Good morning, Ms. Meadows."

"Emma…" she insisted, as she had each time she'd come into the post office.

His flush intensified. "Ah, Emma… I'll get your mail for you."

"I'd appreciate it."

He returned with a handful of envelopes of varying sizes—bills, personal correspondence, advertising flyers and a large manila envelope—and handed them to her. When her hand inadvertently touched his, his eyes widened and his jaw dropped. As she walked out of the post office, she could hear his long-suffering sigh behind her, and couldn't help but smile again.

Parking her vehicle in front of the veterinary clinic, she rushed in hoping she would catch Josh between appointments.

There were two people in the reception area, one with a beagle, the other with a Persian cat in a carrier. With Josh nowhere in sight and the examination room door closed, she knew he had to be with a patient.

"Hey, Emma," Sherri greeted as she emerged from a back room.

"I need to see Josh for a minute." Her gaze

shifted to the people waiting. "Would it be possible," she implored in a quiet voice, "before his next appointment?"

Sherri smiled at Emma reassuringly. "I don't see why not. He's a little ahead of schedule, as unusual as that is." She gestured toward Josh's office. "Wait in there, and I'll send him in as soon as he finishes with Mr. Robertson's Buddy. He shouldn't be long."

"Thanks, Sherri."

"No problem. Could I get you a coffee or something cold to drink while you wait?"

"No, thanks. I'm fine." As Sherri closed the door behind her, Emma settled in the chair in front of Josh's desk and idly leafed through a veterinary supply magazine.

She couldn't remember feeling this good— *this optimistic*—in a long time.

When the door opened and Josh entered, she rushed to him and threw herself into his arms. Josh stumbled under her unexpected weight. "Is everything okay?"

As Emma knew she was generally more reserved with her emotions, and especially so with the recent distance between them, no wonder he looked surprised. She framed his face with her hands and dropped a quick succession of kisses on his brow, his cheeks and his mouth. "Oh, things are a lot better than okay! Thank you! Thank you for believing in me and encouraging me."

The confused, uncertain look on his face made him just that much more adorable.

"Okay. You're welcome for...?"

"I called Arlene and she likes my work! So much so, that she wants me to work for her firm exclusively," she blurted out.

A mixture of emotions played across his face, but then joy and maybe something akin to pride settled on it. He lifted her off the ground and spun her around. "Congratulations! That's terrific news. What does it involve?"

"I have no idea," she laughed. "I don't have the details. Arlene suggested we have lunch to discuss it."

Grinning at her, he said, "All right, but I'm taking you out to dinner tonight to celebrate. Okay?"

"It was just a call, Josh."

"Doesn't matter. She recognizes your capabilities and wants to meet with you to talk terms. That's cause for celebration."

She was touched that he would see it like that. "Okay. I'd love to."

"Great. I have to get back to my patients, Emma, but I'll pick you up at seven. Does that suit you?"

"Perfectly!" She took his face in her hands once more and gave him what she wanted to be a heart-stopping, hormone-elevating kiss. It must have worked, as he didn't immediately follow her out. She hoped it was because he needed some time to settle before he resumed his appointments. The thought made her smile.

On a whim, she opened his office door again and stepped back inside. With her eyes locked on his, she whispered, "Thank you, Josh, for not ridiculing or dismissing me. It means a lot to me." Surprising them both, she reached for his hand and, with her eyes steady on his, added softly, "I love you."

Speechless, Josh could only stare at her as she turned her back to him and walked out of his office a second time.

Still in a state of euphoria, Emma drove home. She wasn't a complete failure. Someone who knew her history liked her work and wanted her to do more of it. And—entirely unexpected—she'd fallen in love again! If she was honest with herself, she'd known for some time that she was falling in love with Josh. She'd just been too afraid to admit it... until today.

And it felt wonderful!

She was going to take a long bath and then

pamper herself to look as good as she possibly could for dinner with the man she loved.

The man I love, she repeated to herself. It sounded good to her. It sounded right. *And he loves me, too.* Which made it perfect.

When she got home, she placed her mail on top of her desk in her office and let the dogs out, before she went upstairs to soak in the tub.

True to his word, Josh arrived at seven. Winston trotted happily in to greet his pals. Though they hadn't discussed where he was taking her, they both appreciated the celebratory nature of the evening and had dressed accordingly.

Emma had decided to wear a long A-line skirt in a deep russet, with a soft, cream-colored cashmere sweater and high-heeled brown boots with a matching leather jacket. She'd left her hair straight and loose, but she had formed two thin braids on either side at her temples and secured them together at the back of her head. The color she'd put on her eyelids picked up the rich tone of the skirt, and her lipstick was a pale cinnamon gloss that accentuated rather than overpowered the natural hue of her lips.

She was pleased when Josh told her that he

thought he'd never seen her look more beautiful.

He'd chosen a wonderful Italian restaurant in the town of Kingston. Emma had veal parmigiana, and Josh selected the osso buco. He delighted her by ordering a bottle of Dom Pérignon, in keeping with their festive mood.

"I'm going to do it!" Emma declared during their meal.

"The work for Elite?" he asked, apparently not following her.

"No. I'd like to adopt one of the Hanson pups and train him to be a service dog. I've done the research. They even have grants and I've applied for one. Whether I get it or not, I'd like to do it."

Josh's smile faded.

"What? What's wrong? You don't think I can do it?"

"No. It's not that. The Hanson pups all have homes."

"Oh." Now that she'd made up her mind, Emma felt the disappointment acutely. "Well, maybe next time." She loved the idea and she comforted herself that she wouldn't give up. There would be more pups.

They finished their dinner with tiramisu and lattes. The slight tension between them in recent weeks seemed to have completely evaporated. Josh appeared both proud and excited for her, and Emma found herself falling even more in love with him.

The temperature had cooled significantly by the time they returned to the cottage, and there was a light snow falling. The silvery sweep of moonlight and the brilliant sparkle of the stars filtering in through the vestibule's windows provided the only illumination as they said good-night.

THERE WAS A new tenderness to their caresses, a new dimension to the sensations, a new quality to their kisses. When he told her again that he loved her, she gave back the words of love without reservation.

"You make it very difficult for me to leave you," Josh conceded with a small shake of his head. "How am I supposed to just walk out the door after that?"

"Look at it another way," she countered with a mischievous gleam in her eyes. "It'll give you something to think about until tomorrow."

He laughed. "Trust me. I didn't need that kiss to keep me thinking of you." After a final hug, he whistled for Winston.

As Josh let Winston hop into his truck, a

thought started to form in his mind and he mulled it over as he drove home.

Yes, he accepted he was in love with Emma. He'd known that for a while. But now he also knew absolutely that he wanted to spend the rest of his life with her. She'd finally admitted to him that she loved him, too. It got him reflecting beyond the present.

Marriage, he thought with a jolt. He'd never considered marriage with any woman he'd dated before Emma.

Yet, there it was. He wanted to *marry* Emma. He felt it with a quiet confidence—an unquestionable certainty.

With the offer of steady work from Elite Consulting, hopefully there would be no incentive for her to move back to the city to resume her career. And even if she did?

They'd find a way to work around it. Couples had to deal with greater obstacles.

The challenge, he knew, would be to get her to trust enough in their love to be willing to marry him. He pulled into his drive with a smile on his face and determination in his mind.

EMMA WOKE WITH a feeling of sheer contentment. She wandered into the kitchen to get a cup of coffee while she let the dogs outside.

Mug in hand and the dogs at her heels, she headed to her office. Only then did she realize that she'd neglected to open her mail. Her excitement from getting the call from Arlene and—more importantly—admitting she loved Josh had caused her to forget just about everything else.

The item that caught her attention was the large manila envelope. It was light and thin. There was no name, personal or corporate, with the return address. Just the address itself. She didn't recognize the street name, but noted uneasily that the zip code looked familiar.

A ripple of apprehension coursed through her. She searched her contact list, just to be sure.

The zip code was American Freedom Munitions' head office location. *This couldn't be good.*

With a sigh, she slid her letter opener under the flap. She reached inside and found— nothing.

She opened the envelope wider and peered inside. Nothing. That's odd, she thought.

What's the likelihood that someone intended to send me something but forgot to place it inside the envelope before sealing it?

Then again, what's the alternative? Someone sent me an empty envelope?

Curious, she booted up her laptop and did a search for the return address. She repeated the search to be certain, but got the same result. The address didn't exist. The street name existed but not the number. There was a large break in the numbering on the side of the street where the return address would have been. More than a little disconcerted and with her curiosity piqued, she did a satellite street-view search of the location. The area appeared to be a large green space, a park perhaps. Zooming in, her fingers jerked away from the keyboard. She pushed back in her chair.

It was a cemetery.

She set aside the envelope and tried to put it out of her mind. She didn't want it to dampen her good mood.

She took a sip of her now cold coffee and started work on the latest assignment she'd received from Arlene. Although she had trouble concentrating at first, her focus gradually shifted to the task at hand. By midday she had effectively blocked the empty envelope out of her mind.

JOSH AND WINSTON arrived at Emma's shortly before six and followed her into the kitchen so they could get dinner started. He leaned back casually against the counter, legs crossed at the ankles, one hand tucked into the pocket of his jeans, the other holding a glass of red wine. He admired yet again how much more confident she seemed since he'd first met her.

"How was your day?" he asked.

He could see that giddy sense of excitement she still had over the fact that her work was valued and, hopefully, her financial situation would be resolved, too, and was happy for her.

Emma glanced over her shoulder and grinned. He felt an altogether different sensation blow through him, nearly bringing him to his knees. He'd never felt such an all-consuming love before, and wondered if he'd live through it, if she decided she didn't want to marry him.

He set down his glass, pushed away from the cabinets and walked over to her. "I'm very proud of you." He placed his hands on the counter on either side of her, effectively blocking her in, and nuzzled her neck. He'd just have to make the most of every moment they had together and not worry about what might come next.

"And you smell wonderful." He turned her toward him. Taking her hand into his, palm up, he raised it to his lips and placed a kiss in its center. "So, do you know when you and Arlene will get together?"

"She suggested some dates for us to have lunch in the city. Could I leave the boys with you when I go? I doubt it would take too long, but I don't want to worry about missing a feeding or walk time with them."

"Of course." He stepped away to give her room to finish their dinner, and he started to set the table.

She turned off the stove and plated their meal. "It's been a lot to absorb, and—and it's been a strange day."

"Strange? In what way?"

Carrying the plates to the table, she paused. "Something odd happened."

"You got another contract offer in the mail for exclusive freelance work and there's a bidding war for you?" he teased as they sat down.

She smiled. "No. But it did have to do with mail. I received an envelope and there was nothing in it."

He looked up from his meal.

"No big deal if not for this," she continued. "The return address is from the zip code where American Freedom Munitions has its head office. When I searched the address, I found that it doesn't exist. There's a cemetery in the location that corresponds to the street address."

Josh put down his cutlery. "You need to tell Chad about this."

Emma let out a nervous laugh. "I'd hoped you'd tell me it was someone's silly mistake and nothing I should worry about."

"I'm sorry to disappoint you."

"You think I *should* be concerned about it?"

"I don't want to alarm you unnecessarily, but the scientist in me doesn't accept coincidences, and this one sounds like a big one."

"So what's the point of it?"

"I can't dismiss the idea that it's a message. First your ex-fiancé calls to try to scare you off, and now it seems that someone wants you to know that *they*, whoever they are, know where *you* are." He held her gaze. "It might be nothing. But we can't dismiss the possibility that it's a form of intimidation, as perhaps the incident in the forest was intended to be."

"Intimidation for what purpose?"

"They know you'll be a key witness for the prosecution with respect to the criminal negligence charges against Morgan. Maybe they hope you won't testify."

"I can't do that!"

"Well, then maybe they hope your testimony won't be as convincing." He leaned over and took her free hand. "It's probably nothing, but I'd rather we err on the side of caution. I'll let Chad know."

"Maybe I'm just jumpy because of what Daniel said about being cautious."

"Maybe, but Daniel made an important point. I'll fill Chad in and I want you to be very careful. Call me if anything worries you."

"Okay." She moistened her lips. "This discussion is making me nervous. What's Chad going to do about an empty envelope? He can't trace it, can he?"

"Unless the person sending it had previous run-ins with the law and had their fingerprints on file, there probably isn't. I just want Chad to know what's going on. Try not to worry about it," he said, but knew he'd be having another beer with Chad as soon as he was available.

"All right." She picked up her cutlery but only toyed with her food.

If he'd lost his appetite, he supposed she had every reason to have lost hers, as well.

EMMA AGREED TO meet Arlene Greenberg for lunch at Le Meurice on 52nd Street in New York City.

Emma was both nervous and excited as she drove to the city. It helped for her to keep thinking of the positive feedback Arlene had given her on her assignments. Josh's support and unquestionable belief in her bolstered her confidence, too.

Arlene was already sitting at a corner table when Emma arrived at the restaurant. She smiled as she walked toward the table, and Arlene rose to greet her.

Arlene's handshake was firm and warm. Emma was relieved that her hand was cool and dry, conveying confidence as opposed to the nerves she felt rioting under the surface.

"It's a pleasure seeing you again, Emma."

"I'm grateful for the opportunity." She paused. Her smile broadened. "And for your confidence in me."

Arlene lifted a bottle of Perrier from the table and, at Emma's nod, filled her water glass. "Emma…" she began, but paused as the waiter approached. He offered cocktails, which they both declined, and ran through the specials. With the waiter's departure, Arlene continued, her voice business-like. "I'm not going to play games with you. It's not my style. I prefer to be direct."

Emma's breath caught. Had she decided to back out? Had she set up a luncheon meeting to tell her she was *not* interested in having Emma do work for Elite Consulting after all? No. Although Arlene's statement had her nerves jumping even more, she did her best to not let it show.

"As I said over the telephone," Arlene continued, "I've been very pleased with the work you've been doing for us. So much so that, as I said, I want a bigger role for you and one that's exclusive to us."

Emma smiled hesitantly.

"Believe me, Emma, this isn't altruism. We've grown sufficiently enough to expand and I've decided that we need another client executive. You'd be a great addition to our team, and I believe we'd work well together."

Emma could feel her mouth drop open and there was a roar of blood rushing in her ears. "A client executive? I don't understand."

Arlene smiled at her encouragingly and outlined the role in broad brushstrokes. The job itself sounded similar to the role she'd had at Tyson, Myers and Smith. If she accepted it, she'd no longer be able to hide behind a computer; she'd have to interact with clients again.

"I'm honored," Emma said, at a loss for what else to say.

When the waiter came back to inquire if they were ready to order, Emma hadn't even glanced at the menu, nor did she think she could eat much under the circumstances. She ordered a Caesar salad, and Arlene ordered the salmon special.

As they ate, Arlene gave Emma additional insights into the company, its clients, its revenue and growth projections. Arlene went on to summarize the terms of the offer.

"Your offer is very generous," Emma acknowledged.

"You'll have an office overlooking Central Park, and company paid parking, should you choose to drive to work," Arlene added.

Office and parking? Emma hadn't thought about the details, but, of course, as a client executive Arlene would want her to be in their offices in New York City, not working from Sanctuary Cove. She'd known that at some level, but had pushed it to the back of her mind. If she had to move back to the city, she could at least afford to keep the cottage, but it would again be for weekend use only. She thought of Josh, and what that would mean to their relationship.

By the time they'd finished their meals, Emma's head was spinning, and part of her— that nagging insecure part—wished she didn't have to face the decision that was before her.

They declined dessert but each ordered a coffee. When Arlene lapsed into silence, Emma sensed she was looking for some sort of response from her. An indication of what she was thinking. Suddenly, Emma felt the lunch was a big mistake. She didn't know if she could accept the offer, but her doubts had nothing to do with her belief in her own capabilities this time. They had to do with what she wanted out of life, where she wanted to live and, most importantly, what was between her and Josh.

Finally, Emma thanked Arlene and assured her that she'd give the matter serious consideration and get back to her as soon as possible.

After they said goodbye, Emma climbed into her X5 and her first thought was of Josh.

They had a lot to discuss.

CHAPTER TWENTY

JOSH HAD ALSO spent the day in New York City.
He purposely picked the same day Emma had
her meeting with Arlene Greenberg, so she
wouldn't know he wasn't in Sanctuary Cove.
He had Sherri reschedule all his appointments
and take care of all three dogs, so he could
have a full day. He wanted to ensure Emma
had no knowledge of what he was up to. He
was nervous enough about what she'd think,
without her being aware of it in advance.

It hadn't taken much to get his sister, Angie,
to be his accomplice. A day of shopping in
NYC and the added inducement of Josh buying her lunch had sealed the deal as far as
Angie was concerned.

Having accomplished what he'd set out to
do, Josh dropped off Angie at her apartment
in Westchester on his way back to Sanctuary Cove.

"Thanks again, Ange," he said as he gave
her a hug. "Don't know how I would've done

it without you. I'm grateful that I didn't have to find out."

"I'm glad you asked." Her eyes misted. "I'm so happy for you, Josh. I haven't spent much time with Emma, but I look forward to doing so in the future. From what I've seen, you're perfect for each other."

He grinned. "Let's hope the lady agrees."

Angie chuckled. "She's a bright girl. How could she not? Mom and Dad will be thrilled."

"Hey, remember you promised not to say anything until I've had a chance to break the news to them," he reminded her. "Don't say anything to Ross, either," he said, referring to their brother. "Promise?"

She rolled her eyes. "It won't be easy but, yes, I promise."

Josh thanked Angie once more and waited as she let herself into her building.

He climbed back into his Yukon and started the engine. He pulled the small silver box out of his pocket. Flipping the lid open, he grinned at the sparkling brilliant-cut, one-carat diamond. He lifted the ring out of the box to have a closer look.

The exquisite diamond was simply set in a thin, white-gold band encrusted with smaller diamonds.

Classic, not elaborate or ostentatious. He

was glad he'd had the benefit of Angie's input, as he'd been thinking of something quite different. After looking at what must have been a hundred engagement rings, with Angie's guidance he had easily decided on the ring he now held. And it was exactly right for Emma. He replaced the ring, closed the lid of the box and slipped it back into his pocket.

Now all he had to do was put the wheels in motion for the rest of his plan to get the ring on Emma's finger. As he headed north on Interstate 87, he contemplated how best to do it.

He decided to start those wheels turning that night.

"How did your meeting with Arlene go?" Josh asked Emma as soon as he arrived at her cottage.

"Oh, good. Great. I guess."

He looked at her carefully, trying to gauge her mood. She didn't seem upset, but she didn't seem overly excited, either. Reserved was the best way he could think to describe her demeanor. He didn't know what to make of it. "Do you want to talk about it?"

"Oh, I want to discuss it with you. Get your opinion, but let me think about it a little first."

"Okay. But know that I believe in you and want what you want."

She gave him a weak smile. "I appreciate it."

It wasn't until after dinner that Josh decided to start working on his plan. "It occurred to me it's been quite a while since I've taken any time off," Josh said casually as he and Emma were loading the dishwasher. "I've been thinking it's time to take a break from the clinic and get away from Sanctuary Cove for a few days."

"Oh?" Emma looked disappointed and he tried not to be happy about it, as he took it as an indication that she'd miss him if he went on his own. "Where are you thinking of going?" she asked.

He reached for her hand and raised it to his lips. "Not me. Us. If you're willing. I'd like to take you away for a few days. A mini-holiday of sorts, before we have too much snow to contend with."

The smile that spread across her face warmed his heart. "That sounds nice. What do you have in mind?"

He'd thought of and quickly rejected the idea of going to New York City. While it would have been a great place to spoil her with a five-star hotel and a variety of restaurants, he understood that the city held painful memories for her. He wanted a place all their own, with no history for either of them, where they could make their own memories. "There's a wonderful place, the Seacliffe Hotel, in Newport, Rhode Island. It has an excellent restaurant and a full-service spa, if you like that sort of thing, and the area offers a lot to do. We could go hiking, shopping, snowshoeing—weather permitting. Whatever you like. How does that sound?"

Emma threw her arms around Josh's neck and gave him an enthusiastic kiss. "It sounds wonderful! What about the dogs?"

"Sherri would be happy to dog sit while we're gone. She could stay here or at my place with them, whichever you prefer."

"When do we leave?" she asked excitedly.

EMMA HADN'T SAID anything further to Josh about her meeting with Arlene. Josh assumed she'd talk to him about it when she was ready. For his part, he was eager to give Emma the ring and making that happen was his focus. He was able to arrange the trip sooner than expected. Based on his schedule at the clinic and Sherri's availability, they settled on a four-day trip at the end of the following week. They left in the morning. The early December air was crisp, and snowflakes were lazily drifting to the ground.

The small silver box was nestled inside Josh's coat pocket.

The three-and-a-half-hour drive went quickly and they arrived in Newport before noon. They entered the gorgeous, fifteen-acre grounds of the Seacliffe Hotel. As they made their way around a bend in the drive, the main building came into view. It was clad in stone and surrounded by rolling lawns, mature trees and generous garden beds. As a backdrop, there was a spectacular ocean view. In addition to the main hotel, the property was dotted with a handful of small, self-contained cottages that Josh had briefly considered. He concluded that both he and Emma had enough seclusion living in Sanctuary Cove. He'd wanted something different. Something special. He'd settled on the two-bedroom penthouse suite in the main building.

A uniformed doorman greeted them as they pulled up to the front entrance. He arranged to have their car parked and their bags seen to, and a bellboy escorted them to their suite.

Josh loved seeing the glow of pleasure on Emma's face, as she took it all in. She stood in the middle of the room and turned in a slow circle, smiling hugely. Delighted by her reaction, Josh knew he'd made the right choice.

The room was decorated in warm, neutral shades with the occasional splash of brilliant color in the form of a throw pillow or a painting. The ceiling was high and vaulted, nearly a story and a half, creating an airy expanse of space. There were two enormous picture windows flanking a stone fireplace. The stonework for the chimney rose from floor to ceiling, the windows on either side soaring up alongside, affording unobstructed views of the grounds and the ocean.

Beyond the windows was a wide terrace overlooking the coastline.

A well-stuffed sofa and armchairs were arranged conversation-style facing the fireplace and view. To the left of the living room was a cozy dining area and an archway leading to an efficiency kitchen. To the right was a small work space with a desk, chair and lamp, and a corridor leading to the bedrooms and main bathroom.

"This is wonderful! Thank you for bringing me here," Emma exclaimed.

Josh circled Emma's waist with his arms and dropped an affectionate kiss on top of her nose. "I'm glad you like it. What do you want to do?"

"I can't decide if I'd rather go out and explore Newport or stay here and enjoy the suite."

He brushed his lips over hers. "Let's make time for both."

Bundled in warm clothes, they walked along Ocean Drive to Main Street. They held hands as they strolled past quaintly decorated shops and charming cafés. Many of the stores were already getting into the Christmas spirit. Occasionally they would stop to window-shop or enter a store and browse.

Josh bought Emma a silly knit hat in the likeness of a pink mouse. She bought him a large ceramic St. Bernard with a small first-aid kit attached to his collar. They stopped at a pizzeria for lunch and shared a large pepperoni pizza. Midafternoon, they headed back to the hotel, happy and tired.

Emma took a bubble bath in the enormous tub of the ensuite of her bedroom. When she joined Josh in the living area, bundled in one of the hotel's thick and luxurious bathrobes, he'd already started a fire and had a bottle of champagne chilling in an ice bucket. They sipped their drinks as they sat on the sofa and watched the lightly falling snow outside.

To Josh, this time together was the prelude to what he'd planned for that evening. He'd been giving how he'd propose to Emma a lot of thought since he'd bought the ring.

He'd made reservations at a French restaurant. He'd order champagne and would devise a ruse to have her go to the ladies' room. Maybe tell her she had a smudge on her nose. While she was gone, he'd place the diamond in her champagne flute and then hope she'd notice it rather than drink it! He'd then tell her he loved her, wanted to spend his life with her and ask her to make him the happiest man in the world by agreeing to marry him.

They both dressed warmly, as they'd decided to walk rather than drive to the restaurant. Josh fingered the small silver box in his jacket pocket as they left the hotel room.

In no hurry, they strolled along Ocean Drive again with Emma comfortably tucked under his arm, her head resting against his shoulder. Although his pulse was racing with anticipation, he felt a wonderful sense of contentment, knowing that Emma was the love of his life. As they neared the shops and restaurants, the lights, activity and noise intensified. Downtown Newport was a popular place on a Friday night, and they weren't the only couple choosing to stroll to their destination.

Josh smiled as they passed a young couple so thoroughly immersed in each other and clearly in love, they were oblivious to everything around them. An elderly pair, probably in their seventies, followed, holding hands and as comfortable with each other as their many years together warranted.

Had he ever noticed couples in love before?

Josh had never considered himself the sentimental sort. It had taken falling in love with Emma to see the whole world in a different way.

He tightened his arm around her and felt a serenity seep through him as she snuggled closer. It was because of how near he was to her—how connected—that he felt her stiffen. Glancing down at her, he saw a wounded expression on her face as she stared across the street.

Following her gaze, he saw a man of about six feet with meticulously styled sandy-brown hair with a slim brunette on his arm laughing up at him as they walked out of a restaurant. Glancing back at Emma, he noted that her attention remained focused on the couple, her face tense and despondent.

Her emotional withdrawal was palpable.

He gave her a gentle squeeze. "Emma, what's wrong?" He had to nudge her and repeat the question, but taking a closer look at the couple, even he could see the man's strong resemblance to her ex-fiancé, Richard.

Emma gave her head a slight shake and looked up at Josh. "Nothing. Nothing, really. My mind was playing tricks on me."

He saw a shimmer in her eyes. Not quite tears but close. "Emma…?" He couldn't believe how much it hurt him to think that just looking at a man who resembled her ex-fiancé would affect her so deeply. Reading up on emotional abuse after his first discussion with Angie about it, he'd been astonished to discover the lasting hold abusers could have over their victims. He'd assumed Emma had moved beyond Richard. Her face pale, her eyes round and large, he had to wonder if she was truly over the guy.

He shifted his gaze back to the couple now strolling on the other side of the street, and cursed the fates for having just spoiled the moment for them.

Once they reached the restaurant, Emma had regained some of her animation, but the sparkle was absent from her eyes.

They were seated at a table in a small alcove overlooking the water. He had the perfect table, the perfect setting to propose to the woman he loved.

But with considerable regret, Josh decided

to hold off on ordering the champagne…and hold off with the proposal. It no longer felt right. He didn't want Emma to be preoccupied with her past when he asked her to share the future with him.

Over cocktails, Emma chattered on about the night sky, the boats in the harbor and many other topics—almost as if she feared silence. He placed his hand on top of hers and interrupted in a quiet but firm voice. "Do you want to talk about what's bothering you?"

She pulled her shoulders back and he could tell she about to deny there was anything wrong, but then seemed to sag. She withdrew her hand from his, glanced down at her glass and sighed. "I… I'm sorry. I don't want to ruin our evening. I don't even know how to explain it." She lifted her gaze to his. "Have you ever felt déjà vu?" At the shake of his head, she looked down again and continued. "Well, that's what I felt on our way here. Just before I left New York City, I saw Richard with another woman." She hesitated again. Swallowed hard. "It happened just a couple of weeks after we split. Granted, we were no longer together, but for him to have moved on so soon…"

When their appetizers were served, she remained silent and then continued. "A couple I saw on the street just now? It was like seeing Richard and that woman again. I truly thought it was them."

"I'm sorry he hurt you, Emma."

A strangled laugh escaped her. "Yeah. Me, too. I wouldn't have expected it to still affect me the way it did. I'm really sorry, Josh."

"You *will* heal," he assured her. "But it takes time." And as he said the words, he slid his hand in his jacket pocket and fingered the silver box again, with disappointment and more than a little frustration this time.

"You haven't told me much about your lunch with Arlene Greenberg," Josh prompted, wanting a change in topic.

A nervous smile flitted across her face, and she took a sip of her wine. "It went well."

He raised an eyebrow. "That's it? You were counting on her giving you steady work. Is that going to happen?"

"Oh, you could say it would be steady."

"That's good, isn't it?" It was like pulling teeth. She didn't look happy. She looked uneasy, and he had no idea why. He prompted her again, and this time she explained to him what had happened.

"She presented you with a contract offer to be a client executive?" he asked.

She nodded. "Yes."

His first thought was that she'd have to move back to the city. There was no way she could do the job from Sanctuary Cove. His words about wanting for her what she wanted came back to taunt him. "Congratulations," he said with forced cheer, as a fist grabbed hold of his heart and squeezed. "Why didn't you tell me sooner?" he asked in a quiet voice. He had a sneaking suspicion why.

"Because—because I didn't know what to do about it."

"And now? Have you decided?"

"No, not yet."

And with those words, Josh realized that it was probably for the best that circumstances unfolded as they had, and he hadn't proposed to Emma. As much as he hated the thought of losing her, her decision about the client executive offer would be crucial to determining the direction of their future together.

CHAPTER TWENTY-ONE

At home in her own bed, Emma woke to the first significant snowfall of the season. Enormous, fluffy flakes drifted gently down. They melted as they hit the open water, but a glistening blanket of white covered the ground. She grinned at the sight.

Texting Josh, she asked that he come over with Winston as soon as he was finished at the clinic. When he arrived, there was already an accumulation of a good four inches of wet, heavy snow.

Barely giving Josh time to say hello, Emma put on her jacket, scarf, hat, gloves and boots. The dogs picked up on the easy sense of play and were also eager to get outside. Their excitement intensified as Josh reached into the vestibule closet and pulled out a rubber football. As soon as he opened the front door, the dogs streaked out.

The air was crisp but not bone-chillingly cold. The flakes clung to their hats, jackets and the dogs' fur. The dogs ran in circles around them until Josh sent the football soaring. In a flurry of flying snow, they raced after it. With one dog or another catching the ball, they chased each other before the triumphant dog would finally return the ball to Josh to start the game all over again.

Josh and Emma made their way along the driveway to its crest before turning back to walk along the snow-covered clearing. When Josh called Emma from behind her, she spun around and a soft ball of snow struck her squarely on her chest.

The dogs got into the spirit as Josh and Emma tossed snowballs at each other, or for them to chase. Emma's aim was accurate, and she was hitting Josh as much as he was hitting her. He must have decided he had had enough snow down the collar of his coat as he seemed determined to put an end to the fight—by tackling her in a patch of fresh snow.

They were both breathless and laughing as she lay sprawled across him. After a long kiss that made Emma's head spin, they brushed themselves off and headed back to the cottage.

When they reached the large granite rock that was Emma's favorite vantage point, she stopped. The stark tree branches and the near black water were in sharp contrast to the blanket of white. In the still air, the dogs' playful yips and barks were the only sounds to be heard.

This spot always made her pensive and it reminded her that she owed Josh an answer about Arlene Greenberg's offer. Since their dinner in Newport, neither of them had spoken of it, but she understood it was on Josh's mind as much as hers.

Emma had considered whether it would be possible for her to continue to live in Sanctuary Cove, and stay in the city a couple of days a week, even if she didn't know how she'd work out the logistics of that with the dogs. It would be a lot of commuting. But she needed income and, right now, Elite Consulting seemed to be the only viable, steady source. But to leave Sanctuary Cove behind for weekends only again? In a few short months, it had become home. More so than the house she'd occupied in the city, or her condo before that.

And a lot of that feeling of home—of belonging—had to do with Josh. How could she leave *him* behind? Her heart ached at the mere prospect of it.

It wasn't an easy decision.

Emma turned to look at Josh, needing to feel the connection.

He smiled down at her and drew her into

his arms. "You look pensive. Want to tell me what's on your mind?"

"Oh, the offer from Elite Consulting." She saw his eyes shutter. Clearly, she'd been correct in her assumption that she wasn't the only one struggling with the decision she had to make. But if she didn't accept, what would she do for income? Would she be able to get more freelance work, sufficient to keep her solvent? And if she was honest with herself, Arlene's offer presented an opportunity for her to prove that she *wasn't* a failure. She *could* do the job. And maybe that was even more compelling than the financial aspect.

Josh gave her a gentle kiss, but Emma felt the distance between them and wished she hadn't said anything about the offer.

They walked back to the cottage, the dogs, happy and exhausted, following them.

While Josh stoked the fires and Emma was making hot chocolate, the phone rang. Emma glanced at the call display.

"It's Daniel," she informed Josh. "I better take it."

Daniel didn't waste any time.

"Because of the fatality, the AFM executives are going to be hit with additional charges."

"Oh…" Emma glanced at Josh. He went

to her and placed a reassuring hand on her shoulder.

"Emma, you need to be careful." Daniel's voice was emphatic.

She thought of the empty envelope and of Max being injured. Of not going into the forest alone any longer. "I have been and I've also made the local police aware."

"That's good. I was going to suggest you do just that. We've experienced some other strange occurrences and I *know* I'm being followed. The police are taking it seriously now, too. Emma, they don't think it's Morgan. After Private Laurence's funeral and the scene with his father, they think it might be him. Mr. Laurence has called me a couple of times. Left garbled and threatening messages, and the police in his hometown have some reports of recent violent behavior. The death of his son—his only child—might have unhinged him."

"That's terrible, Daniel. It makes it even more tragic if Mr. Laurence is doing it. Do you agree with the police?"

"I don't know. The fact that it's happening at all is bad enough, but to think that not only has Mr. Laurence lost his son, it's driven him over the edge… Emma, please be careful," he repeated. "Have your local police contact the

NYPD again if they need verification of what we've reported."

"All right, Daniel. I appreciate the heads-up."

Emma felt the keen edge of despondency as she hung up the phone.

Her sigh was audible and prolonged. Josh simply took her into his arms.

"Daniel's call was to warn me again to be careful. He's certain he's being watched. The police now think so, and they suspect it could be Private Laurence's father," she told him.

"We'll update Chad. Do you want me to stay with you for the time being?"

She thought about it for a moment, but she didn't want to believe there was any great risk to her. "I appreciate the offer, but I'm okay for now." She glanced at the dogs. "Besides, I have Max and Theo. They might not be watch-dogs, but they're an effective early warning system."

"Okay, but keep your cell phone with you at all times, please. If anything strikes you as being out of the ordinary, promise to call me or Chad immediately?"

Emma nodded, and let out another huge breath. "This is so much bigger than I ever thought it would be. It's so beyond me."

Josh slipped a finger under her chin, lifted

her face to his and lowered his lips to hers. "Just know that you're not in this alone. I'm here for you."

MORE SNOW FELL OVERNIGHT. With everything that had been going on, Emma had barely thought of Christmas, but it was fast approaching.

The snow finally slowed by midafternoon. Emma shoveled her walkways and stopped to chat with the man who plowed her driveway. She was just about to strip off the old jeans and sweater she was wearing to take a long, hot bath, when she was startled by a knock on the door. It was much too early for Josh to be stopping by and she wasn't expecting anyone. The dogs' behavior indicated they didn't know whoever was there.

The knock sounded again. She grabbed the phone, just in case she needed it, and glanced out the front window. There was a courier truck parked in her driveway. She rushed to the front door and opened it to the uniform-clad man holding an envelope.

"Ms. Meadows?" he inquired.

"Yes. That's me," she confirmed.

"Quite a place you've got here," he noted, glancing around. "You must be in a big rush to get this," he said, handing her the envelope with the Elite Consulting logo on the top left corner. "We don't usually deliver to such remote locations. There must've been a hefty tab associated with this delivery."

"Uh-huh," Emma agreed, only half listening, wondering what Arlene would be sending her. She felt a pang of guilt over not having gotten back to Arlene with an answer. She'd been procrastinating, pure and simple.

Emma took the envelope into the great room and tore it open. She drew out a letter. Appended to it was a draft contract. She read the letter quickly and scanned the agreement. "Oh, my God!" Apparently, Arlene wanted to nudge her along, because she'd sweetened the offer. Arlene was offering her a partnership! In addition, the base salary and the incentive plan were far more generous than what she'd had at Tyson, Myers and Smith.

She was terrified and elated all at the same time. *She could be a partner!*

The job itself sounded like everything Emma had dreamed of when she'd been climbing the corporate ladder at her former employer.

She needed to see Josh.

She slid the papers back into the envelope, called the dogs, grabbed her coat and keys and headed out the door and to her X5.

Emma was surprised to see no cars in front of the clinic when she arrived at Josh's, considering the time. Not even Sherri's, meaning he must have closed the clinic early. Without thought, she rushed into his house, the dogs at her heels, the envelope clutched in her hand, excitement and nervous energy radiating from her.

"Josh! Josh, you'll never believe what just happened!" she called out as she dashed into his living room—and came to a sudden halt. Max and Theo also slid to a stop beside her.

A lovely middle-aged woman, with dark brown hair and bright green eyes, sat on the sofa. She wore a smoke-gray silk pantsuit and held a martini glass in one hand. A tall man, with shortly cropped black hair, elegantly peppered with gray, stood casually by the fireplace. He wore navy pants and a steel-blue sweater over white button-downs. He swirled the amber liquid in his snifter as he watched Emma with amusement dancing in warm brown eyes.

"Oh. I'm sorry to intrude." Emma felt awkward and wished she'd changed out of the worn jeans she'd been wearing to shovel snow. Catching a glimpse of herself in the mirror over the sofa, she noted with dismay that her hair was tousled and, of course, she hadn't bothered with makeup.

Winston trotted up to greet her and his pals, and she tried to gain strength from the little pack surrounding her. "I didn't know Josh was expecting company," she stammered.

When the man gave her a bemused smile, recognition dawned. She was looking at an older but equally attractive version of Josh. These people weren't merely company, and suddenly she wished she could simply vanish.

Oh, my God. Why didn't Josh tell me his parents were visiting?

The man placed his drink on the mantel, stepped forward and extended a hand. "I'm Steven. Josh's father," he said, confirming what she'd already surmised. "This—" he cast an affectionate glance toward the woman on the sofa "—is my wife, Elizabeth."

Emma shook his hand.

"And you are?" he prompted.

"I'm Emma. Emma Meadows." At his inquiring look, she added, "Um…a friend of Josh's."

Elizabeth rose to join them. "It's lovely to meet you, Emma."

"Josh had to walk over to his clinic," Steven explained. "One of his patients had an emergency while on vacation and the vet treating the dog needed to verify some of his history. Josh'll be right back. Will you join us for a drink?"

All sorts of excuses ran through Emma's mind. She chastised herself for being a coward. She was good with people. She knew she wouldn't have had a problem meeting Josh's parents if she'd not been taken unawares, and if she'd considered herself presentable. If she was serious about Josh—which seemed to be the case more and more each day—she would have to do her best, regardless of the circumstances. "Yes, that would be nice, thank you," she replied, and ran her palms nervously across the fabric of her jeans.

Steven took a step toward the kitchen.

"It's all right. I'll get it," she said hurriedly. "Can I freshen up your drinks?"

They both declined, and Emma escaped the room with the dogs trailing behind her.

In the privacy of the kitchen, she finger-combed her hair to bring it to some semblance of order. She shrugged out of her coat, folded it over the envelope and left both on a chair. After pouring herself a glass of wine, she took a moment to tuck the shirt under her sweater more snugly in her waistband and straighten the collar. Resigned that it was the best she could do, she took her wine and rejoined the elder Dr. Whitmore and his wife in the living room.

JOSH DEALT WITH the emergency consult. He locked the clinic door behind him and, turning, sighted Emma's SUV in his drive.

"Damn." With his parents' unannounced visit upon their return from Europe and then the emergency call, he hadn't had a chance to let Emma know they were visiting. Since he had picked them up from the train station after they'd called him upon their arrival, there was no car in the driveway to alert her that he wasn't alone.

And he wanted very much for Emma and his parents to get along. Not just get along but *like* each other.

He was willing to bet that Emma wouldn't be pleased about the impromptu meeting. Not only that, but he also hadn't had an opportunity to tell his parents about Emma and his plans.

As a result, Josh was certain he would fare no better with his mother, as she'd be disappointed he hadn't told her he was seeing Emma. He'd debated it in his own mind, but had decided it was too important a discussion to have over the telephone when they were an ocean away. "Too late to rectify it all now," he mumbled under his breath as he shoved his hands in his pockets, hunched his shoulders and headed home to face the music.

Opening his front door, he was greeted by the sound of laughter, two soft and feminine voices, and a deeper rumbling one that he would know to be his father's anywhere. Maybe it wasn't going to be so bad after all, he thought optimistically as he walked into the living room. Then he saw Emma's attire and knew without a doubt that it might be fine right now, but he would definitely hear about his oversight later. He liked her casual, but noting the dirt stains and tears on the jeans Emma was wearing, he knew she'd be uncomfortable.

He shrugged in resignation. He might as well make the most of the cheerful mood while it lasted.

All three dogs rose and raced over to greet him. And three pairs of eyes, each with a message to convey, turned toward him. Ruffling the dogs' fur, he decided he might as well start from a position of strength. With a forced smile, he strode into the room. "I see you've met."

He placed a brief kiss on Emma's lips.

Cowardly, perhaps, but he retreated to what

he knew would be safest ground—behind his father's chair—and rested a hand on his father's shoulder. There was a tickle at the base of his neck at the questioning look his mother sent him and Emma's unfathomable one. He'd have felt better if Emma's eyes had been flashing anger. At least he would've known where he stood.

"Yes, we have," his mother responded.

"Your parents were sharing stories from your childhood," Emma added, smiling.

Josh winced inwardly. He could only imagine the stories being told, as he readily acknowledged he hadn't been an easy child. Hopeful that the anticipated storm wouldn't materialize, he joined his mother on the sofa, taking a sip of her martini before handing the glass back to her.

To his relief, the conversation flowed, and Josh was entirely relaxed as it neared dinnertime.

"I'm taking my parents out to dinner. Why don't you join us?" he asked Emma.

She glanced down at her clothing ruefully. "I appreciate the invitation, but the way I'm looking right now, your options of restaurants would be drastically limited."

"Then we'll stay in," he said quickly.

"Or we're more than happy to wait, if you'd like to change," Elizabeth offered.

"I appreciate it. I really do, but I'm sure Josh would like some time alone with you after your lengthy absence."

They tried to convince her otherwise, but ultimately she won out.

As she was getting ready to leave, Steven gave her a kiss on the cheek and Elizabeth embraced her warmly.

Emma retrieved her coat and the envelope from the kitchen. Now was not the time to share her news with Josh. He walked her out, and she rose to her toes and gave him a kiss. "They're wonderful people, Josh. You're a very lucky man to have such fantastic parents."

"I'm glad you think so." He brushed his lips across hers, stroked a thumb over her cheek. "I'm sorry I didn't have a chance to warn you they were here."

"I just wish I could've made a better first impression."

"To put your mind at ease, they like you. I know my parents. My mother can speak volumes with a single glance." Then a thought occurred to him. Christmas would be the ideal time to propose to Emma. Celebratory. Memorable. "Would you join us for our family

Christmas celebration? I know my parents would love to have you with us. You'd get to see Angie again and meet the rest of the clan."

"Ah, would your parents be okay with it?"

"Absolutely." He could tell she was nervous. "You can think about it, if you want, but it would mean a lot to me…and to my parents. I'm glad you met them. Are you sure I can't talk you into joining us for dinner?"

She shook her head. "Thanks, but no."

He watched her SUV thoughtfully until it turned out of the driveway. He sure had it bad for Emma, he mused. He had been patient enough. He'd have to put that diamond ring he'd bought to use soon.

CHAPTER TWENTY-TWO

THE SNOW RESUMED OVERNIGHT, bringing the accumulation to nearly eighteen inches. Yet the morning dawned clear and bright. The warmth of the sun combined with the bite of the wind had caused a thin, glittering crust to form on top of the newly fallen layer of snow.

Emma padded downstairs in the yoga pants, T-shirt and heavy wool socks she'd slept in. She fed Max and Theo, and opened the door to let them out to play. She put the kettle on and stoked the fire to fend off the chill inside the cottage. With her first mug of coffee in her hand, she glanced out the kitchen window to check on the dogs.

Emma thought about Josh's invitation to join him and his family for Christmas, and it appealed to her. She wanted to be with Josh. She knew he was giving Sherri time off over the holidays, and the clinic would be closed. With Christmas on her mind, Emma took the morning to put up some holiday decorations.

Midday, she decided to take a break and call

Arlene. She owed her that much, even if she was still undecided. She didn't want to seem any more unprofessional or nonresponsive as she already had. But what was it that she wanted? And how could she manage it without negatively affecting her and Josh.

Arlene was very persuasive on the phone. In addition, Emma would need the money in the not too distant future. When she hung up, she knew she had to decide and soon. Thankfully, Arlene gave her a bit of breathing space. She was taking a three-week cruise over the holidays.

But she made it clear that she expected to hear from Emma upon her return.

Emma got back to the decorating after lunch, and she was just hanging an evergreen wreath she'd bought at Chadwick's on her front door when Josh drove up.

The dogs raced over to him and Winston, and Josh gave each dog their fair share of attention. "Looks terrific," he said as he eyed the wreath.

"I thought it was about time to start decorating. I was going to set up and decorate the tree next."

"Would you like some help?" he asked as he shrugged out of his coat in the vestibule.

With mugs of hot chocolate to warm them

and Christmas music playing softly, they got to work. They had just hung the last of the decorations when the phone rang. Josh took the empty mugs into the kitchen while Emma answered.

Emma tried to ignore the chill of anxiety that slithered up her spine upon hearing Daniel's voice and masked it with a forced cheerfulness. It wasn't personal. She liked both Daniel and Jenna. It was simply what they were involved in. Every time Daniel called, it seemed to be bad news for her.

"How are you and Jenna?" she asked.

"We're getting caught up in the Christmas spirit," Daniel responded.

Emma glanced over at her beautiful tree. "Yeah. We are, too." She was certain he hadn't called just for small talk.

As if reading her mind, Daniel continued. "I wanted to let you know that the court date's set for the trial," he said and gave her the details. "With the information you provided, the senator is facing some serious charges, including criminal negligence causing death and another of causing injury. Charges have also been laid against Stewart. You having seen Stewart with the senator prior to the award of contract will add weight for the prosecution. You'll be contacted by the prosecuting lawyers with the official notification, but I wanted to let you know personally. Thank you for all your help, Emma," he added, sincerity ringing in his voice. "We couldn't have accomplished what we have without you. The end is in sight now. Before spring is over, this will be behind you."

Emma thanked Daniel and asked him to give her best wishes to Jenna for the holidays. They didn't expect to speak again until the preparations for the trial began in earnest in the New Year.

Spring seemed very distant when the trial stretched ahead of her.

As much as she and Josh tried to recapture the festive spirit, the mood was shattered.

For the days leading up to Christmas, Emma redoubled her efforts to not think about the impending trial.

Josh was so attentive and loving it would've been impossible for her not to be caught up in him and the holiday season. It just made it even harder for Emma to consider the decisions she would soon have to make about the Elite partnership offer. She hadn't been able to find the courage to discuss the mere possibility of her moving back to the city, and knowing his life was in Sanctuary Cove. How would she be able to tell him, if that's what she decided to do?

Pushing those thoughts aside, Emma helped Josh decorate the clinic. They went for sleigh rides and caroling with Sherri and some others. Even Sheriff Chad Atkins joined in the merriment.

Josh and Emma shopped for Christmas gifts together and—for each other—separately.

They drove to New York City and went to Rockefeller Center to take part in the festivities and to watch the lighting of the huge tree, made all that much more magical by the lightly falling snow. They took a carriage ride through Central Park, bought roasted chestnuts from a street vendor and purchased all sorts of silly gifts for the dogs.

And Emma found herself falling more deeply in love with Josh.

Josh and Emma decided to have their own private Christmas celebration at Emma's the evening of December 23, before joining Josh's family the next day. Since it was their first Christmas together, they wanted to enjoy some quiet time on their own.

It also gave Josh the opportunity to propose in private, and then be able to share the wonderful news with his family the next day.

When Josh arrived with Winston in tow, Emma led him into the kitchen so she could finish her final preparations.

She already had a bottle of champagne chilling on ice in a silver bucket.

"Should I do the honors?" Josh asked, pointing to the bottle. She nodded and he uncorked it, the loud pop causing all three dogs to scramble up and over to them.

He filled two flutes and handed one to Emma.

She rested her hand on his arm. "I'd like to propose a toast." She raised her glass to his. "To the most wonderful man I've ever known." Her voice softened and her eyes sparkled. "To the man I love."

Josh's heart soared as they clinked glasses and drank before she leaned forward to claim another kiss. He knew now more than ever that tonight would be the perfect time to propose to her. Just after dinner, he'd do it.

He nuzzled her ear and whispered the words back to her. They sat in the great room to enjoy the warmth of the fire and the sparkle of the Christmas tree. When Emma snuggled up next to Josh on the sofa, he was still trying to regain his balance. This was an Emma he hadn't seen before. He liked her confidence and playfulness, but wondered about the cause.

Before he had a chance to ask her, she began to toy with her champagne flute. "I wasn't planning on getting into this tonight, but I suppose I might as well now."

Watching her fidget and avoid eye contact, Josh sensed he wasn't going to like what she was going to say. With apprehension trickling through him, he waited for her to continue.

"I was going to tell you the afternoon I came to your place and met your parents. With them there, it wasn't the right time."

The trickle turned into a flood. "Tell me what?"

She finally raised her gaze to his. The luminous silver of her eyes seemed to hold a question…or a plea.

"Arlene Greenberg sent me a contract. A firm offer."

Josh had mixed feelings. He hoped that it helped her with her self-confidence, but what would it mean for them? "So you'll have steady work?" he asked in a quiet voice.

"Yes, I will. If I accept the offer."

Josh's emotions were on a roller-coaster ride. She didn't look thrilled. "Are the terms not what you'd expected?"

"The terms are fine. Very generous, in

fact...but the offer is not for a client executive position. It's for a partnership."

The melodious strains of Bing Crosby's "White Christmas," the crackle of the fire and Winston's soft snoring were the only sounds for long moments as Josh tried to make sense of what Emma had just said.

Finally, it was Emma who spoke again. There was pleading in her eyes now. "When I first saw the offer, I was over-the-moon happy. I couldn't *believe* that the owner of such a prestigious firm would want me as a partner. It made me feel wanted. Validated. It was the opportunity I didn't know I was needing to prove myself again. That I wasn't the failure Richard and Morgan and even my former boss had made me believe I was."

Josh could see the outcome as clear as day. She'd become a partner, but that meant her moving back to the city...and that equated to his losing her. He just couldn't see himself living there.

"Josh," she said on a whisper, laying her hand on top if his. "You do realize that without your support—your belief in me—I wouldn't have gotten to the point of receiving such an offer, let alone considering it. As bruised as I was after everything that happened, without you I wouldn't have thought myself worthy or capable of taking on some of the assignments that I have been for Arlene. Certainly not a role like this."

He turned his hand under hers and laced his fingers with hers. Good for him, he thought wryly, for having achieved his goal of helping her rebuild her confidence, but this was not the outcome he foresaw...or had hoped for. "And now? What are you thinking now?"

"I don't know. Josh, in my initial excitement, I didn't think about what it would mean. I was just so thrilled that she wanted me as a partner." Her voice dropped to a whisper again. "I'd have to move back to the city, and use this place just on weekends again. When my workload allowed."

That's what he'd been dreading. "When do you have to give her an answer?" He couldn't believe he was able to sit here and carry on the pretense of a normal conversation, when he felt as if a block of ice had formed around his heart and it would splinter into a million pieces if she accepted the offer...and left him.

Emma nodded. "Arlene is on a three-week cruise. She asked that I let her know when she gets back early in the New Year."

He released her hand. "Well, whatever you decide, I'll back you."

"But—"

"Think about it over Christmas, and we'll talk after. For now, let's focus on the holiday."

He could see she was baffled…and possibly hurt. But he just didn't want to contemplate her leaving right now, when his mind had been on them spending the rest of their lives together. Would he be able to survive in the city, if he had to? He had some thinking to do, too.

The evening passed quietly. They finished making dinner together. They had lobster and steak, passing on the more traditional turkey, as Josh had assured Emma they would have enough of it to last them until next Christmas when they visited his family.

Josh came over again early the next morning to open their gifts to each other. He'd bought Emma a stunning pair of diamond earrings, an angora sweater the exact color of her eyes and a lovely wooden carving of a caribou for her great room. Emma gave Josh a watch, a new medical bag to replace his too-well-worn one and an original painting of an area landmark by a very talented local artist.

They enjoyed a leisurely breakfast of scrambled eggs, bacon, home-fried potatoes and toast before getting ready to drive to Westchester to Josh's parents' house. Sherri arrived just as they were ready to go, to take care of the dogs while they were gone.

Josh had worked hard to not dwell for the time being on the decision Emma faced. He truly wanted what was best for her, and he'd decided it wasn't fair for him to raise the prospect of marriage until she'd made her decision.

While he had to again resign himself to not asking her to marry him just now—and depending on her decision—perhaps never, he didn't want there to be a dark cloud over their time with his family.

Large, black wrought-iron gates stood open and welcomed them at the entrance to the Whitmore property. Josh drove up the long, tree-lined drive. The grounds were covered by pristine, glistening snow, and the trees were decorated with a myriad of small white lights.

Emma craned her neck left and right to take it all in.

Josh glanced over at her with a half-smile. He was so used to his family's home, he tended to forget how imposing the property and house could be to a first-time visitor. He reached over to take her hand and reminded himself again of his determination not to let the circumstances cast a pall over their celebrations.

They followed a bend in the drive, and

the house first came into view. It was a large structure of weathered stone with copper eaves, fascia and soffits and a slate roof. Extensive gardens, the skeletons of the shrubs now shrouded in snow, flanked the drive to the front entryway. Wide stone steps led to a double-story covered portico supported by graceful columns. The front doors were massive and of a rich, deep brown wood with etched glass inserts and sidelights. Large urns, overflowing with Christmas-themed floral arrangements sat on the stairs and portico.

Josh parked his Yukon in front of the garage next to a late-model Jaguar and the blue Mercedes convertible Emma knew to be Angie's.

With bags of gifts in one hand, Josh draped his other arm around Emma's shoulder as they climbed the steps. "Ready?" he asked.

"As ready as I'll ever be."

"Then let's go." He dropped a kiss on the tip of her nose before leading her inside.

Josh watched Emma take it all in as they stepped into the spacious marble-floored entryway. He tried to see it through her eyes. The grand furnishings. The scent of fresh-cut flowers in a large urn on a sideboard. A subtle odor of lemon he associated with furniture polish, along with the delicious aromas of cooking wafting through the open archway to the kitchen. And they heard the cheerful voices of his family, arguing, laughing, with the clatter of kitchen tools and the sound of Christmas music in the background.

Josh helped Emma out of her coat and hung it up. He then took her hand and led her in the direction of the sounds and scents, into the large, open-design kitchen-family-room combination filled with people. The room was bright, with white tile floors, white cupboards, rose-colored granite counters and enormous appliances.

Separated by a railing and a step down from the kitchen was the family room. With hardwood floors, bleached-wood paneling, spacious sofas and a good-sized flat-screen TV, it invited lounging or conversation. Both kitchen and family room were decorated for the holidays with garlands, lights and sundry trimmings. A beautifully bedecked Christmas tree dominated the corner of the family room, its base crowded with brightly wrapped presents.

Josh's mother, Elizabeth, was adeptly slicing vegetables while carrying on a lively conversation with Angie, his brother, Ross, and Ross's wife's sister, Olivia. Sitting in the living room was Ross's very pregnant wife, Gwen, Josh's cousin, Alex, and Josh's father. Olivia's and Alex's relations lived out of town and consequently they were always welcome to join the Whitmores for the holidays, if they couldn't get home to celebrate with their own families.

Angie was the first to notice their arrival. Placing her wineglass on the kitchen counter, she rushed over and warmly embraced each of them. She cocked an eyebrow at Josh after a surreptitious glance at Emma's ring finger. In answer, he gave a nearly imperceptible shake of his head. Angie cast her eyes to the ceiling but didn't miss a beat in welcoming Emma and taking the initiative to introduce her to everyone present.

Josh loved seeing Emma look so animated and relaxed, as she chatted with his parents and Angie. She seemed to immediately connect with the others, too.

Once all the fixings were placed in the oven to join the turkey, the entire group moved to the family room. When dinner was ready, they opened another bottle of wine and moved to the dining room. The dinner lasted well over two hours, but the time passed quickly. When Josh and Emma had a moment alone, she confided that she couldn't remember feeling quite so much at home or welcomed. Josh was pleased how well she fit in with his family. He reached in his pants pocket, closed his hand over the small silver box and tamped down the regret that the ring was there, rather than on Emma's finger.

After dinner, everyone lingered at the table, enjoying plum pudding and coffee. Emma helped Elizabeth, Angie and Olivia clean up. Eventually she and Josh made their way up to the bedrooms they'd been given for the night—for him the same bedroom he'd occupied as a child. Emma's was a room down the hall.

"Merry Christmas, Emma," Josh said outside her room and placed a kiss on her forehead. He thought about how much he wanted her to be his wife. To spend his life with her, building a family and making memories. As much as he wanted it, he wondered if it just wasn't meant to be.

CHAPTER TWENTY-THREE

WITH THE HOLIDAYS behind them and Senator Morgan's court date looming, Emma's involvement in the preparations for the trial ramped up. She felt the pressure mounting.

As she had innumerable times before, Emma wished again she could simply walk away from it all. Not Josh, of course. He was her rock.

Although she'd accepted a few more assignments, she'd put off Arlene again, this time using the trial as an excuse. In her heart, she was leaning toward not accepting the partnership offer. She was honored, but she couldn't see herself back in New York City. She wanted her future to be here in Sanctuary Cove and, if she could have her wish, with Josh. The one compelling point weighing in favor of her accepting was the steady paycheck. She was running out of money, which was the only reason she couldn't simply say no. Emma hoped that Arlene would still give her freelance work, if she turned down the partnership. If only her application for training service dogs would come through. At least she'd have some money coming in, even if not a lot. More importantly, she'd have something meaningful to do that she believed she'd truly enjoy.

Thankfully, Arlene was sending her assignments.

She was already engrossed in one by nine o'clock that morning when Daniel called with terrible news.

She tried to contact Josh but he was with a patient and couldn't be disturbed. She left a message with Sherri and drove immediately to New York City.

Daniel met Emma in the lobby of the Lenox Hill Hospital. Jenna had been admitted early that morning with multiple fractures to her leg and hip as a consequence of being hit by a cube van on her way to work. Her condition was stable, and Emma learned it could've been a lot worse, if not for the quick thinking of an alert bystander, who'd pulled her back.

Due to the heavy sedation after Jenna's surgery, the police had yet to get her statement; however, they'd interviewed several eyewitnesses.

With the information they already had, the police suspected Jenna had been targeted. The physical evidence at the site corroborated the witnesses' statements about how the van seemed to have been heading straight for Jenna. It was white with no identifiable markings. Those who thought to check said the license plate had been obscured.

The police were still investigating and were not prepared to jump to a conclusion. But Daniel's belief was that the intimidation had escalated to a new and much more dangerous level. Daniel revealed to Emma that Ferguson, AFM's previous CEO, had disappeared again and the prosecutors had not been able to find him. If they couldn't locate Ferguson by the time of the trial, Daniel was the only person who knew what he'd confided to him.

"Could it have been Mr. Laurence?" Emma asked.

Daniel shook his head. "No. The police eliminated him as a suspect. He suffered a breakdown and has been admitted into a treatment center, where he's been for the past two weeks."

"Could someone have done it on his behalf?"

"The police dismissed that idea. I trust their judgment. He's not an evil man. Just a broken one."

Daniel was obviously tortured by the knowledge that Jenna lay in the hospital bed, bruised and broken because of him.

Emma sat with him at Jenna's bedside for a long time. They didn't speak much. There was nothing to say. They understood that with the trial just weeks away, and both of them key witnesses, the risk would increase.

Emma had a long time to mull that over as she drove back to Sanctuary Cove. She didn't question Daniel's assertion that Jenna's accident was connected to the Morgan case. She was inclined to agree with him and the police were investigating that angle, too. She was dismayed that the acts of intimidation had turned to violence.

Emma thought about her own situation. As a witness for the prosecution, would they try to hurt her? She and Daniel were two witnesses who had solid evidence that only they could testify to. Still, she doubted they'd go after her, especially with the attention the incident with Daniel's fiancée was attracting, both from the media and the police.

She thought of the cut Max had sustained in the woods and her skin chilled. They'd never found the person responsible for it. Would they try to hurt one of her dogs again, then? God, she could never forgive herself if that happened.

She just wanted to get home and have a very large glass of wine and a hot bath. Glancing at the clock on her dash, she felt guilty about having left the dogs alone so long. The bath and wine would have to wait. She had some making up to do with an extended walk. After the walk, she would take the bath and see if the wine could dull the sharpest edges of her anger and frustration.

They went after Jenna. Not Daniel, she reminded herself and brought the X5 to a stop before she reached the crest of her driveway.

What if they tried to get to her through Josh? She and Josh were now known to have a relationship. "Oh, no," she whispered as she dropped her head into her hands. Another unbearable thought. If anything happened to Josh because of her, she couldn't live with that, either.

She wouldn't take chances. She'd do what she could to make sure he stayed safe.

But how? she wondered frantically.

She would have to put things on hold with him, she realized, until all this was over. Regardless of how slim the probability, she was *not* prepared to risk Josh getting hurt because of her. As much as she loved him, she'd have to keep her distance for now. She thought about telling him outright. Explaining the situation and her concern for him, but she knew him well enough that he'd assure her he'd be careful but wouldn't accept a temporary separation.

She'd have to be the one to put the distance between them. She just hoped that they could pick up where they left off when the whole mess was over and done with. As much as it broke her heart to think there was a chance they couldn't, keeping Josh safe was her priority.

With that thought in mind, she continued down the drive.

And she saw him. Josh was in the yard, playing with the dogs in the snow. He should've still been at the clinic. The love that swelled inside her as she watched him threatened her determination.

He waved as the dogs raced off to greet her. She parked her SUV and exhaled heavily before getting out.

She greeted the dogs, buying time to figure out how she should handle Josh. Straightening, she dragged her fingers through her hair as she glanced over at him.

He leaned in to brush his lips across hers. "When I got your message, I thought the dogs could use some fresh air and you'd appreciate some hot food when you got back."

Guilt warred with frustration within her. She hated the thought of hurting him. Tears stung the back of her eyes, but she refused to let them spill over. "I appreciate your leaving work early to let the boys out for me," she said as they walked toward the cottage. "I'm not really hungry, though." That was a lie and she hated it, but the next words would at least be the truth. "What I really want is a bath and a glass of wine."

"All right." His smile faded. "We can accommodate that, too, in our agenda for this evening."

She stopped and turned to him before they reached the porch stairs. She desperately wanted to simply slip into his arms. Instead, she took a determined step back. "Josh, you're missing the point. I'm grateful for what you're doing—want you do for me—but I need to be alone tonight. I just need some space."

He gave her a long, appraising look. "Something happened and you don't want to talk about it. I respect that. But a relationship is a two-way street, Emma, and not just when it's smooth sailing. I've started dinner and I'd like to finish it." He turned and walked up the stairs, followed by the dogs. He glanced back down at her as he opened the front door. "If you tell me to go, I will. If not, it's your call if you want to join me for dinner or not." The lines on his face softened. "I'd like it if you did."

She stood, speechless as the door swung closed behind him. This time, she dragged the fingers of both hands through her hair and groaned.

When she walked into the kitchen, she was greeted by flickering candlelight and soft music playing from her sound system. Josh stood at the stove, his back to her, and was stirring something that smelled delicious. There was a glass of wine on the counter.

He looked over his shoulder and motioned to the glass with the wooden spoon. "I poured your wine. You can pull up a stool and keep me company while I finish this. My preference. Or you can take it upstairs with you to have a bath." He checked the clock on the stove. "You have about a half an hour before dinner is ready."

She picked up her glass, paced away from the island, paced back again and took a long drink. She spread her arms. "You don't have to do this, Josh."

"I know I don't have to. If I *had* to, I probably wouldn't enjoy it nearly as much." He lifted his beer and took a drink.

"Then why?"

"Because I want to."

She took another large gulp of wine. "Okay." She paced some more. "Okay," she repeated but her tone was no more accepting. Her mind was working furiously.

She hissed out a breath.

"You're going to tell me, sooner or later, what happened today. It might be easier all around if we got it out of the way," Josh said without turning around, his voice casual.

Emma plunked her glass down on the counter and folded her arms across her chest. She walked to a window and stared out. When she spoke, her voice was raised and her temper was raw. "I don't want you here, Josh. I can't do this."

The wooden spoon made a clattering sound as he dropped it into the saucepan. She spun around and locked her gaze with his. His eyes were dark, his expression enigmatic. In all the time she'd known him and after all that had happened, she'd never seen him lose his temper before. She could see he was on the verge now. He was obviously waiting for her to make the next move.

Emma lowered her arms to her sides, raised them in appeal and said emphatically, "Really, Josh, I don't want you here."

He seemed to have a quick and silent debate

with himself. He closed the gap between them with three long strides. "I'm here for you, Emma. Whatever the problem is, I'm here."

The ragged sigh that trembled through her lips spoke volumes. She closed her eyes and placed her hands on his chest, but her fingers clenched into fists. She wasn't sure if it was in anger or frustration. She'd recognized the same feelings in his eyes, along with hurt.

She looked up in surprise when he stroked a surprisingly gentle finger across her cheek. His eyes on hers, he brushed a loose strand of hair off her temple and tucked it behind her ear. "Talk to me." The simple words, laced with concern, broke through her crumbling resolve.

Emma nodded, admitting the truth would be best. "I was in New York City today." She turned away and stared out the window, the darkness relieved only by a smattering of starlight. "I went to Lenox Hill Hospital."

He stepped in front of her again. "Are you okay?"

"Oh, me?" She glanced at him briefly. "I'm fine. I met Daniel there."

When she saw him relax a little, she picked up her glass and drained it. "Daniel was there to see Jenna."

"Why is Jenna in the hospital?"

"She had an accident. Except the police don't think it was an accident and neither does Daniel."

"Is she okay?"

"She will be, but she's banged up. She was hit by a cube van. The police say it could've been more serious if not for a man who pulled her back from the curb when he saw the van barreling toward her." Emma fidgeted with the hem of her sweater and then folded her arms over her chest again. "He probably saved her life." Her eyes stung with unshed tears. "It wasn't an accident, Josh. I'm certain of that."

JOSH WAS APPALLED. If it was true, that things had escalated to this level, Emma was in danger, too. He thought he understood what she'd been trying to do. He wanted to protect her, to reassure her, but knew he had to tread carefully to prevent her from continuing to try to push him away. He kept his voice calm, matter-of-fact. "I'm glad to hear she'll be okay. How's Daniel taking it?"

"Not well, as you can imagine. He feels responsible."

There it was, he thought, the root of it. He skimmed a hand along the length of her hair. "Emma, he isn't responsible and you know it. The person who *is* responsible is the guy driving the van. Even more so, the person who paid him to do it, if that's what's happened."

Her eyes were a turbulent, stormy gray. She blew out a long, uneven breath. "Yes. I know," she said, but without true conviction. "I tried to tell Daniel the same thing. It didn't help. His view is that if not for him, it would never have happened to her."

"And you couldn't convince him because you don't entirely believe it yourself." His words were soft but the force of their meaning drew her gaze back to his.

He framed her face with his hands. "It's not going to work, Emma. You can't push me away. I'm sticking."

She lifted her arms. "You didn't see Jenna in the hospital, the dark bruises on her face, around her eye, the scrapes along her arms and the large cast. You didn't see Daniel, ravaged by guilt. I don't want to be responsible for—couldn't live with—anything happening to you."

He took her chilled hands into his. "Nothing will happen to me, Emma. Even if it did, you wouldn't be the one responsible. Hear me out," he said when she was about to object. "I make my own choices and I choose to be with you—not just when it's convenient. What we need to do is ensure nothing happens to either of us. I know your instinct still is to keep me distant and safe, but look at me." He gave her a moment to do just that. "It would be futile to try."

Emma pressed a hand over her stomach. "Josh, you've become so vital to me in so many ways," she said softly. "Without even realizing it, I've come to trust you and rely on you, when, after Richard, I couldn't see myself trusting again."

Those words meant more to him than she'd ever know. He sensed the change in her and was glad for it. He felt the release of tension much like a balloon deflating, and he drew her into his arms and kissed the top of her head. "Nothing will happen to us, and it will all be over soon. Trust me, Emma."

Josh was already formulating plans to ensure he could deliver on his promise, starting with updating Chad. But first things first. He tilted her face up to his.

Her lips curved and her eyes were a clear misty gray again, before her eyelids fluttered closed as he lowered his head to kiss her.

CHAPTER TWENTY-FOUR

EMMA COULD'VE SLEPT through the bright slashes of blue lightning against the obsidian sky, but the deep rumble of thunder woke her. She lay still for a while, enjoying the soothing sound of the patter of rain on the windowpanes. The steady rhythm of it lulled her and she nearly drifted back to sleep.

Until the thunder cracked once more.

Her eyes flew open. *That one was close*, she thought, not with any degree of fear but as an observation. The dogs—as always taking their cue from her—weren't bothered by the onslaught. Theo groaned and rolled over to his other side. Max lifted his head, sniffed the air and, apparently satisfied that all was well, dropped his head back down between his outstretched paws.

She shook her head and smiled. The world collapsing around them wouldn't disturb the dogs.

Despite the earliness of the hour, she climbed out of bed.

Today was the start of the trial.

With a yawn, she stretched, slipped her feet into slippers and pulled a thick sweater over her T-shirt. She padded out of the room, the dogs, immediately alert, following her.

She scooped the kibble into the dogs' dishes while they impatiently danced in place. Setting the bowls on the floor for them, she then stoked the fires. By the time she'd finished, so had the dogs with their breakfast. Shrugging into a heavy raincoat and pulling a ball cap over her head, she followed the dogs outside.

Emma was grateful for this quiet time alone. Watching the antics of the dogs, it was good to smile—at least for now. She took her time with the walk despite the weather. She didn't mind the rain. In fact, she welcomed it as a portent of the end of winter.

Emma thought of spring and hoped the trial would, indeed, be over by then. She desperately wanted it to be behind her. Yet she dreaded the start. Not only the pressures of giving testimony and being cross-examined, something that the prosecutors had taken great lengths to prepare her for, but also the circus-like media attention that would go with it because of Senator Morgan's notoriety. To add to her trepidation, she didn't want to see Richard, either, in such a public and confrontational manner. She'd been warned that the defense would use Richard's testimony—and his personal relationship with her—to try to discredit her.

Although she could still feel a pang of sympathy for Richard for having lost out on the chance to lead the defense in such a high-profile case and the prospect of a partnership along with it, she was relieved she wouldn't have to face him in cross-examination.

Her sense of tranquility gone, with a deep sigh, she headed back toward the cottage.

JOSH WAS UP EARLY. He knew it was an important day for Emma. When he arrived at her cottage and she and the dogs weren't there, he surmised they were out for a walk. He started breakfast. Watching through the kitchen window for her, he saw her approach. He could almost see the tension build in her as she neared, the way her posture transformed. Shoulders slumped, hands buried in her pockets. He wished there was a way to spare her from the ordeal she was about to face, but the lawyers had been clear. It was unavoidable. She would be called to the stand.

He turned back to the stove to stir the scrambled eggs. He was flipping the bacon when Emma entered the kitchen, her long hair damp despite the ball cap she wore, raindrops clinging to her eyelashes. He handed her a mug of coffee.

"Good morning. And thank you."

After she'd taken a long drink, he pulled her into his arms and asked her how she was feeling. The question was rhetorical, but he thought it might help her to talk about it.

She let her head rest in the crook of his shoulder. "As well as can be expected, I suppose." After a few long moments, she drew back, reached for her coffee and took another sip. "I'll get through it. I'll be fine," she assured him.

"I'm sure. But knowing doesn't make it easier for either of us. I can't help worrying about you until it's over."

Doubt and apprehension clouded her eyes to a pewter gray. "What about the possibility of appeals? By either side, depending on what the verdict is? It could stretch out for years." She tore her gaze away and looked out the window at the rain-drenched landscape. "I just want it to end," she whispered.

The possibility of appeals had occurred to him, too. "Let's get through it one step at a time," he suggested pragmatically.

He turned off the burners and served their breakfast. She surprised them both by clearing her plate rather than toying with her food. When she was done, she pushed away her plate and rested her crossed arms on the table. "Josh, I don't know how to thank you for being here for me. I can't even begin to explain how much it means. I've always prided myself on my independence, what I saw as my ability to confront any challenge and deal with it head-on. To not rely on anyone else for things that really mattered." She glanced down. Her voice dropped to a whisper. "But I'm realizing that Richard had taken a lot of that away from me."

She uncrossed her arms and reached out to rest a hand on top of his. "And I've been struggling to get it back, but I've discovered two things," she continued slowly. "First, that my independence was a matter of necessity as opposed to personal choice. Before you, other than my parents, I never had anyone I could truly rely on. Consistently, unquestionably. Second, that relying on someone is not a weakness or some other lack in oneself. Rather, it's a matter of profound respect for another. The ability to trust and believe in the other person to the extent that you open up and give part of yourself. Josh, you have taught me both these things, and I can't thank you enough."

Touched, he raised their joined hands and brushed his lips over her knuckles.

"Josh, I love you."

He pushed back his chair and rose, pulling her to him. Once he was sure his voice wouldn't betray him, he responded. "I love you beyond reason. I'm here for you no matter what the cards hold."

"I know that, and it gives me strength that I badly need. That I can get through this."

JOSH WAITED DOWNSTAIRS while Emma chose with care what she'd wear for the first day of the trial. He knew she wanted to present herself as professional, but not hard. The lawyers and jury consultant had said that it was important that she connect with the jury, and come across as credible and confident. As a genuine person wanting to do the right thing, rather than someone who wanted the limelight or to bring a powerful man down.

They knew that Senator Morgan was a master orator, and his success in politics had largely been due to his uncanny ability to connect with the average person. She would just have to be better.

She opted for a soft gray suit. The color and tailored cut of the jacket were businesslike and professional. The skirt, flowing to just below her knees, gave it a feminine look.

When they heard Sherri's car in the driveway, Josh helped Emma on with her coat and shrugged into his own.

"Wow, it's weird seeing that cop car at the foot of your driveway," Sherri remarked as she hung up her raincoat.

Chad had insisted on a visible police presence. He'd said that he wasn't prepared to take any chances after the incident with Jenna.

"Get used to it," Josh advised Sherri. "They plan to keep at it until the trial is over."

"Huh! My own protective detail! Maybe I'll take him a cup of coffee later," Sherri said with a grin.

The rain had stopped by the time they left, but the sky was a dull gray and a thin fog crept along the ground. They drove to New York City with little conversation. Josh held Emma's hand most of the way.

Approaching the courthouse, they could see that the media was present in full force. Josh glanced at Emma encouragingly. "It's almost over."

She gave a short laugh. "No doubt, but it's between now and then that concerns me."

They had prearranged parking, and Josh found it without difficulty. As a result of the media attention and the incidents leading up to the trial, they were met by a uniformed police officer. Emma was escorted to a room used for sequestering witnesses, while Josh was led to the courtroom. He took a seat in the row behind the prosecution desk. Jenna was already there, and Josh surmised Daniel would have been sequestered as well. Even though they'd arrived early, the courtroom was already crowded. The senator was big news.

Josh watched as Senator Morgan sauntered into the room.

There was no other way to describe his entry. He was dressed sharply, his silver-gray hair perfectly groomed, and an easy, relaxed smile on his face. He moved to the defense table with the comfort of someone about to take a chair at a dinner party rather than a trial that could see him go to jail for a substantial portion of what remained of his life.

The senator shook hands and greeted a few people seated behind the defense table. He looked like he was campaigning, the way he was working his side of the room, before finally taking a seat next to his lawyers. When the lawyer immediately to his left leaned in to whisper in his ear, Morgan actually laughed. Josh glanced at Jenna and knew she'd witnessed the display as well. He wondered if the senator was a consummate actor or if his arrogance was so monumental that he didn't feel threatened by the proceedings about to commence.

He worried about Emma and thought that for her the day would drag on. They'd been told by the lawyers that the proceedings would involve opening statements to establish context, and the examination and cross-examination of initial witnesses. It was during the afternoon recess that Josh was told that Emma wouldn't have to take the stand that day. Josh didn't know if she'd feel relieved that she could breathe easier for the day or be disappointed that she wouldn't yet be done with her part. He leaned toward the latter.

After the break, Daniel took the stand. Josh thought he was a highly credible witness. He handled some challenging questions exceedingly well, especially during cross-examination. It was only when Daniel looked in Jenna's direction that his composure slipped.

Watching the jurors, Josh tried to assess their body language and facial expressions. He believed Daniel's testimony had gone a considerable way to sway their opinion.

He just wanted it to be over for now so that he could talk to Emma. They'd planned to remain in the city during the trial. They had rooms at the Paramount Hotel for four nights in case they needed to stay that long. They were planning to go home for the weekend even if the trial continued the following week.

After a brief overview from the lead prosecutor as to where Emma was on the witness list, they returned to the hotel. Daniel and Jenna joined them for dinner, but they purposely avoided the topic of the trial.

After dinner, Josh escorted Emma to her suite and said good-night.

EMMA WAS SHOWERED and dressed by the time the alarm clock sounded the next morning. This time, she wore a deep royal blue suit with a powder-blue blouse. Black pumps and a matching belt completed the outfit.

She was standing by the living room window, looking over the city and drinking a cup of coffee, when Josh knocked on her door. His wolf whistle at seeing her made her smile. "I appreciate the sentiment, but not exactly the reaction I'm hoping for from the jury."

Josh took a moment to scrutinize her more closely. "How are you feeling?"

"Good." She nodded. "But nervous."

They shared a light breakfast before Emma

went to meet with the lawyers in a room they'd booked in the hotel.

Emma and Josh entered the courtroom a couple of hours later along with the prosecution team, and Emma was momentarily disconcerted. The crowd was much bigger than she'd anticipated, and it was noisy, as the courtroom had not yet been called to order.

Although she knew Richard would be present, she felt the shock when her eyes locked briefly with his. He gave her what she interpreted as a condescending smirk before he looked away. They must have decided against using him as a witness, she concluded, for him to be in the courtroom. She resolved not to let his presence throw her.

When she was called to the stand, she glanced at Josh and their eyes met. She thought she saw pride in his, and it gave her courage.

She believed she did well with her testimony, but cross-examination was another matter and the trepidation built before it started. The defense lawyer's strategy of beginning gently to lull her into a sense of complacency before hammering her with questions aimed to discredit her testimony backfired on him.

She accepted the change in his rhythm without any discernable unease. Her responses remained well paced, succinct and, she thought, compelling. She was certain that the nerves she felt were not apparent on the surface. She hoped she appeared poised and confident.

She was on the stand when the court recessed for lunch and was called back when it resumed. When her testimony was complete, it was near the end of the day, so the court adjourned. Emma, Josh and Daniel met with the prosecution team briefly. When Emma inquired about Jenna's absence, Daniel explained she was feeling the strain of her recent injuries and had gone back to their hotel room to rest.

Emma was told she didn't need to be present for the remainder of the trial. But she had so much invested in it that she and Josh decided to stay anyway. They wanted to be present to hear the verdict.

The next day, the senator was finally called to take the stand. Emma held Josh's hand tightly during the entire testimony and was astonished at the senator's performance. The senator was clearly playing to the jury, the media and the general audience. He looked like he was enjoying himself.

With the help of his legal counsel, he portrayed himself as a man terribly wronged. As a victim of a vicious attack motivated by greed and envy. He characterized himself as a man who'd dedicated his life to serving his country. In a thinly veiled reference, he implied that Daniel had pursued the matter out of self-interest and for personal gain.

It dismayed Emma, as she watched the jurors, that they were falling under Morgan's spell. He seemed to be spinning a web of sympathy and righteous indignation that he should be the target of something so unscrupulous. "Surely the jurors would be smart enough, decent enough, *fair* enough, to see the truth and do the right thing," he suggested. Morgan's testimony was followed by closing arguments from both sides.

And then it was over.

The matter was now in the hands of the jurors.

For Emma, it felt almost anticlimactic. Emma, Josh, Daniel and Jenna waited together with the prosecution team in an anteroom in the courthouse. At lunchtime, an assistant got sandwiches and soda for them. They mostly just picked at their food. No one was hungry.

The longer it took for the jury to decide, the worse the odds for the prosecution, the lawyers had cautioned. A hung jury was also a possibility.

Checking her watch yet again, Emma noted

that nearly four hours had passed. Was that long? she wondered. Too long for it to mean a conviction? How could anyone not see the truth of the matter?

The pressure of waiting was taking a toll on her. A brisk knock on the door caused her to jolt. After a cursory conversation between one of the legal team and the court bailiff, the lawyer announced that the jury had reached a verdict, and it was time for them to go back to the courtroom.

Emma followed the legal team with a sense of apprehension, feeling almost as if the verdict in question would apply to her, determining *her* fate. Josh kept a reassuring hand on the small of her back. She was grateful for it, as even the light contact helped ease her trepidation.

Once everyone was seated and the courtroom called to order, the bailiff retrieved the folded piece of paper held by the head juror and presented it to the judge. Emma could hear shuffling behind her, a short cough and a soft whisper of fabric against fabric as someone must have crossed her legs.

All eyes were on the judge as he unfolded the slip of paper and scanned it. He shifted his gaze to hold Morgan's for a moment that seemed endless to Emma. The judge's face was inscrutable. Then he refolded the paper matter-of-factly and handed it back to the bailiff to return to the head juror.

The head juror was called upon to deliver the verdict. He was a tall, distinguished-looking man, with a full head of closely trimmed blond hair and dark-rimmed reading glasses. He adjusted those glasses as he glanced down at the piece of paper he held in his hand.

He cleared his throat.

Emma felt almost as if matters were unfolding in slow motion. She watched the head juror as he pronounced each word slowly and deliberately.

"On all counts, we, the jury, find the defendant…guilty."

The final word hung in the air and seemed to ricochet in Emma's consciousness as the courtroom was suddenly thrown into furor.

Senator Morgan shot out of his chair. His face was distorted and red with rage. Two members of his legal team also jumped to their feet and attempted to subdue him. He brushed them off. It seemed that everyone else in the courtroom had also risen, unsure of what was happening.

Morgan looked to the judge, then the jurors. "This is outrageous," he yelled with such vehemence that he was easily heard above all the racket. He continued even as the guards attempted to restrain him. "It's a travesty! You can't do this to *me*. I will appeal the decision and *win*."

Though the guards forced Morgan's arms behind his back and locked the handcuffs into place, the senator fought them every step of the way. His eyes burned with hostility as they bored into Daniel's, then Emma's. His voice became more moderate but was still laced with venom as he directed his next comments specifically at them. "This is all your fault. You'll be sorry you started this. That you dared to go up against me." He gestured with his chin toward Jenna. "You haven't seen anything yet. You'll all be sorrier than you can imagine."

The sound of the side door slamming behind Morgan after he was dragged through it by the guards reverberated around the room. In contrast to the clamor and activity around Emma, she stood still and felt an unbearable chill descend upon her. Despite Josh's hand resting at the back of her neck, she felt alone and very cold.

Morgan had said it wasn't over, and Emma knew it was a fact. He was going to appeal and would likely be out on bail. His comments made it clear to her who'd been responsible for the acts of intimidation—and likely Jenna's injury. Morgan might well be facing additional charges now, as a result.

Her hope of putting it all behind her once the trial was over had been a foolish delusion. Although the din in the courtroom hadn't subsided, the sound of soft weeping penetrated Emma's consciousness. Glancing toward the sound, she saw Daniel sitting next to Jenna, his arm around her, his head bent as he spoke into her ear. With his other hand, he covered both of Jenna's as they jerked nervously on her lap. Jenna nodded occasionally in acknowledgment of Daniel's words, but continued to hang her head, eyes closed, tears coursing down her face.

Emma understood Jenna was terrified of becoming a target again, or feared for Daniel.

She'd have to live in fear for herself and those she loved and cared about, for how long, no one could say. The police couldn't protect them indefinitely and not everywhere they went.

Emma turned to Josh and slipped into his embrace. His eyes looked as hollow as she felt. He placed a kiss on her brow. "Let's go home. There's nothing further we can do here. Not now."

She didn't trust herself to speak. She nodded in response. Josh released her but kept one arm firmly around her shoulder. As they passed Daniel and Jenna, Emma reached out to place a hand first on Jenna's shoulder and then, for a longer moment, on Daniel's. "I'm sorry" was all she said, before she and Josh walked out of the courtroom.

CHAPTER TWENTY-FIVE

WEEKS HAD PASSED since the trial, and Emma's apprehensions had not subsided. The legal wrangling continued and Emma found herself looking over her shoulder and expecting the worst to happen. She no longer had around-the-clock police protection. The small-town police force couldn't afford it. The best they could do was periodic drive-bys.

One positive was that her application to train service dogs had been approved. She was happy and excited about it, and was ready to start as soon as a puppy suitable for the program could be found. Josh had promised her she'd have first choice from the next litter he'd deliver at the clinic.

She still hadn't given Arlene an answer and Arlene hadn't given her new assignments for some time. She tried not to worry about what that meant for her from a cashflow perspective. She'd have to make a decision soon and take steps, one way or the other, to secure a steady source of income.

For respite, she spent most days working outdoors and she'd made considerable progress with her spring cleanup.

When she heard the phone ring one afternoon, she rose from the edge of the flower bed she was working on, yanked off her gardening gloves and rushed to where she'd left the cordless phone nearby. She didn't bother to check the display as she grabbed it after the third ring.

"Emma, am I getting you at a bad time?"

She recognized Daniel's voice and held back a sigh. She knew he had to be calling about Morgan. "No. I'm just outside in the garden," she stated. The unease that seemed to form a knot in her stomach of late intensified at the odd note to Daniel's voice. She lowered herself to sit on the grass.

"Emma, I'm sure you can guess that I'm calling about the senator."

The knot in her stomach hardened.

"I received a call from his lawyer."

Oh, God! Was he being released on bail?

"I'm not going to sugarcoat it. Morgan's dead."

She thought she couldn't have heard Daniel correctly. She was struggling to understand what he'd said.

"Emma, did you hear me?"

She switched the phone to her other ear. "What? What did you say?"

"I said he's dead. Morgan's dead."

"Dead?" The single word was a whisper.

"Yes. He died yesterday evening."

She ran her fingers through her hair and rose to pace along the edge of the grass. "Are you sure?"

"Yes."

"How did it happen?"

"I was told there was another prisoner with him. An inmate who'd been a soldier and was suffering from psychological issues. Apparently he'd heard about what Morgan had done and the consequences. He flew into a fit of rage and strangled Morgan. We can only surmise that it was retribution for the soldiers who'd suffered because of the defective rifles. By the time the guards and medical staff got to Morgan, there was nothing they could do. He was pronounced dead at the infirmary."

Emma stilled, trying to absorb what Daniel was saying. "This means…?" What? She wasn't sure what this meant.

"There will be no appeal," he replied.

She dropped down onto the grassy ground, elbows resting on her knees. She was appalled that she was feeling a sense of relief over a person's death.

"What about the others? Innes, Hughes and Stewart? What will happen to them?"

"Hughes has accepted a plea bargain. He will testify against Innes and Stewart. Their trials will proceed. With Hughes testifying, it's likely you won't be required to."

"It's over, then?"

"It's over, Emma. It's tragic about Morgan, but it's over. You did a good thing. A *very* good thing by coming forward. All the defective rifles have been accounted for. AFM will likely be out of business."

"I don't know what to say." She covered her face with her free hand, rubbing her fingers over the spot on her forehead where a headache was brewing. "It doesn't seem possible."

"Not only is it possible, it's true. Is Josh with you?"

"No." She checked her watch. "He's still at the clinic."

"Call him. It really is over, Emma."

Emma swiped at the moisture on her cheek with the back of her hand.

"Thanks for calling, Daniel."

"No problem. Emma...?"

"Yes?"

"It wouldn't have been possible without you. Let's stay in touch."

Emma ended the call but sat motionless.

With Morgan gone, she no longer had to live in fear of his threats. She no longer had to dread the prospect of an appeal and a drawn-out legal process.

Was it really true? Could she go on with her life and focus on what was important to her?

With that thought, Josh came immediately to mind. She loved the dogs, her cottage, the idea of training service dogs, but it was Josh who was most important to her. She smiled as she picked up the phone.

First she called Arlene. Apologetically, she explained that she was grateful for the opportunity she'd offered, but she just couldn't move back to the city. Arlene said she'd presumed as much, but it staggered Emma when she said that if she couldn't have her as a partner, she still wanted her on contract. Exclusively. And she was prepared to pay a premium for it.

In a bit of a daze—but a good one—Emma called Josh next. "What time can you leave work?" she asked.

"I have one more patient waiting. Barring any emergencies, I'm done for the day."

"Good." Her smile broadened. "I would like to celebrate."

"What are we celebrating?"

"Us," she said simply.

After she hung up the phone, she got caught

up in a flurry of activity. She rummaged through her refrigerator and realized that with her preoccupation, she'd been neglectful about her shopping. She settled on steak, potatoes and salad, as she had to acknowledge the pickings were slim. She set the dining room table. She started a low fire. She lit candles and turned on soft music. She hopped into the shower, rubbed scented lotion all over her body and dressed in slim black jeans and a white tuxedo shirt. She applied makeup, sparingly, and dabbed Josh's favorite scent behind her earlobes and on her wrists.

Back in the kitchen, she opened a bottle of cabernet and left it to breathe on the counter. She fed and let the dogs out. Then, suddenly, her energy deserted her.

The realization of all that she'd been through and she was now free of Morgan forever coursed through her system, left her stunned. She leaned heavily on the kitchen counter, dropped her head and let her shoulders slump.

JOSH FOUND EMMA in the kitchen and rushed to her. He placed his hands on her shoulders. "Emma…?" His concern for her was acute.

"It's over," she said softly, as she melted into his arms.

"Over? How?"

"He's dead. Morgan was killed in prison. He can't touch us anymore."

Josh's arms tightened around her, one hand gently cradling her head against his chest. Closing his eyes, he murmured, "We got through it, unharmed, thank God."

When Max's soft whine was followed by a nudge at her knee, Emma swayed. Josh slid his hands down her arms and moved a step back. "Are you all right?"

She took a deep, steadying breath. "Yes. I was feeling great. Then it hit me. It just all caught up with me."

"That's understandable. You've been through a lot." He brushed his knuckles along her cheeks. "The color is coming back to your face."

Her eyes met his. No longer hollow. No longer afraid. "It's really over."

"Yeah, it is," he agreed. "Let's get some fresh air." He held his hand out for hers. She linked her fingers with his as a hesitant smile softened her face.

They walked along the stone path, past the gardens cheerful with the early blooming daffodils and tulips, across the damp grass, beneath trees laden with fresh green shoots yet to unfurl into leaves, and down the gentle embankment toward the lake. The dogs followed, prancing playfully.

Josh put his arm around Emma's shoulder, drawing her to him, as they followed the water's edge, then walked back up the embankment. They continued along the path, skirting the clearing, and finally crossed the driveway and headed toward the cottage. As they reached the large outcropping of granite, Josh stopped and pulled Emma down beside him on the rock.

The early evening sky was clear and calm, the deep-blue water of the lake still. The heron called out as it skimmed above the lake's mirrored surface.

Emma sat with her knees drawn up, her head resting against Josh's shoulder. "I told Arlene I couldn't accept her offer."

"You did?" He hoped he hadn't imagined what she'd just said. "How did she take it?" he asked, needing the confirmation that it was true.

Emma laughed. "She wants me to keep working on assignments, but exclusively for Elite. And she's prepared to put me on a long-term contract."

"How do you feel about that?"

"Great. I can work from home. From Sanctuary Cove. That's part of the deal. It's non-negotiable."

Josh felt as if a two-ton weight had been lifted from his shoulders. His hand slipped into his jacket pocket and he fingered the silver box he'd kept there since they'd stayed at the Seacliffe Hotel.

They watched the sun's slow descent and in its wake, the wash of glowing crimson and gold.

With Josh's eyes on hers, he lowered his head and kissed her. When they drew apart, Emma's lips were rosy red, her eyes brilliant in the dimming light, her love for Josh, shinning in their depth.

He kissed her again, tenderly. "This is not how I had intended it, but it occurs to me that perhaps it's the way it's meant to be."

He smiled as he saw her baffled expression. He stroked his index finger along the furrow in her brow, smoothing it gently, before reaching into his jacket pocket again.

Pulling out the silver box, he held it out to her. Raising the lid, he watched her eyes go wide, her lips form a small *O*, and the contradictory emotions play across her face. He prayed silently that she would trust him, believe in him, now, most of all.

She lifted her gaze from the box to meet

Josh's. Her lips quivered, the corners curving upward into a shaky smile. Her eyes glistened.

Josh's smile broadened. He held the glittering solitaire engagement ring out for her to examine, before taking her left hand in his. "I've been carrying this ring with me far longer than I care to admit. As hard as it's been for me, being absolutely sure, knowing how much I want to spend the rest of my life with you, how much I want you as my wife, I've held off." He laughed. "The box has been burning a hole in my pocket, as I plotted and planned and waited until the time would be right. Until it could be all about you and me. There were moments when I thought I'd never get the chance to put this ring on your finger, but I never stopped hoping that you would know without reservation that I'm here for the good times as well as the bad.

"I had planned something a little more romantic, a little more traditional." He flashed a grin, his heart racing. "But here we are. Frankly, this is your special place, and it just *feels* right."

He placed his palm on her cheek. "Emma, I love you and I want to spend the rest of my life with you." He held her gaze, searching for any misgiving in her eyes. Seeing none, he took the final step. "Emma, will you marry me?"

Emma's eyes were wide and shinning. "You've given me everything—unwavering support, strength of conviction and, most importantly, unconditional love. I don't have a single doubt, Josh. Yes, of course, I'll marry you!"

Her laughter echoed across the lake to blend with the cry of the loon and the joyous barking of their dogs, as she threw herself into his arms.

* * * * *

If you enjoyed this novel, you'll love Kate James's THE K-9 TRILOGY*:*

WHEN THE RIGHT ONE COMES ALONG
WHEN LOVE MATTERS MOST
WHEN I FOUND YOU

Available now at Harlequin.com.

And watch for Kate's next book, coming in July 2017 from Harlequin Heartwarming!

Get 2 Free Books,
Plus 2 Free Gifts—
just for trying the
Reader Service!

Get 2 Free Books,
Plus 2 Free Gifts—
just for trying the Reader Service!

HOMETOWN HEARTS ♥

YES! Please send me **The Hometown Hearts Collection** in Larger Print. This collection begins with 3 FREE books and 2 FREE gifts in the first shipment. Along with my 3 free books, I'll also get the next 4 books from the Hometown Hearts Collection, in LARGER PRINT, which I may either return and owe nothing, or keep for the low price of $4.99 U.S./ $5.89 CDN each plus $2.99 for shipping and handling per shipment*. If I decide to continue, about once a month for 8 months I will get 6 or 7 more books, but will only need to pay for 4. That means 2 or 3 books in every shipment will be FREE! If I decide to keep the entire collection, I'll have paid for only 32 books because 19 books are FREE! I understand that accepting the 3 free books and gifts places me under no obligation to buy anything. I can always return a shipment and cancel at any time. My free books and gifts are mine to keep no matter what I decide.

262 HCN 3432 462 HCN 3432

Name	(PLEASE PRINT)	
Address		Apt. #
City	State/Prov.	Zip/Postal Code

Signature (if under 18, a parent or guardian must sign)

Mail to the **Reader Service:**
IN U.S.A.: P.O. Box 1867, Buffalo, NY. 14240-1867
IN CANADA: P.O. Box 609, Fort Erie, Ontario L2A 5X3

Get 2 Free Books,
Plus 2 Free Gifts—
just for trying the Reader Service!

HARLEQUIN *super·romance*

HSRLP17

READERSERVICE.COM

Manage your account online!

- Review your order history
- Manage your payments
- Update your address

> ### *We've designed the Reader Service website just for you.*

Enjoy all the features!

- Discover new series available to you, and read excerpts from any series.
- Respond to mailings and special monthly offers.
- Browse the Bonus Bucks catalog and online-only exculsives.
- Share your feedback.

Visit us at:

ReaderService.com

Get 2 Free Books,
Plus 2 Free Gifts—
just for trying the
Reader Service!

HARLEQUIN
HEARTWARMING™

Get 2 Free Books,
Plus 2 Free Gifts—
just for trying the Reader Service!

Love Inspired HISTORICAL

YES! Please send me 2 FREE Love Inspired® Historical novels and my 2 FREE mystery gifts (gifts are worth about $10 retail). After receiving them, if I don't wish to receive any more books, I can return the shipping statement marked "cancel." If I don't cancel, I will receive 4 brand-new novels every month and be billed just $5.24 per book in the U.S. or $5.74 per book in Canada. That's a savings of at least 13% off the cover price. It's quite a bargain! Shipping and handling is just 50¢ per book in the U.S. and 75¢ per book in Canada.* I understand that accepting the 2 free books and gifts places me under no obligation to buy anything. I can always return a shipment and cancel at any time. Even if I never buy another book, the two free books and gifts are mine to keep forever.

102/302 IDN GLQG

Name _____ (PLEASE PRINT)

Address _____ Apt. #

City _____ State/Prov. _____ Zip/Postal Code

Signature (if under 18, a parent or guardian must sign)

Mail to the **Reader Service:**
IN U.S.A.: P.O. Box 1867, Buffalo, NY 14240-1867
IN CANADA: P.O. Box 611, Fort Erie, Ontario L2A 9Z9

Want to try two free books from another series?
Call 1-800-873-8635 or visit www.ReaderService.com.

* Terms and prices subject to change without notice. Prices do not include applicable taxes. Sales tax applicable in N.Y. Canadian residents will be charged applicable taxes. Offer not valid in Quebec. This offer is limited to one order per household. Books received may not be as shown. Not valid for current subscribers to Love Inspired Historical books. All orders subject to credit approval. Credit or debit balances in a customer's account(s) may be offset by any other outstanding balance owed by or to the customer. Please allow 4 to 6 weeks for delivery. Offer available while quantities last.

Your Privacy—The Reader Service is committed to protecting your privacy. Our Privacy Policy is available online at www.ReaderService.com or upon request from the Reader Service.

We make a portion of our mailing list available to reputable third parties that offer products we believe may interest you. If you prefer that we not exchange your name with third parties, or if you wish to clarify or modify your communication preferences, please visit us at www.ReaderService.com/consumerschoice or write to us at Reader Service Preference Service, P.O. Box 9062, Buffalo, NY 14240-9062. Include your complete name and address.